SAMHAIN SCREAMS

Want more thrilling anthologies from Black Beacon Books?

The Black Beacon Books of Mystery
The Black Beacon Book of Ghosts
The Black Beacon Book of Horror
The Black Beacon Book of Pirates
Steampunk Sleuths
Tales from the Ruins
A Hint of Hitchcock
Murder and Machinery
Shelter from the Storm
Lighthouses
Subtropical Suspense

How about a novel or a collection?

Flicker by Cameron Trost
Dark Reflections by Paul Kane
Fortitude by Karen Bayly

www.blackbeaconbooks.com

SAMHAIN SCREAMS

Edited by

GREG CHAPMAN

and

CAMERON TROST

**BLACK
BEACON
BOOKS**

Samhain Screams
Published by Black Beacon Books
Edited by Greg Chapman and Cameron Trost
Cover art and internal illustrations © Greg Chapman
The Day You Die card illustrations © S. B. Watson
Copyright © Black Beacon Books, 2025

Black Beacon Books
blackbeaconbooks.com

ISBN: 978-0-9756118-2-1

FOREWORD

Halloween: it really is the spookiest time of year.

And so much more.

When I pitched this anthology to Cameron Trost at Black Beacon Books, my aim was to create a book worthy of the season—no, the lifestyle—that I, and so many horror authors and artists and fans live by.

When I was a kid, an Australian, Halloween was something I could only dream of, akin to visiting Disneyland. It was all jack o'lanterns, and scarecrows and witches and slashers. A cavalcade of spookiness that was just out of reach and only lived inside my mind.

Growing up, Halloween and spooky stuff wasn't forbidden, so much as it was kind of frowned upon. Gradually, after seeking out 'spooky stuff', I came to learn more about the season and its connection to horror films and literature. Through those films and books, I found

Halloween was indeed about pumpkins and corn fields and crones and masked psychos, but I also realised there was more beneath the surface.

Having fully embraced the spooky stuff as an adult (and someone who has actually visited Disneyland), I've come to appreciate Halloween's superficial qualities as a creative spark for my writing and art. Last year, I was fortunate enough to visit the US for Halloween, taking in New Orleans, Salem, MA and Sleepy Hollow, NY. Walking the streets in those cities for spooky season was my true Disneyland. Hell, my Christmas.

Yet beyond the trick or treating and costumes, and scares, the season has a deeper meaning. Its roots hark back thousands of years to Celtic myth and lore, which speaks of Halloween—or Samhain—as a time of harvest, renewal—and remembrance. It coincides with the changing of the seasons and a fading of the veil between life and death. As a writer, exploring those roots appeals to me so much more than the stock standard pumpkin, witch or knife-wielding maniac and thankfully, it appeals to many other writers as well—including the authors you're about to read in SAMHAIN SCREAMS.

The stories within this book capture those roots perfectly. Not only that, they're creepy as hell. They're more than worthy of the season. Sure, they have monsters and pumpkins and slashers, but each one also strives to delve deeper; each one parting the veil to remind you in the most horrifying of ways, that Halloween isn't just a spooky time of year—it's a time to wonder and be terrified of what lies on the other side.

Happy reading and Happy Halloween.

Greg Chapman
Brisbane, Australia

Black Beacon Books would like to thank our patrons, whose passion for great fiction and independent publishing helped make this anthology happen.

If you'd like to join the team and reap the benefits, subscribe on our Patreon page at: *patreon.com/blackbeaconbooks*

The five patronage tiers are
Shipwreck Survivor, Moonlight Smuggler, Sea Witch, Assistant Keeper, and *Lighthouse Keeper.*

Indian Corn
Jacy Morris

Grandpa sat around the fire, dressed like a tiger, black, grease-painted whiskers blending in with the orange and white stripes painted on his face. He poked at the fire with a stick, while the little kids all danced around the flames, their fuzzy tails bouncing from side to side.

For Halloween, Dany had dressed like a cat, though she would be ditching the family-friendly costume for something a little more scandalous in no time at all. She was too old for ghost stories by the fire, though she loved the way Grandpa told his stories.

On the radio, music played, something new and popular, and totally forgettable—*The Jackson 5* maybe? But Grandpa didn't care what was on; he just liked background noise and so the radio played on and on. To his right, a woven basket sat upon the ground, cobs of corn jutting up from its depths. The sight of those ears of corn almost made Dany want to stick around while her sister and cousins danced around the fire, plucking up popcorn as it bounced out of the fire, waving them in the air to chase away dust and heat, and then shoving them into their mouths.

But she had places to be, was getting older now, didn't want to sit around a fire with little kids and her grandpa, even if she did love them. She wanted to be out with her friend Mercy. But Mercy was not a sit-around type of person. She wouldn't understand Grandpa's stories or popcorn without butter.

'Going somewhere, huh?' Grandpa asked.

He looked up at her, the firelight glinting in his eye. He nodded his head, knew he couldn't keep her here. He'd always been weird about Halloween, refused to take any of them trick or treating.

'You're dressed as an animal, at least,' he said.

The youngest of Dany's cousins, Jayden, stopped chasing Hadija around the fire, came skidding to a dusty stop. A gust of wind blew puffed the fire, sending smoke streaming east. Leaves tumbled across the flattened grass of their well-used backyard. Inside, Dany's parents and aunts and uncles cackled, laughing like a challenge to the world to come and take their good time away from them.

'Why do we have to dress like animals?' Jayden asked.

Dany couldn't help it. She rolled her eyes and settled in to hear the story Grandpa had been telling one night a year since as far back as she could remember.

Grandpa nodded, tried to play the part of the grave Indian storyteller.

'Sit,' he called to the children, and they obeyed without complaint, dropping down on the fire-warmed dirt and making sure their animal tales didn't accidentally catch on fire, which had happened before to Hadija a few years ago.

Grandpa jabbed at the fire once more with a stick he'd previously used to spear a hot dog a half-an-hour ago. Flames shot up, making the orange stripes on his face glow. 'Do you know the history of Halloween?' Grandpa asked.

'Noooo!' all the kids said, though they had all heard this story before. This was how it always began. Every year, someone complained about having to dress like animals when everyone else was out there dressing up like musicians, or vampires, or zombies. Not in Dany's family.

'Well,' Grandpa said, 'guess we oughta fix that. Halloween is a universal thing. Now, not everyone has the same traditions, but we all know when the world thins. Cultures around the world celebrate

12

this night. Oh, some dress up in costumes. Some visit graves and leave offerings. Some go running around looking for candy and playing jokes. But we, our people, have always done something different.'

Grandpa's voice sounded the way the tobacco he smoked smelled. Hard to explain how a sound could equal a smell, but Grandpa's voice did. Dany turned her head, waited for her ride to come driving up the road. From inside, more cackling and the firecracker snap of an aluminum can being busted open.

'On this night, the others come. And they're hungry. Oh, they're just about as hungry as hungry can be. Because where they live, there's no food, no bite-size Goodbars. No single-serving Sweet-Tarts. All they got to eat is pain and regret.'

'Who are they?' Jayden asked, he eyes large in his raccoon-painted face.

Grandpa scrubbed a hand across his stubbled cheek. 'The lost.'

He fell silent, jabbing that stick into the hissing coals.

'Now, the lost, when the world thins, they get to come out and eat, and do you know what they want to eat?'

'What?' the children asked, their eyes big, their hands nervously wringing the faux-animal tails clutched in their hands.

'People. Not because they like it, but because they miss it, because they want to remember what it's like to feel, to laugh, to love, to scream. They think if they can eat it, they can be it. So we hide in plain sight.'

'As animals?' Hadija asked, even though she already knew the answer—they all did.

'As animals. Before the reservation, when we were free and could do as we'd want, we would mix up the pigments, decorate each other, become squirrel, beaver, or bear and the lost would walk among us, none-the-wiser. This is why, when other people are dressing up like their favorite wrestler, we are the creatures of the earth, because the lost are hungry, and if they get ahold of you, well, then you'll be lost as well.'

Dany knew the story for what it was—absolute bullshit. She'd asked around, even did some research in the library, and had found no hint of this supposed tradition, which meant her Grandpa had made it up with his wild imagination.

13

Grandpa reached down and pulled an ear of corn from the basket, the lawn chair creaking underneath him. With his gnarled, brown hand, he placed the ear of corn in the fire.

'Do you know the legend of the corn?' Grandpa asked, though he didn't need to. They all knew it already.

The corn hissed and steamed in the fire, and Dany predicted what Grandpa would say before he even said it. He told of the relationship between the tribes and the corn, how corn was both a gift and a curse. How on nights like this, they would use the corn to keep away the lost. As she stared into the fire, the corn finally popped, and the children jumped, whooping in fright. Dany's young relatives hopped to their feet, rushing around the fire and plucking up the tasty morsels. They waved them in the air to cool them off and remove any dirt before popping the popcorn into their mouths.

A horn honked from the front of the house. Dany rose and said, 'That's my ride.'

Her Grandpa reached his arms out to her, and she bent down and kissed his whiskered cheek. 'Be safe,' he said.

'I will.'

#

Dany flopped into the passenger seat of her best friend's ride, her skirt riding up.

'Don't be a slut,' Mercy said.

'Fuck you.'

Mercy threw it in reverse, and they backed out of the driveway, the taillights making the tall, fall grasses glow red. Mercy spun the wheel, and they sped through the Oregon countryside.

'You bring the stuff?' she asked.

'I brought it. But you should just wear that. You look cute.'

'I don't want to look cute. I want to look sexy.'

'Because of Brad?' Mercy mocked.

'Shut up.'

'Listen, Brad will like you no matter what.'

'Just pull over up here.'

Dany knew Mercy knew the spot. They'd pulled over here and smoked joints and cigarettes for most of the year. The pullout was far enough away from her own house and far enough off the road that no one would find them. But it was still close enough to not be a pain in the ass—a teenager's dream.

'Where is it?' Dany asked.

'In the bag.'

Dany torqued her torso and reached into the backseat of Mercy's Chevy Nova. Her hand fell on a cloth gunnysack, and she pulled it up, accidentally smacking Mercy in the head.

'Ow, watch it, bitch!'

Mercy had the foulest mouth of anyone Dany had ever met, besides herself, of course, which made them perfect friends.

With the headlights turned off, Dany stepped into the darkness. She moved away from the road and stood in front of the car, allowing its rusted, olive-green body to hide her from the road. She threw the bag on the hood, and Mercy leaned out the window and said, 'Watch the paint job!'

'What fucking paint job? It's all rust.' If Mercy's car had been a dog, they would have taken it out back and put it out of its misery.

She spread the opening of the bag open and pulled out her real Halloween costume, not this kiddy shit her family insisted she wear. She peeled her skirt off, rolled down her stockings, still keeping them neat for when Mercy dropped her off. She would have to change back, didn't want to get caught in a lie by her grandfather. She peeled off her top, and this is when Mercy turned the headlights on, exposing Dany's naked body, the brown of her skin washed out by the headlights. To add insult to injury, Mercy laid on the horn.

'Mercy!' Dany screamed.

The lights clicked off, and furious, Dany finished dressing. When she pulled open the door, she threw the bag at Mercy's face.

'Ow! You hit me with the buckle.'

'That's what you get.'

'Nice titties. Brad's gonna love 'em.'

Dany sat in the car, feeling half-naked. She *hoped* Brad loved 'em. She wasn't freezing her ass off out here for nothing. 'Turn on the heat.'

Mercy did as she was told.

On the radio, *The Monster Mash* played for the thousandth time that day. Dany rolled her eyes, couldn't help but think of her

Grandpa. His stories weren't so different from this song, a little corny, but awesome when you're younger. When you're a kid, the idea of monsters partying together is like an explosive in your mind. When you're older, you kind of get sick of it, want to be doing more adult things.

Mercy backed the car out on the road, and they headed to the party.

#

They pulled up to the cornfield—a Howell High School Halloween tradition. A blinking construction light showed them where to turn, and Mercy swerved left, bouncing off the road and guiding her Chevy Nova through already flattened stalks of corn.

'Won't the farmer know we're out here?' she asked.

'Shit, the old man who owns the field definitely knows what goes down here. Hell, the old pervert probably hides in the corn with his hand down his overalls, whacking it to people like you.'

'Ew,' Dany said. 'But seriously though, are we going to get in trouble?'

'Relax, Dany. My brother says they all know. Everyone's just happy we're in one place, and not out cruising the streets drinking and driving.'

'You're not going to drink, are you?'

'Maybe one or two,' Mercy said.

'Just don't get so loaded you can't drive. If I don't come home tonight, I'll be grounded for life.'

Mercy rolled her eyes. She didn't need to worry about getting home at night. Her parents didn't seem to care about their kids at all. The Thomases were known for being wild and lawless, all five of them, and though Mercy was the youngest, she had picked up several bad habits from her older brothers, one of them being sometimes she got a little too loaded for Dany's taste. But she was fun, so there was that.

The corn corridor—Corridor!—opened up into a large circular clearing, cars parked around the edges. In the middle of the circle, people milled around a fire contained in a burn barrel. The flames reflected off the gleaming silver sides of a keg and the red cups

16

clutched in everyone's hands.

Suddenly, moths danced in her stomach, and she wanted nothing more than to ask Mercy to turn the car around so she could go home, eat popcorn off the dirt, and listen to Grandpa's stories.

The car came to a bouncing stop.

'You ready?'

'No,' Dany said.

'Aw, don't puss out on me now.'

'Maybe we should go.'

'Are you kidding me? When you look like that? You ain't always gonna look this good. Trust me. I seen my mom naked, and it ain't pretty.'

Dany nodded.

When she reached for the door handle, Mercy put out a hand to stop her and said, 'Just don't let Brad get any jism on my car seats.'

'Gross,' Dany said. And then she stepped out of the car, the cold washing over her skin, exposed in far too many places. The heels of her boots sunk into the earth.

'Woooo!' one of the big-bellied football players yelled upon seeing her.

She blushed, hoped the firelight didn't show it.

Mercy stepped out of the car dressed in perhaps the sluttiest witch costume anyone in the world had ever worn. Maybe it wasn't even a witch costume, but an old-timey hooker outfit. She lit a cigarette, and together, arm in arm, Dany and Mercy did the rounds.

Dany tried not to look desperate, tried not to peer around the boys who were talking to them so she could find Brad. While Mercy ate up the attention, Dany wasn't nearly as comfortable in her own skin.

Red cups found their hands, seemingly of their own volition, and they talked and joked with the people from school. The other girls, all wearing more clothing, sneered at them, which wasn't different than any other day. The world lets you know when you're trash, and they don't let you forget about it.

She was tilting the cup up to her lips and choking down the beer when she spotted him standing off the side, his arm around...a princess, a plain old boring princess with blonde hair.

Dany hated her hair, hated they way the princess gazed up at Brad. She knew the girl, knew she was "popular".

17

Mercy noticed where Dany was looking and elbowed her in the ribs. 'Look at that slut.'

Dany knew her friend was just trying to make her feel better. The girl in the princess outfit, Sarah Heffner, was the furthest thing from a slut in the school. She was wholesome, the good cheerleader, sang in the church choir—all that shit. If that was the type of girl Brad was interested in, then she knew she had no chance.

She tilted back her beer, draining it even though it burned going down and sat like a rock in her stomach. Mercy grabbed the empty cup from her and said, 'I'll be right back.' Good friends were like that, knew when you intended on destroying yourself and were only too happy to help out.

Dany couldn't tear her eyes from Brad and Sarah. Jealousy bloomed in her heart, a small bud at first. Then Brad watered that bud with that winning smile of his, those perfect white teeth, his sandy brown hair ruffing in the wind. The bud had grown to a healthy stalk when he leaned down to Sarah and placed his lips to hers. Sarah, sweet wholesome Sarah, opened her mouth and accepted his tongue in her mouth. Brad draped a hand over her shoulder, and they wandered off in the direction of the cars, by which point, that stalk had sprouted ears of corn, each cob covered in hateful kernels of jealousy, ready to pop off at any moment.

Mercy appeared, a foaming Dixie cup full of beer in her hand. She handed it to Dany, and foam ran down the edge, dripping onto the flattened cornstalks.

'He's not worth it,' Mercy said.

At that point, Barney Conrad, dressed like Luke Skywalker, appeared, waving his stupid plastic lightsaber around like it was his cock. His pale skin was flushed with alcohol, and he said, 'Whoa! Sick costume!' He sang, 'Wonder Woman!' at her in a falsetto voice, and though she was too hurt to reciprocate his interest, she smiled at him and drank her beer, piling that foamy cold liquid on top of the other beer already warming in her belly.

Barney draped a hand over her shoulder, stared down at her cleavage, until Mercy punched him in the shoulder.

'You know what would happen if you put your Lasso of Truth around me?' Barney asked.

'What?' Dany responded, her head becoming lighter.

'I'd tell you I loved you, and you'd know I meant it.'

Dany rolled her eyes, and somewhere in the apex of her bemused eye-rolling, she caught sight of Brad's jeep rocking up and down on its shocks.

The kernels of her jealousy popped, and she shrugged Barney off.

'Hey! Was it something I said?' he asked, his arms out to the side.

'Buzz off, Barney,' said Mercy.

He spun around, waving his stupid light saber around once more, looking for the next girl to test one of his terrible lines upon.

Dany drained the last of her beer and then wandered off toward the corn.

'Hey, where you going?' Mercy asked.

'I have to pee,' she said. She didn't, but she said that so Mercy wouldn't think something was wrong, wouldn't think she was hurt and tag along to make sure she didn't slit her fucking wrists in the cornfield. Dany just needed a moment alone to process. Also, now that she thought about it, maybe she did need to pee.

The autumn cornstalks, their outer leaves gone dusky brown, brushed against her skin, rasping like a knife drawn across a whetstone. She pressed further into their safety, allowing them to block off the world. They towered over her, and after several minutes of trudging, she worried she would become lost if she kept going. She stopped and listened, heard the laughter of the party in the clearing. Feeling confident she could find her way back, she pressed through the stalks. They slashed at her skin, scratching and furrowing her cold flesh. But she didn't mind. Dany much preferred physical pain to the emotional type.

When she could barely hear the party, she squatted down and did her business in the cornfield, shivering as the cold air kissed the parts of her body she normally hid under clothing. When she finished, she stood and buried her face in her hands while trying not to cry. Of course, trying not to cry is one of the quickest ways to ensure waterworks, and soon Dany was bawling her eyes out.

And for what? Some stereotypical smalltown heartthrob? Some cornfed jock with charming good looks and a Jeep and a future that didn't include working at the diner in town?

What would he have ever wanted with me anyway?

As her face lay buried in her palms, Dany became aware of an absolute quiet around her. No corn leaves rusting in the wind, no laughter in the distance—nothing. *Strange*. Dany lifted her head and discovered herself bathed in blue light.

'Is someone there?' she asked.

The blue light stopped, seemed to turn toward her, blinding her with its glare.

'What—'

The light rushed at her, and she screamed as she discerned a shape within the light—a skeletal body, its desiccated skin drawn tight across its skull. It reached out to her with fingers like claws, the skin pulled back from the fingernails to expose the bones underneath.

She turned and ran, the heels of her red Wonder Woman boots stabbing into the soil. She glanced over her shoulder once, and ran right over a corn stalk, the shaft poking up between her legs until she pressed forward, shoving it to the ground. In that one glance, she spotted others—a dozen or more—hurrying through the cornstalks.

Dany screamed in the night. The cornstalks kept their silence.

Onward she ran, the corn whipping her for her stupidity.

Her grandfather's stories came to her as she fought her way through the field. In her mind, she imagined his raspy voice trying to calm her. Dany glanced up, spotted the faint glow of the burn barrel's flames in the distance. She ran in that direction, the lights of the dead slashing their way through the corn, carving furrows through the field.

Ahead, one of the lost attempted to cut her off, its cracked skull visible where its scalp had been peeled away. A greedy hand reached out to her. Its mouth opened as if to say something, but Dany jigged to the right, pressed forward, starving for the light of the fire and other people.

They encircled her now, drawing tight like a snare around a rabbit's paw.

'No,' she moaned.

The beer in her belly sloshed, the alcohol pumping into her brain, making it hard to think straight. Combined with her horrible boots, she didn't think she was going to make it, and then she burst out into the clearing. She spun around to peer behind her, to see if those blue lights still pursued her.

She wanted them not to be there, but they were, and there were more of them now.

'They're coming!' she called.

'Who? The cops?' Barney asked.

'The cops!' the other kids called.

And like that, a panic ran through the kids of Howell High School. They abandoned their beers, tossing the red cups onto the flattened cornstalks even as they dug the keys from their pockets.

Mercy rushed up and grabbed Dany by the arm, dragging her to the car. A Ford pickup narrowly missed running them over, and then they were diving into Mercy's rust-bucket of a Chevy Nova.

She fumbled with her keys as the cars all around them bolted. Jamming the key home, she twisted her wrist, and the engine choked, gasping and gasping.

'Come on, Mercy,' Dany moaned.

'It won't start.'

Their breath and fear fogged up the windows, but the fog couldn't hide the spectral blue outside.

'They're coming!'

'Shit, if I get busted, my dad's gonna take the skin off my ass.'

You don't have to worry about that, Dany wanted to say, but she couldn't. Mercy would find out it wasn't the police she had to worry about all too soon.

Dany reached out with her hand and swiped at the passenger seat window. Through the small circle she made, she spotted the only other car remaining in the clearing—Brad's turquoise blue Jeep, still rocking on its springs.

'It's not fucking starting!' Mercy howled.

'Brad's still here,' Dany said as the blue lights surrounded his Jeep, the shapes within moving slowly, surrounding it.

'Forget Brad,' Mercy said, stomping on the brake pedal, on the gas pedal, on the floorboards, anything to get her car working.

The lost faded through the Jeep, and Dany reached out to Mercy and grabbed her arm to get her to stop for a moment. From within the Jeep, screams. The vehicle didn't stop rocking, just kept moving—side to side, up and down.

'What is that?' Mercy asked, fully aware for the first time that these weren't cops moving through the corn, sneaking up on an unsuspecting group of minors. They were something else.

'The lost,' Dany said.

Through the glass windows, the screams of Brad and Sarah reached their ears. For a moment, the blue light flared inside the Jeep, blinding Dany. Then the screaming stopped.

'We gotta run,' Mercy said.

'You run,' Dany said. 'I can't run in these boots. These stupid fucking boots.'

Dany rummaged around in the back of the Nova for the bag, felt the cloth on her fingertips. From Brad's Jeep, the lost emerged, began heading in their direction. Dany began peeling her clothes off, didn't care if Mercy saw her naked or not.

Mercy didn't run, though she should have. Dany wanted to warn her, but all her focus was on her grandfather's words, on the stories he had told her since she was little. She pulled her boots off as the turquoise light intensified, wriggled out of her Wonder Woman booty shorts, and then she was spinning her cat costume around in her hands, wondering how to get inside it.

The turquoise light washed over her, allowing her to see better.

Mercy screamed as one of the creature's hands pressed through the windshield, electric blue and terrifying.

Dany slipped the skirt on, wrapped her cat tail belt around her waist. With her fingertips, she traced the scratches on her arms and legs, dragged her own blood across her face to create red whiskers.

The lost entered the vehicle, hunkering down to feed. Dany closed her eyes and screamed.

Mercy screamed along with her, and kept screaming and screaming, until the screams turned into nightmarish gurgling.

Dany opened her eyes because somewhere, deep down inside, she knew someone would ask her about this, about what had happened to her white friend. *Why did you kill her?* they'd ask, even though she had done no such thing. And when she opened her eyes, she watched as her lost ancestors, her lost relatives, scalped and left to rot in the open air, fed on Mercy, their hungry teeth ripping through her body as if it were cake, taking great chunks of her flesh away. Blood fountained from a hole in Mercy's throat, splattering the Chevy Nova's interior. The lost fed and fed, and when Dany's friend stopped gurgling, they peeled back and turned to her, sniffing with the holes where their noses should be and studying her with their empty eye sockets.

Dany couldn't meet their stare, so she closed her eyes once more, waited for their teeth to sink into her. But when she opened her eyes, they were gone.

She sobbed, reaching a hesitant hand out to Mercy but drawing back, not wanting to get Mercy's blood on her, because that would mean she was responsible. When she could stand the sight of Mercy's dead body no longer, Dany exited the car, walked over to the burn barrel, and kicked it over.

Barefoot and bloody, she strode from the field until she found herself standing on the side of the road. The dry corn stalks burned like birthday candles, turning the field into a flaming hell.

At the edge of the fire, the kernels of a few overlooked cobs of corn popped. Dany rushed to pick them out of the dirt and pop the steaming morsels in her mouth.

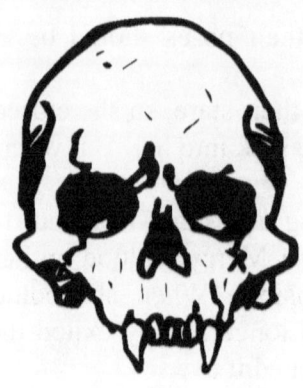

The Last Pumpkin
Mia Dalia

It took weeks to figure out that what they had was a pumpkin patch. Months, really, if you take in the time right after their midsummer move here when they were convinced the greenery in their makeshift backyard was purely decorative.

It was all so brand new—this suburban life, the quiet, the in-your-face presence of nature. Ted was rearranging the bookshelf by the window, imagining his name on the well-worn spines, when he happened to glance outside and notice that the patch had sprouted a gourd. They were delighted. Lucy proclaimed it to be zucchini and Ted, not knowing any better, agreed.

It didn't look like any zucchini they'd ever seen in the produce aisles, but according to the internet, it came in all shapes, including this peculiar butternut squash one. Lucy took it off the vine and made it into a stir fry. The flavor was pleasant but much too light, even for a zucchini.

The next gourd rounded itself up into the shape of a small watermelon. It even sort of looked like one. The innards of it were all different—stringier. Lucy turned it into a hearty stew, carrots, onions, and all. It lasted them for days.

They emailed pictures of the gourds to friends, like proud parents, sharing their discovery with delighted bewilderment of people getting to know and love their new home.

No one thought it was a zucchini. No one knew what it was.

When the third gourd came up, this time the size of a large watermelon, perfectly round and striated green, Lucy left it alone and googled it extensively. What you couldn't learn on the internet wasn't worth knowing, she joked.

What she learned was that they had a pumpkin patch. And one last pumpkin left. The previous owners must have planted it. Either way, Halloween was Ted and Lucy's favorite holiday, and they found the patch to be serendipitous. They waited for their last pumpkin to turn orange with the wink-wink-nudge-nudge glee of an inside joke.

They were like that, as a couple. Unburdened by kids, untethered by pets, living in a world for two; lovers, best friends, partners-in-crime. This house was a culmination of a decade's worth of plans and aspirations. It was almost everything they ever wanted, and they treated it like a cross between a dream come true and a brand-new toy.

A pumpkin patch right outside their window was an unexpected and lovely bonus.

The window technically belonged to a dining nook, but Ted had taken to setting up his writing station there. Unlike Lucy, he didn't have a proper office. Not yet, anyway. He was waiting to achieve enough success to warrant one.

Since the move, he wrote wherever the mood struck him, trying out different set-ups until the convenience of the already-there table and the delicious warmth of the sun streaming through the window had anchored him in the dining nook.

The writing thing was new to Ted. Or, rather, Ted was new to it. Having lost his day job and having never been a fan of it in the first place, he decided to follow every motivational poster ever made and pursue his dream. *Do what you love and you'll never work a day in your life*, they said. Well, his bank account for the last year looked like a bank account of someone who wasn't working all that many days.

In reality, Ted was making strides, though. He'd had several short stories accepted in small publications and had just about secured a publisher for his debut novel.

While Lucy (saintly, Ted thought) was bringing home the proverbial bacon, Ted was doing his best to earn her faith in his talent, churning out petite macabres one after another.

Their couple dynamics, however unconventional, worked for them. Things made sense. The sun shined. And there was a pumpkin ripening into Halloween-orangeness right outside.

'Coffee?'

'Yes, please.' Lucy stretched and cracked her spine. She was still adjusting to their new mattress.

They shared their morning brew in companionable silence for a while watching the world outside, then talked about what their days held.

'He emailed again,' Ted said, shaking his head lightly.

'The weirdo?'

Ted grinned. 'Technically, he's my number one fan.'

It went with the territory, they supposed. Fame, no matter how slight, attracted attention. Some of it was the wrong kind.

They had set up a website for Ted, a place where he could list his publication credits and talk about his work, and soon enough emails began arriving.

'But *I'm* your number one fan,' Lucy pouted cutely.

'You are.' Ted winked. 'Of course, you are. Nothing wrong with a little friendly competition.'

They joked about it because taking the emails seriously would creep them out. The emails *were* creepy. Possibly unintentionally so, but who could tell? The internet rendered most communication tone deaf and nuance free. And with the sort of stories Ted wrote…

'What's he saying now?' Ted and Lucy had gendered the emailer as a *he*.

'Let's see.' Ted grabbed his reading glasses and pulled up the message on his iPhone.

I think about you all the time. Think about what's going on in that head of yours. I mean it in the nicest sense. Something about the idea that we can look at the same things and see something so different boggles my mind. That latest story of yours…it made me afraid to use the toilet at night. I had to get a nightlight. Haven't had one since I was a kid. Kudos, Ted, you've regressed me. Happy nightmares. Your #1w/bullet.

That's how the fan always signed off. Lucy, being a Google devotee, looked up the phrase's origin. It wasn't a threat as she was afraid it might have been. The "bullet" in the phrase simply referred to an icon placed next to a song that makes rapid progress in the charts.

'When he starts signing off #1w/knife, we'll start worrying,' she half-joked.

'Nah, we won't worry at all.' Ted pulled her into a hug and kissed the top of her head which conveniently came up to his chin. 'He's just some lonely weirdo with exceptional taste in indie horror and lamentable social skills.'

Ted had never been much into technology. Social media appealed to him purely as a source of self-promotion, so he never posted any personal information out there. It made the world feel remote, just how Ted liked it, with him being a mystery among the mysterious.

They were both private people, only just now getting to know their new neighbors. They relished anonymity so much that Ted had almost ended up publishing under a pseudonym, but at the last minute decided against it. He hadn't made much of himself prior to taking up writing and rather liked the idea of having his name associated with something he was proud of, an accomplishment all his own.

Ted kissed Lucy again, taking in the taste of strawberry ChapStick-flavored coffee on her lips, and wished her a lovely day. Then he got back to writing.

#

Clay spent his mornings drinking tea and watching his neighbors leave for work, partly wishing he had someplace to go, partly glad he didn't need to. The tea was a leftover affectation of his British mother, from all the years they lived together before she went into a home. Nowadays her mind wandered and strayed too far for even the simplest of conversations. Sometimes she thought Clay was his father, a man who abandoned them decades ago, a ghostly presence from faded photographs. Sometimes she thought Clay was the orderly she suspected of stealing. Either way, he got the brunt of her ire. When what he wanted, what he missed, was company.

Living on his own was strange, like there was suddenly too much space and too much silence. The excess suffocated him. Put him in mind of those percussion instruments with beans rattling around a dried-out gourd. He was the bean. Existing in an echoey solitude.

Like many lonely people, Clay spent entirely too much time on the internet. He had never been a sound sleeper, frequently haunted by nightmares. It made him curious about the nightmares of others. Horror had always been his guilty pleasure, ever since his mother let him watch *Psycho* with her. He'd been young then, perhaps too young, and the movie left an indelible impression.

The parallels were hard not to draw, a young man living with his mother as his entire world. Clay too went a little mad sometimes, but it was nothing, not really…

When he found Ted Maxwell's story online, it was a revelation. Something about the spin the author put on the haunted house trope really spoke to Clay. Reminded him of his nightmares, specifically the one where he was lost in an old, dilapidated manse and every turn yielded no exit.

Clay tracked down and read every single Maxwell story after that. He found the man's website and learned all there was to learn about Ted Maxwell, which wasn't much. But he didn't need the internet to tell him things because he had an ace up his sleeve: Ted Maxwell was Clay's neighbor.

That's how he found out about Maxwell's writing in the first place. Brought in the wrong package from their shared porch. Googled the name out of curiosity. Et voilà.

Clay had no illusions about his social graces; he wasn't the sort of person to go introduce himself to the neighbors, to make friends, but he did have an inquisitive nature and an active imagination and had spent countless hours fantasizing about becoming friends with Ted Maxwell.

Alas, the man seldom left the house and when he did, it was with his wife. Clay couldn't start a conversation in real life, so he turned to the internet. He started emailing Maxwell. There was never a response, but he thought maybe Ted was just shy, like him.

He'd wait.

When Clay saw a giant pumpkin blossoming right under Maxwell's window, he recognized a perfect opportunity to make contact.

#

Ted Maxwell considered himself a connoisseur of nightmares. He dreamt them, read them, wrote them. A lifelong horror aficionado. And yet the thing before him turned his blood to ice. Something about it—the violation—was profoundly unsettling in a way his writerly brain couldn't even describe.

Lucy's screams brought him out; he was deep in a story but came running.

Someone had carved their pumpkin. They were saving it for the weekend, to have a shared project. Been looking forward to it for weeks. They had a mischievous design in mind, something from one of Ted's lighter stories. Nothing like this.

This pumpkin was a nightmare. Carved with crude expertise to resemble Ted's face. It was etched there, unmistakably, eerily, and, lit up from the inside, it gave Ted a demonic countenance.

Lucy had her hands pressed to her mouth; her eyes were large with fear. Ted put his arms around her, turning her away. He found himself unable to look anywhere but at his evil doppelganger.

Ted wanted to find humor in the situation, but levity failed him. The way the pumpkin innards were arranged around the gourd, their red dye that looked unsettlingly like blood…it wasn't funny at all. He led Lucy inside, then came back out, stomped out the gourd, gathered the remnants into a trash bag, and binned it.

They had a long talk inside, deciding against calling the cops, but for getting a security camera system. For the first time since taking up writing, Ted had a serious think about his life choices. Fear, it seemed, was only fun to write about. Real life was a different story altogether.

#

I thought you'd love it. It's Halloween; I guess everyone's entitled to one good scare. You've given me SO many. I'm sorry.

29

Clay sent the email, but he felt more angry than sorry. His effort failed. He'd never be friends with Ted now. Never know what went on inside his mind, where the stories came from. Unless...

The anatomy books lied, Clay learned the hard way. Carving up a person's head was way different from a pumpkin. Harder, messier. Breaking into the house was easy enough, but this...this took work. Clay had to tie them both up. The woman was screaming, so he gagged her. She stopped making noise after a while—Clay hadn't checked on her, didn't want to know what her silence meant. Maxwell's brain refused to yield its mysteries. It was bloody, mushy, unpleasantly juicy, and slippery. Gray-pinkish with white fibers at first, it was now turning shades of an ugly bruise and Clay still didn't know what made it tick. Guess he never would now, he sighed.

There was a loud knocking echoing through the house. Trick-a-treaters, Clay figured. It was, after all, Halloween. His mother eschewed the tradition, calling it a crass American thing, but Clay had always secretly enjoyed it. He sighed again and went to look for the candy.

The Knock
DJ Tyrer

It happened a few years back, when I was still living on the estate, before I decided to get out and start sofa-surfing. Believe me, there was no way I was going to stay, not after what happened, not when it was due for demolition and good riddance. Not that it has been. It's still there, squatting on the horizon of my life, like the memory of a nightmare, taunting me, daring me to come back.

I've no idea what it's like on there now—I've heard the ongoing housing crisis has had them offering flats to homeless families, fresh meat for that concrete hell—but when I was there, it was almost deserted. Mainly, we thought, due to the threat of demolition: those who could move out did, while nobody else was being moved in. Only, so many seemed to be doing moonlight flits, disappearing without a word to friends or neighbours, that it began to feel as if it were some sort of black-hole that sucked you in and never let you see the light of day again. Literally, I mean, not just the metaphorical sinkhole that every sink estate is, sucking away hopes and dreams and leaving nothing but empty lives numbed by drugs and booze.

Not that my life was empty, despite the usual soul-destroying rounds of remedial courses and job-clubs offered to the unemployed that did nothing to answer the question of how to land a job in an area where there were none. I was writing. Well, trying to. At least, the writing itself was going okay, when the foggy malaise of depression lifted, but getting published was a dead end. The phone line worked less than half the time, so the internet was out; in the end, I ditched it altogether as I couldn't afford the bills, anyway. The mobile coverage was no better, with my flat in some sort of dead zone; it never worked when I needed it to, although cold callers always seemed to get through. Even the post was hit-and-miss, the posties scared of the estate's reputation.

Submitting stories and getting responses was nearly impossible, even when I could make it to an internet cafe. It's difficult to carve out a writing career when you can't make contact with the editors. My only means of escape was almost as much of a dead end as my life.

I was going nowhere.

The only other person on my floor, my fellow inmate, if you like, was Lindsay, who lived four or five doors down. It was ironic that we lived in these piddly-little bedsits, in cramped misery, when all the others along the corridor were empty. I actually contacted the Housing Association about getting the keys to another flat for additional storage and was told, in no uncertain terms, that there were rules that could never be bent, no matter the situation.

We didn't see each other often, just the occasional nod and 'Hello' going in or out. I was often out on courses during the day and Lindsay worked nights at a takeaway with lousy food I never visited, plus I wasn't that sociable, being happier hunched over my ancient desktop, pecking out a story that would never sell. Nor were visitors of any sort common, especially after the post became erratic and even the postman became a rare sight.

So, it was a surprise, even an alarming one, when there was a knock on my door one evening, just before Hallowe'en.

I nearly didn't answer. Although the night was a couple of days away, that never stopped the trick-or-treaters. Already, I'd had two knocks on my door with nobody there; I was surprised there was no vandalism. Likewise, idiot kids were already chucking fireworks about ahead of Guy Fawkes Night.

But, I did answer, to discover Lindsay on my doorstep.

She shuffled, as if embarrassed, and didn't speak, so I said, 'Hi. Can I help you?'

'Kids,' she said. 'They keep banging on my door.'

I nodded and told her I'd had the same problem.

'I think they've broken into the flat next to mine,' she went on, wringing her hands. 'The one where Mrs Haines lived. I can hear someone moving about in there.'

That brought forth a curse from me. Mrs Haines had left about six months previously, one of those who did a moonlight flit. A formidable old woman, she'd been a bit of a busybody, a gossip, but a decent-enough neighbour. If kids had broken into her place, they could make our lives hell, starting floods by bunging up the sinks, or by starting fires.

I told Lindsay, I'd take a look.

She nodded. 'Thanks.' Her smile was shy, but welcome.

Pausing only to close my door behind me, I went over to Mrs Haines' flat. The door was slightly ajar—they lock automatically when closed, so I guess they wanted to get back in.

Slowly, nervously, I pushed it open. Of course, Lindsay had said 'kids', but that could cover a wide range of ages nowadays, up to strapping eighteen-year-olds. Besides, even the little ones seemed to be carrying knives these days. I didn't want to encounter *anyone*, and I remember wishing I'd brought a weapon of some sort.

But, I needn't have worried, for, as I searched through the flat, I found it was empty.

'Nobody here, now,' I shouted back to Lindsay.

From the front-door, I heard her call out, 'I'm sure I heard them just before I came over.'

'Well, they must've scarpered while your back was turned. Place is a mess, though. Looks like Mrs Haines didn't take much when she went.'

'Really?' I could hear the doubt in Lindsay's voice. I shared it. The old woman had been something of a hoarder and it was difficult to imagine she'd just upped-and-left, leaving it all behind.

'Perhaps she went into a home?' I suggested as I poked about. 'Or, maybe she died?'

'Maybe.' Lindsay didn't sound convinced.

The stuffed bears scattered across the floor seemed to agree with her. I can still remember that room, perfectly. There was tinfoil, a scorched spoon and a lighter on the table, next to the knick-knacks left behind. One wall had been sprayed with some sort of tag, more complicated than the usual sort you see, although I was sure I'd seen others like it round the estate, some sort of gang sign, I supposed: a complex swirl of sinuous twists in red and black that formed a circle.

As I stared at it, it was as if it were beginning to spin, suck me in. I had to look away and blink my eyes over and over to refocus my vision. I assumed the kids painted it while off their heads: maybe it was a money-saver, as who needs drugs when you can just stare at the wall and set your head into a free spin?

With a shrug, I exited the flat and pulled the door locked behind me.

Lindsay looked at me and said, 'Well?'

'Yeah, they've definitely been in there. Hopefully, they won't be able to get back in and will go elsewhere. If you hear them giving the door a kicking, call the police.'

Of course, that assumed they couldn't just trip the lock. Most flats had additional locks in their doors because the ones they came with were easy to open with nothing more than a bit of plastic. That was probably how the kids got in the first time. If the Housing Association had any sense, they would secure the empty flats properly, but then, nobody's ever accused the Housing Association of being awash with sense. I doubted we'd heard the last of the kids.

Lindsay hung awkwardly outside her door, as if unwilling to go inside.

'Any problems,' I said, 'give me a knock. Or...' I fumbled through my pockets for a pen and paper and scribbled down my number, '...give me a ring, assuming you can get a signal.'

She took the scrap and looked at it almost as if she didn't quite know what it was, then nodded and thanked me.

I watched as she slipped back inside her flat, her movements still conveying a hint of reluctance. I wondered if I'd just missed my chance: Lindsay was a decent-looking woman. You don't meet many of them when you don't have much of a life.

After a moment, I went back inside and returned to my writing, although the words didn't want to flow. At first, I found myself thinking of Lindsay, I couldn't help myself, but then, I found my thoughts drifting back to the flat, wondering what had happened to Mrs Haines and why the kids had chosen it of all the empty places. Why choose one next door to an occupied flat? Stupidity? Or, were they deliberately trying to intimidate Lindsay? I resolved to keep a better eye on her, just in case.

And, after that, I began to think about the pattern sprayed upon the wall, the strange coiling pattern of red and black that, even in my mind, seemed to twist and turn, writhing almost as if alive.

Weird.

A sudden hammering on my door tore me out of my reverie. Lindsay?

I ran to the door and, like an idiot, didn't even pause to check through the spyhole, just pulled it open.

There was nobody there.

I looked both ways along the corridor, but could see no one. It was too long, I was certain, for them to have run away. Had they fled to a neighbouring flat? Damn kids!

I walked a short distance either way, looking at the doors of the other flats, particularly the one next to Lindsay, but they were all shut. Which, naturally, told me nothing, if the kids were inside having a giggle at their brilliant joke.

Despite pausing for a minute and listening intently, I heard nothing that offered me a clue and had to return to my keyboard, disgruntled.

The words continued to refuse to flow, so I flopped down in front of the telly, flicking from channel to channel in the hopes of something decent to watch, but all I seemed to find were shows filled with the hip-hop I detest, news programmes about the rising tide of knife crime, and late-night gambling with roulette wheel after roulette wheel spinning into a blur.

So, I retreated to bed and slipped off into dreams of spinning wheels of red and black that transformed into the swirling symbol from the wall of the empty flat, sucking me down into deeper dreams that I don't remember, but which made me shiver, even now, when I try to recall them.

Lindsay called me several times, the next couple of days, to say the kids had been banging on her door, but I never once caught them. Had there not also been a hammering on mine, I might not have believed her. It was as if they could just melt away whenever I opened my door.

'Are you doing anything tomorrow?' Lindsay asked me on her doorstep, after I'd come up empty-handed once again.

'Nope.' I never did anything special on Hallowe'en, just locked my doors, maybe popped in a DVD of an old horror movie, and pretended I wasn't there when the trick-or-treaters came round, praying they didn't gum up my keyhole or smear my door with paint.

'I hate to impose,' she said, 'but, I'm not working and I really don't want to spend the night alone. Could I spend it with you?'

That blind-sided me and, again, I had no idea whether I should read anything into it, but Lindsay had been pretty shaken and I couldn't blame her for not wanting to spend Hallowe'en alone, wondering if the kids would ratchet up the harassment, so I said, 'Sure.'

So it was that, about five, I heard a soft, tentative knock on my door that I recognised as hers.

There had been a constant muffled beat in the background for a while and, when I opened the door, I could hear it more clearly. Somebody was playing the rap by *The Laughing Man* that was big at the time. I couldn't quite make out the words, but as Lindsay slipped past me, I did catch, 'The joke's on you.' It seemed horribly appropriate, as if we were the subjects of some cruel, meaningless gag that was slowly sending us insane.

I slammed the door to cut it off.

'It's been going on like that for ages,' Lindsay said. Her voice wavered with a mixture of stress and tiredness. 'I don't know where it's coming from.' She gave a vague shrug. 'It must be this floor, but I just can't place it.' With a rueful smile, she added, 'It's driving me nuts.'

'You and me both,' I said. 'Come on, let's try and take our minds off it.'

But, although I tried to drown it out, the repetitive thump of the beat continued, a vibration through our bodies more than a sound, each thump like the tick of a clock counting down to something.

Then, we heard *the knock*.

Lindsay looked at me and I shook my head, trying to keep my composure, despite the beat that set my nerves on edge and seemed to merge with the knocking.

'Ignore them,' I said. 'They'll go away.'

They did, but only for a little while.

The knocking returned.

'They want to come in,' moaned Lindsay, hugging herself.

'Well, they can take a running jump. Just ignore them.'

The knocking ceased and even the vibrating beat vanished. I remember I shivered, then. For some reason, their silence was even more unnerving, like knowing something is watching you, waiting to pounce...

We waited.

When they knocked again, it was a real hammering and we could hear the door vibrating in its frame. We exchanged a nervous look: the doors were pretty cheap and it sounded like they were kicking it in.

I got up and ran for the front door and looked out through the spyhole; the juddering ceased the moment I pressed my eye against it, as if they knew I was there.

There were two of them standing outside my door, teenagers or adults, it was impossible to tell as they wore pale jackets with their hoods pulled up, their heads bowed, concealing their faces. For some irrational reason, I found myself praying they wouldn't look up. Their tops were a sort of dirty-beige colour, as if they hadn't been washed in a long time, or else, a darker colour had faded—horrible.

I stared for some time and they just stood there, heads bowed, silent and unmoving.

A noise behind me caused me to turn and I saw Lindsay, wringing her hands, standing just a short way behind me.

'They want to come in,' she said, voice flat and emotionless, her former fear missing. Her eyes, though wide, also appeared devoid of emotion. I would've take a step back, had the door not been there, because I found her oddly unnerving.

As if in response to her statement, they began to hammer upon the door, again, and I felt it shuddering against me.

'Go away!' I shouted. 'I'm calling the police!'

If they heard me, it made no difference and the door continued to judder in its frame.

Pushing past Lindsay, I ran for my mobile, praying that, tonight, it was getting reception. It wasn't.

Behind me, Lindsay repeated, 'They want to come in.'

Turning, I saw she had stepped up to the door and was drawing back a bolt.

'No, don't! Don't let them in!'

Somehow, I just knew that if they came in, something bad would happen, that if I saw their faces... Well, I didn't know what, but I didn't want to find out...

'No!'

Lindsay continued to ignore me and unlock the door.

I ran to her and tried to pull her away, but she shrugged me off.

The door continued to judder.

As she reached for the main lock, I retreated to the bathroom and closed the door. The tiny bolt looked so flimsy, but I drove it home regardless, and fell to the floor beside the bath.

The hammering sound ceased and I heard the creak of my front-door opening. There was a moment of silence in which the air seemed to press heavily down on me...

Lindsay's scream made my heart leap in my chest.

For a moment, I felt as if I were about to faint, thought I must be having a heart-attack, while the bathroom span about me as her shriek seemed to echo within my skull.

There was a wet sound, unpleasant and strange, then nothing, and I cowered back, gripping the toilet bowl for support as I stared, wide-eyed, at the bathroom door.

I expected them to come for me, to kick the door in—the bolt was nothing—one good boot and the couple of tiny screws would tear away from the cheap wood of the door.

I waited and stared and trembled, but nothing happened.

Nothing.

There was only silence, no more, not even the distant sound of fireworks or the music of a Hallowe'en celebration. Nothing. Nothing at all.

I sat there all night. Unable to sleep, too scared, I sat and stared at the door, waiting for them to come, anything...but, nothing happened.

At some point, I realised I was still clutching my mobile and I checked the time—It was gone ten in the morning. After all those hours, they had to be gone.

I have to admit, my heart was racing as I eased open the bathroom door and stepped out into the hall.

They were gone—and, so was Lindsay.

The door was wide open, but the flat was untouched. I'd expected there to be blood, for the place to be ransacked, but, had the door been shut, it might have been as if nothing had happened.

I tried to find her, of course: I knocked on her door, phoned her, checked with her work, even spoke to the police, but nothing— Lindsay was gone.

Another moonlight flit, people said.

And, that's when I packed up and left, decided to try my luck sleeping on the sofas of friends rather than stay there a day longer. It was no Hallowe'en prank, I knew that, and I had no desire to wait and see if they would return for me, discover who they were and what they wanted.

No, I was gone. I just wish I could have gone further. I can still see the towers of the estate, squatting on the horizon of my life like the memory of a nightmare—a nightmare that might not have reached its end.

Halloween Under the Sea
Nick Manzolillo

March 2018

The beach town flickered orange from the jack o'lanterns posted on every street corner and crouching on every doorstep. The summer crowds had all abandoned Silverport, but local children adorned in costumes took to the streets. From the black waters of the harbor, sisters Polaris and Shaula watched as the children marched to each home with a carved and glowing pumpkin by the front door, rang an electric bell with trembling fingers, and said the three magic words.

'Trick or treat,' Polaris whispered, half swallowing water as she bobbed in the choppy surf. The Autumnal winds were blowing, casting brown leaves into the harbor where they sank, floating gracefully down to the sea floor; Polaris made a habit of gathering them and leaving them by the boat anchors.

'They're dressing like us again,' Shaula said, pouting. Some children had plastic fins along their arms and capes flowing behind them in mockery of mermaid tails. Tails that varied from merperson to merperson in real life. Polaris had fins along her legs; Shaula had a tail. Polaris could occasionally venture onto land, barring she didn't get too far from the water, while Shaula could swim thrice as fast.

Polaris had once ventured on land during the Halloween celebration. She couldn't last out of the water as long as the adults. Weakened and having trouble breathing raw air, she'd stood among the children in their manic frenzy. She'd been in the company of goblins, witches, and people from the TV screens that the humans were always watching (Polaris had caught glimpses of them from the port windows of the boats that took moorings in the harbor).

Intruding during the trick-or-treat ceremonies, kids had stopped to marvel at Polaris. They'd complimented her costume. Parents had reached out to touch her scales. Their human eyes had been wide with wonder. The children dressed as they never could during the summer and all the other days of their short lives. Feeling like the invader that she was, Polaris had fled back to the shore, ready to topple over from exhaustion. She had been a liar among them. She had shown up trick or treating without a costume.

'It's flattery,' Polaris said of the children that imitated them. On land, children thought of the merfolk as just stories. In the caverns, miles offshore where her independent clan lived, Halloween and its celebrations were just another symptom of human excess. Polaris's people failed to see the magic above the surface.

'Humans wish they wouldn't drown. I don't blame them. Sometimes I wish we could last on land,' Shaula mused. The elders would pinch her and tilt her upside down if they heard her uttering such blasphemy.

'There's no coordination on two feet. The air makes your chest feel like it's filled with sand,' Polaris said of her brief adventure. Voices echoed across the harbor. The bars were filled with adults in costume who chose to drink poison instead of fussing over sugary treats. The wind blew low along the water, whistling around the sisters.

'They'll want us back soon,' Shaula said, not quite telling Polaris that they *should* get back. She left it up to Polaris to decide. They'd already gotten in trouble last Halloween.

Last year, a gang of children by the docks had been chasing one

41

lonesome boy around. The gang of five all wore glowing fangs while the boy was dressed like some scaled thing that Polaris wanted to say was one of the serpents bred by the deep sea clans, but to the boy was a fire-breathing beast called a dragon. The boy had fallen off the dock and Shaula had seized the opportunity to play a trick on the mean kids in return. Faster than the boy could come up for air, Shaula had grabbed him and pulled him to the shadowy, metal-filled bottom of the docks.

Shaula was one of Tiamat's blessed and could transplant breath to humans. She wrapped her arms around the struggling boy and planted her lips upon his. As she breathed in, the boy went slack. As if sleeping for just a moment, he startled awake, no longer needing to breathe and capable of seeing underwater with at least a fraction of Polaris's sight. The children on the docks above panicked; the sisters could feel their vibrations as they argued amongst one another over whether the boy in the dragon costume had drowned or not.

The boy had looked up at Shaula in wonder like a fresh-born babe. He was cradled in her arms like one, too, the folds of his costume floating up around him.

The children above left in a panic, some of them in tears. Shaula had played her trick and then the sisters got their treat as they dragged the boy to the far side of the wharf, to a beach where people tied up their rowboats and inflatable motor machines. He didn't struggle as they pulled him along; his eyes wide as he took their world in.

As soon as his head broke the surface, Shaula's gift wore off and the boy was an air breather once more. There, the girls kept him on the rocks, in the dark, as they grilled him with questions one after the other. What is Halloween? Why the costumes and the lanterns? Why do they do it on the cusp of fall, during the night Bella Scaleless haunts the sea?

That last question was the only one the boy didn't have an answer for. As it turned out, the mortals didn't know about Bella Scaleless. It was one legend they'd never been privy to. To Polaris it was proof that there were already Halloween traditions in place beneath the waves; her people had just refused to acknowledge them. This year that would change.

'Let's head back. They'll be looking for us now that the sun has left,' Polaris said but Shaula grabbed her arm.

'Let's bring the lanterns back. They were dumped off the docks again. I saw them this morning,' she said. A few older Silverporters had the tradition of carving jack o'lanterns and dumping them off the docks. The boy had told them it was to appease all those who died at sea.

Ordinarily, lit jack o'lanterns lined the dock posts, to guide the dead home. The boy said there was a rumor that a ghost ship appeared in the harbor on Halloween night, but Polaris had never seen it. Her people did have legends about certain tribes out in the ocean communing with the afterlife. Polaris's people weren't like that, however. They hunted and occasionally paid their respects to Silverport's famous glowing shore. That would change.

Polaris and Shaula swam over to the base of the docks, taking two precisely round pumpkins with grinning faces carved into them. Polaris gripped hers by the eyes as they swam back home.

Mother Altair was waiting for them at the borders of the caverns, a hive of chambers that eroded through a limestone shelf along the ocean floor. Polaris and Shaula saw through the dark as easily as sunlight above the water. Mother Altair paced, swimming back and forth by the entrance until she spotted them. Children among the merfolk were rare; the entire tribe raised them and watched out for them. Octopi that were the length of a forearm slid up around the sisters as they entered the protected zone. The octopi, stealthily lurking among the rocks and seaweed making up the ocean floor, usually followed after the sisters. They'd made a habit of ditching the creatures behind, however. The octopuses were terrible at keeping secrets when questioned.

'Organic matter? Hardly edible, I'd say,' Mother Altair bared her serrated teeth at the two jack o'lanterns.

'We wish to light them, like the mortals do above,' Polaris said and Mother Altair swam above them, laughing and shaking her head.

'Stay put now. Bella Scaleless is nearly upon us, and we must all be accounted for.' The elders of the tribe believed that Bella Scaleless was the great ancestor who came back from the underworld to visit all the tribes and ensure that everyone was healthy and respectful to the gods.

The Silverport boy had told the sisters that Halloween was when the borders between the living and the dead were at their thinnest. Hauntings were at their most common during this time of year, and the tribe failed to see what Bella Scaleless truly was. The entity didn't look at the tribe when she glided past. She didn't care about them. She traveled from one corner of the ocean to the next, crossing through the world of the living on her way back to the sea of the dead. Bella Scaleless was a guide.

Within the caverns, there was a hall of curiosities; artifacts from mankind, both recent and ancient, piled in gleaming stacks that the merfolk occasionally perused through. There was much to learn from inspecting their relics, from colored plates of metal featuring numbers and letters that they stuck on the back of their motor machines to strange, human-like figurines that the land children played with. The most treasured artifacts were those successfully stolen by the merfolk, though in the past few decades, the act has become frowned upon. Polaris and Shaula have a secret spot away from the caverns where they stored their successfully stolen treasures.

The cavern was lit up by glowing moss that the merfolk cultivate. While not needed for sight, the pulsing green, purple, and blue glow relaxed them; Polaris found it helped her sleep easier. When she slept close to the glowing moss, she could remember her dreams more easily.

When nobody was looking, the girls scraped off some of the moss from the limestone walls and placed it within their jack o'lanterns. Instantly, the grinning faces pulsed forth light.

Cradling the jack o'lanterns to their chest, the girls tucked away from the rest of the tribe as they waited for Bella Scaleless to arrive. Octopus surrounded them, curiously prodding at the pumpkins. Pushing through the tentacles, Shaula reached for Polaris's hand. They hadn't discussed their plan, but they knew what the other was thinking. The mysteries would be fewer after this year.

Even with night vision, the water grew darker around Bella Scaleless as she drifted overhead. Her rust-colored hair floated to the end of her tail, fanning out around her like the tatters of a cloak. Beneath the strands of rust there were only bones with fins jutting off at the limbs. Bella Scaleless's tail was a scrawny, twisting thing. Bits of muscle and connecting thread held her bones together. The upper portion of her skull, from the nose up, was a bleached skeleton while her white lips held pale, peeling flesh as if her upper half had once been more human than merperson. Silence fell over the tribe as Bell Scaleless passed. Even the octopi stopped their endless scurrying and playing.

The Halloween entity gazed onward, and just when she became a cloud of rusty hair and a gently flickering skeletal tail, the sisters got up and followed, octopi trailing behind them. The sisters swam with their lanterns held out as if the grinning pumpkin faces were the heads leading their bodies.

Once past the tribe's territory, Bella Scaleless picked up speed, gliding with purpose. Shaula, tucking her lantern to her chest, reached back for Polaris's webbed hand. Holding onto each other, Shaula thrust her tail forward, propelling them after the undead entity.

Just as Shaula began to slow down from exhaustion (though she'd never admit it) Bella Scaleless came to a sudden stop. Shaula squealed, pulling Polaris around the specter, terrified of crashing into her. Touching Bella Scaleless seemed deadlier than touching silver.

Bella Scaleless stared down over the side of a drop in the sea floor. A crater stretched out before them and Polaris couldn't see to the other side. Below them was an impenetrable darkness. Even if the sunlight were to miraculously grace the sea at this hour, its rays would have been beaten back by the cluttered dark.

Thinking back on that moment, where Bella Scaleless stared down into the abyss, her dead lips firmly pressed together, Polaris would realize that the entity they'd followed hesitated. For just a few seconds, it was afraid.

Bella Scaleless tilted over the side of the chasm and the black below. Shaula pulled Polaris over to the edge but didn't dive down. They merely watched as the specter slowly descended until she was consumed by the black.

'We've followed her this far,' Polaris said but her sister was hesitant.

'This lantern's too much to carry. I want both my hands ready,' Shaula said, swimming down to the edge of the chasm and placing the glowing jack o'lantern down. Its violet light beamed over the chasm, a lonesome, pumpkin lighthouse lording above the dark. Satisfied, Shaula took Polaris's hand before they descended into the deep.

Bella Scaleless was lost in the inky black that seemed to stick to their scales and fingertips. The lantern against Polaris's chest beamed yellow, providing just a few feet of light to illuminate the two sisters.

'Is this it?' Polaris asked. 'Is this where the dead return?' They hadn't swum *that* far away from the tribal grounds. No scouts or passing merfolk from the other colonies and tribes had ever mentioned the chasm. The true, deepest depths of the ocean were hundreds of miles from the American coast. Perhaps the chasm only appeared during All Hollow's Eve?

'Will we meet the old Queen Ran of Silverport Harbor? Do you think?' Shaula asked, excited and jittery, pulling Polaris along until the starlit sea above was no more.

'She died on land. I don't think all the dead come back on Halloween. Remember, the town boy said it wasn't just the dead that come. The monsters they dress as weren't people or merfolk to begin with.'

'If they think of us as make-believe, then who to say the goblins and horned things are not out there, living as we do?' Shaula asked. 'Perhaps the land holds secrets even from the mortals.'

'Then all we need is proof down here,' Polaris said. Proof that Halloween was just as important in the sea as it was on land. She wasn't exactly sure what would count as proof, though. Mother Altair and the other elders were set in their ways. They honored the season by watching Bella Scaleless, and no more. Polaris wanted more for their tradition than one pale specter.

Clicking noises echoed through the oily black. Shaula brushed closer to Polaris. They gathered over the lantern like the humans did with their fires along the beach. Polaris wished the fungus gave off as much heat as it did light. The cold rolled over them in waves, as if they were being pushed further and further down the gullet of the shadows around them.

Out of nowhere, Bella Scaleless floated within an inch of the sisters; the bottom of her tail fin equal with theirs while she stretched out nearly eight feet, towering above them. Her rusty hair formed a

46

semi-circle around the living mermaids. Finally, Bella Scaleless showed signs of consciousness. She looked down at them with hollowed-out, sightless eyes.

Clicking popped from all around the sisters. Bella Scaleless wasn't the threat. The black of the abyss was; the other world hadn't been prepared for them. Polaris held her lantern tighter.

'We should go,' Shaula said, but they'd come too far. No other merfolk knew of the otherworld, or dared to tell legends of it.

A scythe slowly swept into the lantern's light. The scythe was a fin glistening with sharp spines, and as that fin stretched out of the glow, the face of a shark emerged. The lips of its jaw rotted; every other tooth in its gaping mouth missing, like Shaula's jack o'lantern that she'd left above. The scythe shark floated beside Bella Scaleless, and the darkness around them was too thick. They were surrounded without realizing it.

Another entity lurked behind the sisters. A humanoid figure with arms, legs and a neck that trailed out from the snake-like body stretched from behind the sisters. The mutant humanoid resembled a brittle star, its body had hips and a chest, its head was lost at the end of its preposterously long limbs. In the shadows, the mutant brittle star likely cut off all escape.

Lastly, something made of seaweed with the flexibility of an octopus emerged from below them. Eyeballs, not unlike those of man, opened and closed along its body that seemed to fold and unfold within itself; a less sophisticated jellyfish.

'Most curious for children to follow the prophet of rot,' the monstrosity of seaweed spoke. Its body was purple and oily black, blending into the shadow around them. Maybe the abyss was all this thing; all of the shadows could very well have been a part of its body. Polaris knew of many strange and rare beasts of the sea that were both allies and enemies to the merfolk; these things were new. The dead held secrets.

'We wished to greet you while our worlds are joined,' Polaris said, picking one of the thing's eyes to stare into while she spoke. The scythe shark hovered close to Shaula, its mouth open, its body in a state of perpetual lunge.

'I'm always joined with your world, daughter of Tiamat. It is only now that you may fall into mine.'

'The humans above honor their dead, and your world and all the spirits of the lost. We wish for our people to do the same.'

'The humans above are food,' the lord of rot seemed to snicker. It's voice echoed within their heads.

'We want to convince our people to honor you and your world. That is all.' Polaris turned the pumpkin to face the rotting thing.

'We sent you Bella Scaleless, yet you came. She was like you once. A young thing curious about Samhain. One who longed to breach the hallowed realm and honor those who have become one with the brine. Centuries later, we're still playing with her corpse.'

Bella Scaleless lunged toward the sisters, her jaw opening and closing as if she were a figurine that Polaris stole from the shore decades ago as a child.

Despite flinching, Polaris held Shaula close to her and kept the pumpkin trained on the one below. 'We don't wish for anything from you. If you keep the dead, then keep them as you were. We only wish to honor thee.'

'Honor? With one lantern? A single lantern is more than Bella brought, but do you not see all this dark? Why come at all with only one lantern? You mock our realm.'

Polaris, as a natural-born mermaid, was keen on the art of bargaining and trickery. Even the sharks, the real, living sharks, could be bargained with. For every problem, there was a solution, and for the merfolk, that solution was often a trick. When it came to trick or treat, Polaris considered herself an expert in the former.

The problem was that the abyss had no patience for clever mermaids.

The scythe shark finally closed its mouth, taking half of Shaula's body in the process.

The weight clinging to Polaris lightened; red tinged the glow of the lantern. The rotted one's laughter echoed around her, coming from every direction.

'You honor us with your flesh. You worship us with your lives. We are the jaw that waits to close for eons.' The lord of rot cackled, and Polaris did her best to escape.

She swam up, opposite the rot, opposite the hive mind twitching and pulling at everything around them. Her last glimpse of the shark was of it taking another bite from Shaula's remnant.

A serpent-wide trunk appeared in the pumpkin's glow, and a limb filled with prickly, urchin spines swung toward her. Polaris lifted the lantern as a shield, and the brittle star abomination's limb jerked back. Burned, but not stopped. Polaris pushed upward, knowing with all her heart the direction of the surface, of the air.

Another limb rose up, and this time, it was the brittle star's head, dozens of proboscises opening and closing, filled with needle teeth. It lunged forward, the lantern pushing it back from attacking Polaris's chest. Her flailing, finned ankle kicked into one of the teeth-filled tubes, the pain shocking throughout her entire body, practically exploding out of her head. Polaris angled the lantern down in time to reveal Bella Scaleless's bone face. In the full glow of the lantern's light, her lips twitched. For the briefest moment, there was a mournful smile. The undead mermaid held the brittle star abomination at bay. Her skeletal fingers dug into the center of the thing's proboscis-filled face, its teeth sucking at her bare bone, and that was the last Polaris saw of her.

Bursting out of the crack in the earth, Polaris was bathed in the light of the lantern left by the mouth of the pit. If Shaula had taken it, would she have survived? With her injured foot, Polaris kicked the jack o'lantern into the pit before swimming back to her the tribe. From behind her, she heard shrill squeals of pain. When she dared to look over her shoulder, the roving blackness of the abyss was following her.

The darkness swept away the starlight behind Polaris, but it moved slowly. Eventually, she lost track of it, but she could feel its presence following her. Was it as drawn to the pumpkin's light as it was repelled by it?

Mother Altair and the elders were waiting for Polaris when she returned. Arms crossed and adorned in coral armor, for a moment Polaris wondered if they were more of a threat to her than the abyss. Shaula's death finally seemed real. In an instant, the scythe shark had bitten away the side of her that Polaris had curled against, held, and gone on adventures with her whole life.

'We were moments away from sending out our scouting party on the night of Bella Scaleless,' Mother Altair shook her head.

'It is not Bella Scaleless's night. It is Halloween, and I,' Polaris looked over her shoulder. The star-eating mass of shadow was in the distance across the ocean floor. 'I have made a terrible mistake, but it is not too late. There's a way,' Polaris looked at the glowing jack o'lantern in her hands. The ones at the dock in Silverport were too far away. There was an abundance of glowing fungus in the caverns, however. Treasure, too. Treats of a more significant sort.

As quickly as she could, Polaris explained the threat approaching them. Approximately half the elders sneered at her. She was a child. She wasn't fit to inform them of something they and their centuries hadn't already learned about.

'Shaula's dead. Devoured,' Polaris said, but they still didn't believe her. With all great change came the death of those who refused to adapt. Polaris swam toward the caverns while the roving abyss of rot and empty stomach pushed closer, taking the starlight with it. Mother Altair, surprisingly, followed her.

'What have you done, youngling? What have you awoken?'

'I have awoken something that has always wanted us. That has always been a threat,' Polaris came to these realizations as she said them. She wasn't wrong, no. She was the hero of Halloween, but her people hadn't realized it yet. 'We can right an ancient wrong, and we can start a new tradition, Mother. That's what we will accomplish. All will be well, you'll see.'

Polaris grabbed heaping handfuls of the closest fungus she could find within the mouth of the cavern, not ready to venture further. The glow alone wouldn't stop what was coming.

Other merfolk came to investigate the commotion, and Polaris filled them in on her revelation. Many were wide awake and ready to help, believing Mother Altair's desperation, if not Polaris's own. More merfolk flocked into the cavern, having been convinced the star-eating blackness was a danger to them all. The same elders who had warned Polaris were now terrified. She passed the only true jack o'lantern she had to one of the men, ordering him to set it at the mouth of the cavern. With a little luck, it would give all those who took shelter with her time to prepare.

'Gathering the glow!' Polaris wailed, leading her tide of new followers to the collection chambers. Within were rare giant clams, the sort used to conceal a mermaid's body when they were killed (old age was hardly a threat to their immortal scales). The shell couldn't be cracked and carved like a gourd, but it could be filled with light and painted with a jack o'lantern's same wickedness.

Polaris spread the word; whether it was with seaweed, mud, or squid ink, she commanded that all the giant clams were to be decorated. Human skulls and skulls belonging to land animals such as deer, rodents and birds were scattered along the collection chamber and Polaris decided to fill those hollow things with the glowing fungus too.

Merfolk then adorned themselves in the clothing that had been dragged into the chamber of the centuries, pieces of armor and diving gear, coral and other aquatic armor worn by other merfolk tribes from around the world that had once upon a time come to barter and trade. The collection chamber became alive with last-minute festivities, and while the merfolk moved with twitchy nervousness, Polaris could tell they liked what they were doing. It was eccentric and bizarre, more artful but less soulful than their singing or weaving could ever be.

Amid this new ritual, there came screams from the elders who had refused to flee into the cavern. Their coral armor and spears were nothing against the abyss. Their deaths weren't as quick as Shaula's.

'They're here!' Polaris announced, and despite all she'd seen and escaped from, her fear was the first to subside.

Polaris led her former elders through the surface tunnel. She held a glowing deer skull in one hand and a medium sized clam carved with a sardonic grin in the other. She wore a piece of orange plastic that the human fishermen called a hardhat. Severed octopus tentacles floated by the mouth of the cave. The first jack o'lantern that she had placed held strong.

Behind Polaris rose a group of merfolk wielding skulls and clams, looking more like humans or one of the warring tribes than their humble selves. Polaris couldn't help but smile as she faced the amorphous lord of rot, who billowed on the other side of the lantern, his blackness filling the entrance to their secluded caverns.

'I've brought you the respect you deserve,' Polaris said, reaching forward with her two lanterns.

'You act only out of fear and self-preservation,' the rotted one hissed. However, it moved back ever so slightly from the new glow of the makeshift lanterns.

'Both play a part of reverence, do they not?' Polaris said. She was no longer a child; she felt it the moment she grew up. The merfolk behind her witnessed it, too. She only wished Shaula could be there with her.

The abyss laughed, its voice echoing in all their minds. 'We know your home now. We've been brought to taste your thoughts and fears. Now that you've begun your worship, you will suffer if you do not continue. No matter where you move to. All the oceans are ours. The land is no barrier. We will return. We will come to be appeased.'

Without responding, Polaris set the clam and the deer skull down, then reached behind her to take two more clams from Mother Altair.

'Then let this be our new tradition,' Polaris moved past the original jack o'lantern and offered the lord of rot the two clam lanterns. The seaweed thing sank back into the shadows, only for Bella Scaleless to reappear. Her lips had been torn away. She was all bone now. She took one of the glowing and painted clams and turned away, flowing back down the cavern, the darkness receding with her, mopped up by her flowing, red hair.

Polaris led her people from the caverns; together, they watched the shadows depart. Soon, the starlight trickled back down over the ocean floor. The lanterns were then set around the tribal grounds, roving out to the very borders of their land.

From troublemaker to hero, Polaris found herself shunned. The merfolk stopped looking at her. The elders began to speak openly of exiling her. She hadn't gotten what she wanted, but there would be a tradition now. For centuries, her tribe and perhaps many of the others would celebrate Halloween, and the merfolk who hadn't lost someone as dear as their own sister would ever enjoy it.

Nothing was left of the dead merfolk who had met their fates that night, and there would be no sight of them. Not for another year, at least.

Perhaps next year, Bella Scaleless will be joined by Shaula. Perhaps Polaris will swim after them and leave her lantern behind.

Hauntology
Matthew R. Davis

Like many people her age, eighteen-year-old Poppy Piper had developed a deep interest in dead things. In her case, this didn't extend to anything so morbid as corpses—the bodies in her beloved horror movies didn't count, as they were either warm props or cool prosthetics—but rather to more abstract fields: fashions and trends, bands and genres, times and places. It was hardly surprising, then, that she and Kirsten would choose to spend so much time at the Crosstown Mall, since the old plaza was slowly rotting from the inside out.

The Crosstown suffered from a syndrome that afflicted many malls around the world—retail habits had changed, big box stores had come of age and moved out, and the old shopping precincts were ailing. Poppy remembered the way this place had looked to her ten years ago, walkways bustling with life and outlets seething with trade; she regarded it now with adult eyes and saw that even back then it had been on a slow but steady decline, a drawn-out death that crept closer by the year. It was sad, but if anything, this increasingly obvious decay only made the mall more appealing.

'At least someone's getting into the spirit of things,' Kirsten said this morning as they began their first circuit of the galleria, pointing out the mani-pedi salon's display window filled with black-nailed hands and fake cobweb. Another Friday, nothing to thank gods for since their casual jobs involved as much weekend work as not...but it was also Halloween, and such days felt gravid with potential. Perhaps that was why Kirsten had arrived at Poppy's house earlier than usual, sending a voice message from outside—*shake a leg, sleepyhead. I'm hungry. I love you*—and visibly twitching with impatience by the time her best friend opened the front door to her.

'You know what they should do?' Poppy prompted. 'Halloween tours! Like, close all the shops, dim the lights, and lead people around in a candlelit procession, telling tales from the mall's past.'

'Love it, but...*what* tales? Are they going to talk about the time some kid pissed himself in David Jones?'

'There must be heaps to tell,' Poppy insisted. 'Forty years of history? Thousands of messy, hungry lives passing through every week? People would have *died* here! Any place that's had so many people in it, there would be stories.'

Kirsten conceded the point with a shrug. 'Look at the place, Pops. I wouldn't be surprised if people were *still* dying here.'

The Crosstown Mall was laid out in a long, straight line, allowing visitors to complete a lap from any entry point and experience everything the place had to offer. Once, this had been an impressive sight—Poppy had seen photo prints from her mother's teenage years in the mid-1990s, the polished terrazzo-tile floors gleaming white as mallrat teeth bared in smiles of youthful happiness, the potted palms a vibrant green that distracted from their fraudulence, the skylights shining with all the promise of a bright future. Now the walkways were dulled by the passage of long years and countless feet, the fake plastic foliage yellowed by the critical gaze of the sun through casements always cataracted with dirt. Fully half the shopfronts were vacant and closed off behind stained shutters, where once had thrived music stores and sports emporiums and bookshops and video arcades. These days, the mall's reduced profile boasted such highlights as a jewellers two years into their closing-down sale, a hairdresser whose clientele had aged as badly as its location, and a newsagent whose balding shelves admitted that it sold more lotto tickets than magazines.

Poppy and Kirsten walked by a window of fashion-savvy but faceless mannequins posing with plastic pumpkins that grinned on their behalf, passed the old, black-curtained photo booth that never seemed to be working. Both wore headphones as if taking self-guided tours; in fact, they were quietly listening to playlists of vaporwave tracks built on anonymous muzak or pitch-shifted songs stolen from the 1980s. They found this a more apt soundtrack to the mall experience than the superannuated hits stations playing instore, and the fact that vaporwave itself was regarded as a dead genre—defiantly underground and plunderphonic, its ironic independence had been appropriated and absorbed by the industry years ago—only added to the pleasantly downbeat vibe.

'I love the smell of commerce in the morning,' quoth Kirsten over the low hum of Poppy's headphones. 'And breakfast.'

'Food court?'

'Duh. You wouldn't like me when I'm hangry.'

Poppy liked her a lot better than the other customers she saw on their walk: a tracksuited couple with curls of ink crowding sour faces, pushing a pram as though it were freighted with responsibilities they'd never wanted; a pair of dour women whose morbid obesity had rendered their age unguessable and their gait a kind of orbital perambulation; a grim Indian couple bearing full plastic bags like unwanted burdens, the happy chatter of their two patka-clad boys making no impression whatsoever. Their presence here seemed merely routine, hollow as an empty stomach and habitual as filling it. Poppy found it odd that some people chose to cling to company that brought them no joy—she had known Kirsten Pfeiffer for ten years, their alphabetical proximity pushing them together in primary school, and their bond showed no signs of becoming boring.

She nudged her best friend, sent her a just-because smile that was immediately returned. During high school, Kirsten had leaned into what she saw as her inescapable frumpiness and adopted the adorable aspect of a 1970s academic—A-line skirts, floral blouses, glasses on a chain and all—though her rosy Gen-Z youth lent the look a modestly sexy edge. Poppy had followed the alt-girl route,

55

brushing against goth and punk aesthetics with her clothes—today, Mum's thirty-year-old Bikini Kill t-shirt and a buckled black miniskirt—and whatever tiny tattoos she could afford for her ears and hands. In a post-everything era, fashion was fusion; they might have been amalgams of a thousand young women absorbed by the mall's long memory.

Led by Kirsten's grumbling stomach, they reached the centre of the arcade, where old and often immobile escalators funnelled traffic down into the basement. The downstairs food court had suffered as many losses as the level above; the big fast-food names had migrated outward, leaving a shabby Subway outlet as the only franchise amongst a brace of places selling Turkish, Thai, Chinese, Japanese, and Greek cuisine. Poppy matched Kirsten's orders of a vegetable pide and strawberry boba bubble tea, and then they wandered wordlessly toward the long-closed Crosstown Cafeteria.

The mouth of the mall's inhouse café was shuttered, the windows that comprised the upper half of its walls scratched and dirty. Through that glass could be seen the dim interior, stripped of tables and kitchen and reduced to a dusty void scattered with stacks of unneeded shelving and rubbish left by the removal crew; evidently the room was also used as storage by clothing stores extant or otherwise, for a half-dozen human-shaped figures could be spotted in the shadows by the back wall, still dressed for display and forever frozen in imploring poses. The bottom half of the café wall was panelled with bland promotional images that had accompanied the Crosstown's advertising campaigns around the time of Poppy's birth, beautiful young people of diverse ethnicity drawn together to fake laughter for the camera, captioned with meaningless slogans like F R I E N D S T O G E T H E R and T A S T E L I F E. These had fallen victim to vandalism, slapped with cryptic stickers and carved with blunt blades and inked with crass tags…but one panel always stood out to Poppy and Kirsten.

This grinning young woman was a standard advertising model—teeth inhumanly white, hair luminously blonde, skin suspiciously clear—a human Photoshopped to the point of uncanny blandness, headphones slung around her neck as shorthand for youthful cool. Whatever lay behind her was reduced to blurry bokeh globes of multi-coloured light by the camera's focus on her face. But what

Poppy and Kirsten found morbidly fascinating was her post-closure fate, her advertising afterlife: the woman's eyes had been furiously scratched out by vandals, rendering her smile an eerie leer, and her printed skin was faded and cracked by years of neglect. Waxing sinister, the slogan alongside her was a single ominous word.

H U N G R Y ?

'Thanks for asking, but I'm good,' Kirsten said, raising her paper-bagged pide in salute. Poppy had once photographed her standing in front of this defaced panel as she munched on a sushi crunchy roll, the question mark of the phrase cut off by the edge of the frame— she'd liked the image enough to post it on her socials, but it felt strangely disrespectful, allowing her friend to replace the advertisement's occupant like that. Kirsten had nodded knowingly when she'd expressed this. Kindred spirits required no explanations.

Turning away from the derelict cafeteria and its eyeless eidolon, Poppy and Kirsten returned to the escalator. The upward stairs had broken down yet again, so they ascended its still steps to the ground level and recommenced their aimless amble.

'Being here makes me want to watch *Dawn of the Dead*,' Kirsten remarked between slurps of bubble tea. 'The OG, not the remake.'

'You say that every time,' Poppy pointed out. 'That, or *Chopping Mall*, or *The Initiation*. But for real, I thought about doing a *Dawn* cosplay if we went out tonight.'

'You mean a zombie?'

'Fuck that, I mean Gaylen Ross.'

Kirsten cast her a speculative glance. 'Okay, I can see it. You'd need feathered bangs, though.'

'Right? And where am I going to find a powder-blue turtleneck on my budget?'

'Maybe next Halloween, Pops.' Kirsten's eyes flickered away from hers, fixed on something beyond. 'Hey, wow. Is that thing finally *working*?'

Poppy turned to see that she meant the old photo booth. Barely bigger than a toilet cubicle, it had loitered near the centre of the mall for years, its black velvet curtain always pulled across, its name panel forever obscured by a laminated OUT OF ORDER sign—but today, the drape was drawn back a couple of inches in invitation, and the panel was free to show its face. CROSSTOWN MALL PHOTO

CAPTURE, it said.

'Popsicle, you *know* we have to do this.'

'Oh, totally.'

They squeezed into the confined space and Poppy pulled the curtain to behind them. On their right, a square screen sat below a lens labelled LOOK HERE and above two slots, one for vending photos and the other for reading a credit card, with a brief list of instructions alongside. To their left, another sheet of velvet hung on the wall as a backdrop, this one the deep crimson of a theatre drape. The booth smelled of stale breath and might well have been sitting here before either woman was born.

Poppy sighed. 'Not very flash, is it?'

'Yeah, but look.' Kirsten pointed to the screen, which read 1 CREDIT—TOUCH TO START. 'Our lucky day!'

'Maybe it's not actually fixed, then.'

Kirsten shrugged and touched the screen, summoning up a familiar icon: the Crosstown Mall logo, a cursive M overlaid with a cursive C, all drawn in a single connected line—it always reminded Poppy of the occult, Kirsten of the embroidery on a private school blazer. It was soon replaced by a single word: H A P P Y ?

'None of your business,' Poppy quipped, squeezing Kirsten's hand, 'but yes.'

'Aw, babe.'

The screen now showed the women themselves, caught within a red viewfinder border as if cut off from the world without, and they examined themselves critically as a countdown began.

'3'…'2'…'1'…'CHEESE!'

'Cheese!' they cried, lifting their fingers to add sarcastic air-quotes in mockery of the programme's excessive punctuation. They ran through a quick array of faces as the camera flashed and whirred four times, then collapsed laughing at the ridiculousness of it all.

THANK YOU! PRINTING NOW.

The booth hummed like a dial tone for perhaps thirty seconds, then spat out a four-panel strip of photographic paper. They laughed and sighed over the images like they were distant childhood memories, missives from the deep past of one minute ago.

'Two each,' Kirsten said, 'and if I don't see these in your phone case, we're through.'

'So drastic. Anyway, I need to wee.'

Poppy led them to the nearest public toilets. When she emerged, Kirsten was frowning down at the strip of photos that had so amused her just minutes before.

'What's with the face?'

'Look at these again and tell me if you see anything weird.'

Poppy took the pictures and stared as requested. 'Like what? You're looking snatched as, if that's what you mean.'

'Look behind me.'

As soon as she shifted her focus to the backdrop, Poppy saw what was bothering her friend. In each of the four shots, Kirsten was outlined by a bulging impression in the red velvet. As though someone were standing behind the curtain, close enough to press against her back.

'I don't get it.'

'Me either. You know what it reminds me of?' Kirsten turned her phone to display her research. 'Hidden mother photos. In the 1800s, cameras had wack exposure times. The only way to keep a baby still for photos was for their mother to hold them—but she'd be covered with a blanket or something, so she looked like part of the scenery.'

Poppy frowned. 'I don't think that's your mum, babe.'

'No shit. We were alone, yeah? So why does it look like someone was standing *right behind me*?'

'That's spooky. Did you feel anything?'

'Just hungry.'

Poppy clicked her fingers, excited. 'Oh, wait—I've got a better question. Why is the selfie booth finally working *today*, of all days?'

Kirsten's eyebrows shot up above her glasses. 'You think it's a prank?'

'A hidden figure in an old photo booth, on Halloween? What else could it be?'

'And that's why it was free! Popsicle, you're a genius. Let's go check.'

The return trip to the photo booth took less than a minute. Poppy was half-expecting to find other customers inside, but the cubicle, like the escalator, had returned to its natural state of inertia. The laminated OUT OF ORDER sign hung in its usual spot, smug as any authority.

'What, we broke it?' Poppy said. 'That was quick.'

'That's mad sus.' Kirsten slapped the back wall, her brow furrowed. 'No way through. And we would've noticed if someone was already inside.'

'Unless they were really, really thin. Like, skeletal.'

Kirsten shuddered. 'Not helping, babe.'

Poppy jerked the black curtain back, keen to punish someone for provoking her friend's anxiety. The booth was empty, but when she looked at the red backdrop, she could see the faint impression of what looked like a body on the left side, as though its outline had stained the material. Was that all they'd seen?

'Peekaboo,' she said, and drew the curtain aside fast like a horror movie heroine. Kirsten gasped the way she always did at jump scares.

'What's *she* doing here?'

The woman on the wall grinned back at them, her face as familiar as her scratched-out eyes. The same model from the abandoned cafeteria downstairs—the very same panel, even. Poppy was queasily certain that if she browsed her phone's gallery for a photo of the original, this image would match it perfectly, right down to the rough strokes of the vandalism that had blinded her.

'Okay, that's *weird*,' said Kirsten. She pulled back the other side of the drape and found what they expected: the same word from the basement, only the booth's cramped space meant the question mark was cropped out. 'Why is this here? How can it be exactly the same?'

'Part of the prank?' Poppy suggested, somewhat feebly.

'How does *that* make sense? No one's that subtle.' Kirsten touched the faint outline, unconvinced. 'What's going on here? It really looked like something was behind me, Pops. *Touching* me.'

'I know. Don't hate me, but…haunted photo booth?'

'Ha.' Kirsten didn't sound amused. 'Well, like you said—so much has happened in this place. Maybe the whole fuckin' mall is haunted.'

Unsettled, they left the cubicle and resumed their slow circuit of the galleria. Occasionally they deigned to enter a shop and browse, but it didn't feel the same now—some fundamental certainty had been undermined by the wrong kind of weird. Kirsten let her glasses hang on their chain as she repeatedly polished their lenses, an action Poppy recognised as a nervous tic, and noon wasn't long past before she turned to voice her unease.

'I'm just not vibing today, Pops. I might head off a bit early.'

'I feel you. I've got to get ready for work soon, anyway.'

As they left the cavernous belly of the Crosstown Mall, a weight lifted from Poppy's soul. Since that strangeness with the photo booth, the atmosphere of the place had hung heavily upon her, a sick old leech glutting itself on her good mood. They caught a bus to the end of her street, and there they hugged goodbye.

'I know we talked about going out tonight,' Kirsten said, 'but I could really do with something low-key.'

'Sure. Want to hang out at mine and binge chocolate and old horror movies?'

'Elite! See you after nine, babes.'

Poppy headed home and passed a few minutes with her mother, who was going out for dinner and a spooky movie with friends she'd known since her own mall-punk years. She wanted to ask about her mum's experience of the Crosstown back when it was clean and vital, but she didn't know how to start that conversation or explain why it was necessary. She imagined that grinning blonde model unmarked and clear-eyed, wondered if she'd been less H U N G R Y back when the cafeteria was open, and shook it off.

After a snack and a shower, she changed into a branded t-shirt with black slacks and redid her makeup more modestly for her server job at Gimme the Schnitz. Then came another bus trip, headphones on as she watched the streets stream by. Not wanting to be reminded of the mall, she listened to the Samhain-themed playlist she'd put together with Kirsten: *You Make Me Feel Like It's Halloween* and *(Every Day is) Halloween*, *Bury a Friend* and Carpenter's classic theme, *Zombi* by Goblin, and all sorts of spooky delights that nevertheless failed to raise her saturnine spirits.

Poppy disembarked at the bus stop nearest her work and trudged along the footpath, trying not to think about the day's events. Close by the restaurant was a long-defunct pub, its front wall coated in overlapping layers of posters that advertised long-past tours, events, and Fringe shows—she'd always had an archaeological interest in the strata of paper that peeled and tore away to reveal pieces of a deeper past, had always wondered at the nature of the mural beneath that sometimes showed through when gaps opened in that weathered hide. She cast it a glance from across the road as she passed, then paused and pulled the phones from her head, disconcerted. Was she mistaken, or was there an eye peering at her from between two fraying one-sheets? If so, perhaps it had been vandalised before being covered, because it looked like it had been sprayed over with messy swipes of paint. And so did the other eye, now visible through a ragged hole torn through the many skins of faded tour posters.

Poppy bit her lip and squinted, trying to bring the bigger picture into focus. From where she was standing, she got the nastiest feeling that those eyes weren't sprayed over but scratched out. She thought she could even see the bokeh blurs of out-of-focus lights through holes and gaps in the poster palimpsest, and was that the letters H and U?

'No, no,' she muttered to herself, 'we are not doing this,' and she hurried on down the footpath to Gimme the Schnitz. By the time she began work at three-thirty, she'd convinced herself that her mind was simply getting carried away with strange associations. Perhaps it was an old advertising panel, not a mural, that had been lurking beneath that poster patchwork all those years.

The next five hours passed quickly, with little time for Poppy to think about anything other than which order went to which table. She occasionally spied cadres of children passing by on the footpath outside, all dressed up for trick-or-treating—a pint-sized witch, a clutch of *Pokémon* zombies, a vampiric Chappell Roan—and longed for days when she'd been young enough to do the same; so strange, to feel this old and nostalgic at the age of eighteen. She amused herself with the thought of throwing on a white sheet and joining those groups of kids, hanging around silently until they noticed she was there and freaked out. But then she remembered how she'd imagined that eyeless model following her out of the mall and all the way to work, and the notion grew chilly in her mind.

Clocking out at eight-thirty, Poppy bid farewell to her workmates and began her trek back to the bus stop. With strange ruminations fresh in her mind, she paused over the road from the pub wall and steeled herself for a sight she didn't want to believe. The eyes were still there, along with those other details that may or may not have been what she feared they were, but now that she was paying closer attention, they didn't look quite as she remembered. Perhaps it was because night was falling, but beneath the paint—or scratches—the shape of the eyes looked different...still familiar, but not what she remembered from the Crosstown Cafeteria. Maybe the hidden picture was a mural after all, just some other woman's face, with Poppy's paranoid pareidolia filling in the gaps and stretching red thread between pins that shouldn't be connected to create an image that was not there. Easier to believe that than to contemplate being stalked by a decades-old advertising photo from a defunct eatery.

Poppy took a photo, shot it to her best friend with a query: *I'm just seeing things right? Nothing looking back at me rn???* Kirsten hadn't sent anything since they'd parted in the afternoon, and the last entry in their chat was her voice message from that morning. Trying to think of anything other than the unthinkable, Poppy hurried on to her stop. It didn't help that the Hungry Jack's restaurant across the street from the bus shelter wore its name above the door in red neon and the second word had blacked out.

At home, with her mother out for a livelier Halloween than she was likely to enjoy tonight, Poppy changed into a Deafheaven shirt and that afternoon's skirt over pumpkin-orange leggings, then padded barefoot to the kitchen. Meat was off the menu after serving schnitzels all evening, so she cast a randomised playlist through the Bluetooth speaker atop the fridge as she fixed herself a veggie sandwich. She sat at the counter and browsed her phone as she ate, noting that Kirsten hadn't even read her previous message. Maybe she didn't want to be reminded of the mall, either—but it was bound to come up in conversation when she arrived, and she would be here any minute.

The first song on Poppy's playlist was an old Billie Eilish banger; the second caught her attention by being completely alien, yet somehow familiar. Little more than a camera-click beat backed by a dial-tone drone, it showcased a slowed-down and reverb-soaked vocal typical of vaporwave. Poppy nibbled her dinner as she tried to place it, but it was only when she focused on the pitch-shifted moan of the lyric that she finally understood just what she was hearing.

'*Ssshhhaaakkkeee aaa llleeeggg, sssllleeepppyyyhhheeeaaaddd… III'mmm hhhuuunnnggggrrryyy, III llloooovvveee yyyooouuu…*'

Her half-chewed crust fell from nerveless fingers. A sudden vertiginous sensation as though the walls were closing in and falling away at the same time—life's camera doing a dolly zoom on her stunned face as the horror movie fan realised that she was now *in* one—

'No,' Poppy said. A stupid line, but she had no script to consult for this. Grasping at simple explanations, she checked to see if Kirsten had hacked her Bluetooth to prank her with that mutated voice message. According to her streaming account, the artist was [untitled] and the track was called H U N G R Y.

'Oh, bullshit!' she snapped, panicked. 'Come on!'

She hit STOP on her phone and the speaker fell silent. Almost at once, her doorbell chimed like the announcement tone on a shopping mall PA.

'I *knew* it!' The timing was too perfect to be anything but an elaborate Halloween trick. 'You sneaky wench!'

Laughing off her chills, Poppy skipped to the front hallway. She took a deep breath to look totally unfazed, like she hadn't bought this caper for even a second, then opened the door. Sure enough, Kirsten stood grinning on the other side.

'You think you're so...'

Poppy trailed off, her relief turning cold.

Kirsten was frozen in a silly pose, two fingers on either hand forming air-quotes as though she were a hippie throwing peace signs. Poppy recognised it from the photo booth shoot that afternoon, but what had once been goofy now struck dread into her heart—this display was *too* identical. Her best friend was so unnaturally still that it might have been a photographic blow-up of Kirsten Pfeiffer standing there...and when she hit upon that thought, Poppy understood it was truer than she ever could have believed possible. Kirsten looked as though she'd been badly Photoshopped into this scene, two-dimensional against a 3D backdrop, and the sight was so uncanny that Poppy tried to believe she'd dozed off at the counter and fallen headfirst into a nightmare. But this vision was too pervasive—too lucidly unreal.

Then Kirsten's image blanched paler as if suddenly sun-faded, and her edges split and creased beneath the compressed effects of time-lapsed decades, and some unseen force scratched out her eyes to leave only the scribbled fury of its passing. The lights on lampposts and in loungerooms beyond her went out of focus and became hovering bokeh globes. And six letters appeared in the air beside her, stamped upon reality like a surreal subtitle, their font and kerning so familiar that this felt like a thing that was always going to happen.

H U N G R Y

Poppy screamed at the thing her friend had become and slammed the front door. Backing into the kitchen, she shrieked again when the Bluetooth speaker burst into life, playing that same eerie anti-melody.

'III'mmm hhhuuunnngggrrryyy…'

The front door aged before her eyes, the wood weakening as black streaks of graffiti spread across it, and then the pitted brass doorknob fell off and the whole panel swung in to dangle from one precarious hinge and Kirsten stood there, smile too wide and teeth too white, her dear eyes scratched out and her fingers now looking less like air-quotes and more like hooked talons. She didn't move, *couldn't* move, but somehow throbbed and swelled closer and closer, over the threshold and into the house.

Poppy backed away until she hit the counter and then scrambled along it to the edge, made a desperate dash for the back door. She was almost there, her hand reaching for the knob, when it underwent the same transformation as the front entrance. Tags broke out on panels like an inky rash, wood discoloured and split as if subjected to hundreds of seasons in a single second, but Poppy was already turning the handle. It fell apart in her fingers as the door dropped away, and she was through—

But it was not a single step and cool grass that met her on the other side, and no backyard moonlight shone down upon her. Her bare feet rasped on a dusty tiled floor, the only illumination a cold fluorescence creeping through the slats of a closed shutter and the dirty glass of a half-windowed wall. Poppy's terrified gasp echoed through the dim, vacant space as she realised where she was, if not how she'd come. She stood within the long-closed cafeteria in the basement of the Crosstown Mall.

The atmosphere hung heavy and hungry upon her as she turned to find herself amongst the frozen figures she and Kirsten had spied from outside. This close, she realised they were not mannequins at all, nor were their clothes leftovers from shut-down stores. They were just as bleached of any colour or features, but the poses they struck reaching for the shutter would not have been possible for the fixed joints of shop dummies. And the nearest of them was so familiar that Poppy's heart caught in her throat, choking a scream at the sight of its floral blouse and the glasses that dangled on a chain over its still chest.

The air felt thick as dusty breath, so thick Poppy could barely lift her arms in a desperate plea to the food court now closing for the night just metres away, let alone cry out to the last unsuspecting workers passing the shuttered cafeteria on their way home. Seasoned by so many delicious visits, here she was at last in the belly of the beast: food, caught. Around her, the bones of the mall echoed with an aching appetite assimilated through forty years of hosting humanity, an addiction to all their howling hungers and unfulfilled needs. And then either the windows or her eyes closed like lips, swallowing the light and fixing her forever in place beside her best friend—a camera shutter closing, a black curtain drawn.

We Played the Odds at Whitley
Darren Todd

Mark and Eva had been married for almost five years when she discovered his panic button. She didn't mean to. Not really. Sure, she'd come to bed after trying her first ice bath with every intention of curling up next to him, thinking he'd wake up and tell her to move onto her side or scramble onto the very corner of their king-size bed to escape her. Maybe even fetch her another blanket from the closet, still half asleep. None of that happened.

Instead, she snuggled next to him, the frigid skin of her exposed thigh and arm bumping against his thin cotton PJs. He stirred a little. Only, it wasn't to move away or grumble in protest. He began moaning in his sleep, deep in his throat at first but then moving higher and faster. The sound became something like a dog's whine, all through his closed lips, as if he were locked in place by sleep paralysis.

Not funny anymore, she meant to wake him from what was obviously a nightmare. But when she put her freezing hand on his forearm, he bolted awake, screaming. He kicked off the covers and jerked his head back and forth across the bedroom like their home was alien to him.

'It's okay,' she said, holding her hands up. 'Mark, it's me. It's okay.'

Their dog burst into the room, barking and searching for whatever threat he might face.

Mark scrambled back again when his vision seemed to finally focus on Eva. His momentum sent him flying off the bed; he grabbed for purchase, finding the lamp on his bedside table, the only light in the room. It hit the hardwood floor and either came unplugged or the bulb shattered, sending the room into total darkness.

Then he screamed some more.

The following morning, Eva made him some slippery elm tea to soothe his inflamed esophagus. The screaming had rendered him near mute. Still, while he drank, avoiding her eyes, despite wanting him to take it easy that day, she also needed answers.

Seeming to sense this, Mark leaned back into his chair in their breakfast nook, took a deep breath, and eased out a string of nonsense:

'You ever heard of Sardines?' he croaked.

'Um...like the food? The fish in a can?'

He nodded. 'But I'm talking about the game based on the food.'

'I...no. But that stuff stinks, so I'm having a hard time imagining a game that uses fish.'

'*Based* on sardines. It doesn't use them.' He paused, rubbed his throat, took another swallow. 'Let me back up. Start over. When I was little, there was this neighborhood connected to ours called Oak Hills...'

#

Oak Hills had the good stuff, as every kid in the Eastview Arms apartment complex knew. So they gathered on the edge of the Whitley field not long after getting off the school bus to hash out their plan of attack.

'I've gotta get my bow ready,' Hunter Allen said. 'My dad and I have been working on it all week. Looks just like Legolas' bow from

68

the Battle of Helm's Deep. Even has all the carvings on it.' His curled lip completed the smug bragging. His face drooped when he turned his gaze on Mark. 'What're you gonna be, Mark? A ghost? Can your mom afford the sheet?'

'Asshole,' Mark said, and the others from the neighborhood sucked in a breath. Such language was common among the eighth graders but not as a challenge to Hunter Allen of all people.

'Y'know, my dad can kick your asses out anytime I want,' he said. 'He owns the whole place.'

'*Runs* it, you mean,' Mark said. 'And, yeah, we know. You only mention it every single day.'

Not one of the dozen kids who rode the number nine bus moved, all of them waiting to see how this would play out. Mark was curious himself. He'd been tempted to stand up to Hunter before in the almost two years they'd lived at Eastview Arms; making fun of his mom—even if he was spot on about them having no money—took it far enough to warrant action.

'Whatever,' Hunter finally said, making a farting noise to hammer home his supposed apathy. 'Just be out here at five on the dot if you're coming. All of you.'

'Isn't that early?' Kevin Hendrix asked. 'The babies are still out at that time.'

'You wanna miss the good stuff?' Hunter asked. 'You gotta get to Oak Hills early, man. The high schoolers always toilet paper the rich houses, so they close up at and call the cops on anybody out after that. We don't get there till then, and we get nothing.'

'Yeah, we can't miss the good stuff,' Hunter's little toady, Tony, said. He threw down his backpack to emphasize his point.

'See you guys at five,' Mark said and headed to his apartment.

Mark wasn't wearing a sheet, but nor did he have an elaborate homemade getup like Hunter. That would mean having a dad around, or at least a mom who didn't work two jobs. He'd settled on a cheap Spider-Man suit from Big Lots. Better than his mom's suggestion of using the same stupid Harry Potter robe from last year. He didn't even have the wand anymore. He'd thrown it away when it quit making those electronic swooshing noises.

In previous years, they'd been stuck walking around Skyview Drive, Mayor Ave, and Hermitage—the same loop that the babies made (if earlier in the day). This was the first time they'd cross the field to the notorious Oak Hills, where real bounty awaited. And without an escort, to boot.

An hour later, Mark met a handful of others at the edge of Whitley field, close enough to hear the shushing noises that the high grass made in the breeze. Also close enough for stories about the field to pop up in Mark's imagination, as they no doubt did the other kids'.

'Y'think they're gonna grab one of us?' a feminine voice whispered into his ear. The stupid Spider-Man costume dulled his hearing. The cheap fabric not only didn't breathe at all, making him sweat despite the chill in the air, but it also made a constant swishing, like he was on the phone with someone rubbing up against the mouthpiece.

Mark jumped and spun mid-air, discovering a pirate brandishing a foam cutlass.

'Sorry I scared you, love,' the pirate said, affecting the accent and gruff of Jack Sparrow. A few of the other kids chuckled.

It was Erin, the girl from two apartments down who'd been his saving grace when Mark had first moved in, introducing him around when he'd been too shy to go out on his own. The kids at Eastview Arms played at all hours, either out front—the light traffic along Eastview be damned—or, more often, in the grassy patch butting up against Whitley field.

'Your costume looks great,' he said.

She shrugged. 'I figured I had the hair for it, so what the hell? Did I scare you?'

'No,' he fired back, fast as a gunslinger.

'It's okay to be afraid of Whitley field,' she said. 'You never know when the Whitley twins are gonna claim their next victims.'

He scoffed. 'I'm not the new kid anymore. I heard it all last Halloween.'

'They didn't *take* anyone last Halloween,' she deadpanned. 'Well, that ups the odds this year, right? Like,' she pulled the pistol from her belt and held it to her head, 'Russian roulette. Someone's luck has to run out eventually.'

He huffed. 'Can't play Russian roulette with a flintlock, dumbass, and I'm not scared. Maybe you are.'

70

She swayed on her feet in what Mark had to admit was a damn-fine imitation of the Johnny Depp character. 'Of course I'm scared, mate. I've got common sense. Two kids disappear Halloween night without so much as a trace in twenty years. Then other kids.'

'What others?' he demanded. 'The others are just rumors.'

She swayed some more, head moving back and forth, eyes on his, like a King Cobra attempting to hypnotize him. 'They said the Black Pearl was just a rumor, love. Tell that to the people of Port Royal.'

'Sick costume, Erin,' came Hunter's unmistakable voice, a mix of pseudo-surfer and punk rocker. 'Beats the hell outta Mark's. Yeah, I knew it was you, dude. Wanna know how?'

The last of their group joined them, perhaps only popping out of their apartments once Hunter showed up to lead the charge.

'No,' Mark said.

'I asked myself which costume was the cheapest,' Hunter said.

'No, I get it,' Erin cut in. 'It's from the wrestling match, right? When Peter just threw whatever he had together to make a suit. It's *supposed* to look cheap.'

'Uh, yeah,' Mark said. 'Exactly.'

'Whatever,' Hunter said, tossing the long braid of his wig over his shoulder, a move he'd probably practiced in the mirror.

'Yeah, whatever,' echoed Tony, who—best as Mark could figure—dressed as a hobbit companion to Hunter, with a vest over a button-up shirt, high breeches, and bare feet.

'Dude, aren't you freezing?' one of the other kids asked Tony. The evening was indeed atypically cold and still humid from recent rains.

'He's fine,' Hunter butt in. 'Are we going or what?'

#

They walked in tight formation once inside Whitley field. No more jokes from Erin now. Mark turned to his left as they trudged toward the playground that marked the start of Oak Hills. In the high grass, he spotted the dilapidated remains of a house a quarter-mile away.

'That's the old Whitley place,' Erin said beside him. 'Where the twins lived.'

71

'What happened?' Mark asked. Sure, he'd heard a few things last Halloween, but he'd acted uninterested in the tale both because— even at eleven—he'd figured it was all bullshit but also because it got under his skin. Now, though, packed in with a near dozen other kids, the danger seemed far away.

'No one knows, really,' she said. 'They went out trick or treating and never came home. People from our side and the Oak Hills side said they'd seen them that night, but no one could decide on when exactly. Didn't matter anyway; they were gone.'

'What did the cops do?' Mark asked.

'Jack shit,' Hunter chimed in, having eavesdropped. 'As usual. Never found them, did they? Dad said what do you expect when the same cops take two months to evict deadbeat tenants?'

'Total deadbeats,' Tony echoed, shaking his head as if he'd dealt with the law plenty during his twelve years of life.

'Not really the same,' Mark said.

They spoke no more about it while traversing the well-trod path between Eastview Arms and the Oak Hills playground. Someone had even strung up lights along a series of metal stakes, plugged into an outlet by the playground and triggered only once it grew dark. With the sun still hanging atop the distant mountains, they'd yet to come on. The lights would be carving a comforting path through the darkness by the time they finished trick or treating. Of course, also by then, the ramshackle place the missing twins had occupied would be cast into deeper shadow, invisible from within the light's embrace.

Mark tried to push the twins from his mind once they'd entered Oak Hills. The homes stood two, even three stories high, with two-car garages, expansive, well-kept lawns, and clever decor like giant felt spiders or ghosts rendered lifelike by fans blowing underneath.

'Remember,' Erin said, 'use the sidewalks. You'll mess it up for all of us if you walk across the grass. They're fanatical about their lawns here.'

Hunter grumbled but relented, using only the edged sidewalks as he led the entourage to the first house. Sure enough, nothing but smiles and kind comments. They each scored a full-size candy bar. Mark was in the back, so that meant he was stuck with a Zagnut by the time the lady had reached him, but he didn't mind. Such a bar would have cost him a week's allowance at Edgemont Market down from his apartment.

And so it went for house after house: chocolate bars, wax lips, even one house that gave them homemade candy apples covered in nuts.

These they ate right away, milling about in a street all but void of traffic, which only led to the houses; no shortcuts to Church Ave, sending cascades of vehicles through on the weekends, like back at the complex.

'I'm gonna be so rich when I grow up,' Hunter said, mouth full of apple and face smeared in red.

'Me too,' Tony called, his teeth chattering between bites.

'My mom said rich people put razor blades in the apples to cut up little kids,' Kevin mumbled. He held his apple aloft but had yet to bite into it.

'I'll take it if you don't want it, dipshit,' Hunter said. 'You can tell your mom how much I enjoyed it, too.'

'That's right,' Tony said.

#

The sun disappeared behind the mountains before long, though porch lights of the Oak Hills residents offered a beacon of riches still left untapped, of homes they'd yet to plunder.

At their final street, a man answered dressed as a clown. Most of the adults wore no costume, though they'd encountered a vampire in one and a super tall guy as Frankenstein's monster in another.

'Well hey there, kids,' the clown said. 'I know how you love your candy, but I've got something else you might be interested in, since your buckets are looking pretty flush on sugar as it is.'

He pulled an object tethered to the buckle of his hobo overalls into his mouth and let out a series of sounds that instantly drew everyone's attention, like a crescendo of whoops from a bird.

'It's a siren,' the clown said. 'I've got one for each of you. Or should; I'm running a little low.'

The kids butted against one another to get at the pumpkin bucket of sirens. They were plastic instead of the clown's metal version but came in all sorts of bright colors.

'Just don't keep your folks up all night with them. Or at least, if you do, don't say you got them from me,' and he laughed and gave his own siren another blow.

Somehow, Mark ended up at the end, behind even Howie Kline, the youngest of their crew, who'd barely entered middle school. When he reached inside the pumpkin, he found only the smooth plastic.

'It's empty,' he told the clown.

'Oh, shucks; I was afraid of that.'

'Tough luck,' Hunter said and let out a long series of whoops from his bright red siren.

'Yeah,' Tony said, then blew into his, 'that's tough luck.'

The clown sighed, looking actually sad and not just made up to seem so, then said, 'Tell ya what. Hang out here for a second, sport.'

He disappeared into the house as the kids began to trickle away. Mark felt like following and would have if Erin hadn't hung by his side. The man once again stepped into the glow of his porch light rubbing something in his hands with one of those moist toilettes like Mark remembered seeing at fancy restaurants back before his dad had left. He pulled the towel away and revealed the metal siren, wiped clean, its tether now dangling free.

'You take this one,' the clown said, 'if you don't mind it being second-hand. Every kid deserves one. It's my fault I didn't buy enough.'

Mark took it, mouth hanging open. The towelette and the cool night left the metal cold to the touch. 'Wow,' he whispered.

'Don't lose it,' the clown said. 'Clip it to your costume.'

'Thanks, mister,' Mark said.

'Happy Halloween, kids. Guess I'm closing up shop, since I'm all out. Maybe I'll see ya next year.'

#

They made their way along the street towards home, most of them whooping their sirens except for Hunter, who'd chucked his into his elven knapsack, saying they were stupid baby toys once he discovered that Mark had gotten the metal one. Tony had gone so far as to trade his away for a pack of Nerds.

'Would you guys shut up with those things?' Hunter said, as they followed the lights back to the Eastview Arms. 'If my dad hears them around the complex after hours, he'll file a noise complaint, and if you get three of those you're out on the street.'

The sun had long set, though the sky still reflected some of the day's soft blue. The midnight tones waited perhaps a half-hour away, giving them time to retreat into the safety of their apartments and show off their hauls to parents wary of stomach aches.

The temperature had dropped several more degrees, causing several kids to forgo any dedication to their characters and don gloves, beanies, and jackets they'd brought with them.

'You guys wanna play a game?' Erin asked. They were all lined up along the lighted path, halfway between the playground and home.

'I don't know. Streetlights are already on,' Kevin said.

'And your mommy will get worried?' Hunter mocked, employing a sing-song baby voice.

'No, jack-off. I just said I'd be home now. I'm supposed to help with brownies.'

'Brownies,' Tony scoffed, looking to Hunter for affirmation.

'What's the game?' Mark asked.

'It's called Sardines,' she said. 'It's like hide-and-seek, but better. One person's 'it,' and they go and hide in the grass while we all close our eyes and count to a hundred. Then we split up and go look for them. Whoever finds them, has to hide, too. Lay down alongside them, like sardines in a can. But you do it all sneaky, so the others can't see you. More and more people will join the can of sardines until there's only one left, and they're the new 'it.''

Long seconds of silence hung in the air following her explanation, as if they were processing the rules and not wary over leaving the lighted path and trudging through that high grass, each kid separate from the others.

'I'll do it,' Mark said. One hand clung to the metal siren pinned to his left shoulder, as if drawing strength from a totem. 'Unless Hunter wants to be 'it' first. It's a big field. Kinda creepy.'

'You go ahead, Marky Mark. We might get lucky enough to step on you. And there's nothing brave about lying in grass. But you show us how it's done.'

'Start counting,' Mark said and walked into the grass. At first, he headed toward the dilapidated home without thinking; after all, it was shrouded in darkness by now. He reneged and took the other direction, since the lighted path almost perfectly bifurcated Whitley field.

He walked as quietly as he could, the counting growing softer and softer as he made his way further from the path. Soon, he heard only the sound of his steps in the grass—a crunching noise, as if the dried stalks were breaking off inside already frozen earth. It was cold, but not that cold. He thought he heard laughing, and he whipped his head around. It would be typical of Hunter to cheat and get a head start while the others were still counting. But only silence answered back, followed by the muffled edges of numbers riding the chilly air. Thirty-five, or somewhere around there. Time was running out.

Again, a laugh, like a childish giggle, really. It spiked his fear, but only for a second. What could really happen? Hunter would try to scare him, but then he'd have to lie down next to him. That'd be the worst part—waiting alongside that jerk while he made jibes about how he'd startled Mark.

Still, he walked a bit farther, till he could make out the dark outlines of cypress trees marking someone else's property. He marched in place, as if stepping on grapes. The damp ground turned soupy enough to make suction noises against his And1 hightops.

'Great,' he whispered.

But Peter Parker wouldn't hesitate to lie down on the cold, muddy earth, would he? Not if it meant standing up to a bully like Hunter. In his own way, keeping Hunter and his toady in check made him a friendly neighborhood hero, as well. Guys like him thrived on cowardice and only became bigger assholes if left unchallenged.

So he lay down, the cold ground apparent instantly through the synthetic material of his costume. But if the fabric didn't breathe, hopefully that made it waterproof.

'Ready or not, here we come,' came several voices in concert, though far enough away to sound almost like the moaning of spirits on the wind.

Don't go there, he told himself.

Long minutes of nothing passed. The occasional whoop of a siren or shout of collaboration met him, but the voices still sounded impossibly far off. Finally, the crunching of grass nearby. The steps were hesitant; whoever it was hadn't seen him. They grew more distant a moment before turning and heading closer.

Mark saw him first—a smaller kid, a boy if judging by his profile, though Mark couldn't tell for sure because of the costume. He didn't recognize it right off. Not surprising, since they'd picked up some Eastview Arms stragglers while walking Oak Hills, trick or treaters who'd gotten started late or who were outside of their core group of friends. Maybe kids who thought it better to stay on the periphery when dealing with punks like Hunter. Still, his get-up seemed like it would have stood out. He wore blue jeans hiked up, like an old person might wear them. And a red-and-white shirt tucked into them. A weird, clown-looking mask with red yarn for hair topped it off.

At last he kicked Mark's shoe, looked down at him, and pointed.

'Remember to do it secret,' Mark said. 'So, the others don't notice.'

The kid giggled, reminding Mark of what he'd heard before, then nodded. He looked around and then shot down within the grass next to Mark.

'Did anyone see you?' Mark asked him.

The kid turned to look at him but said nothing. Mark could hear him breathing, the sound rough, croupy, even. Like the kid was fighting off sickness.

Shouldn't be out on a night like this, Mark thought. *Halloween or not.*

'You all right?' Mark asked.

The kid nodded slowly, ragged breath the only sound.

'Cool. Just stay real still,' Mark whispered, 'so they don't hear us.'

Truth was, even though the kid hadn't spoken a word and stood probably a full head shorter than Mark, he hoped someone *had* heard them, came over, and joined the sardine can. Mark couldn't say why the weird clown costume gave him the willies, but it did.

Mark lay back and stared straight up into the sky, which had only recently erupted into a thousand pinpricks of light, without all the streetlights to drown out the stars. He extended his ears out into the field, hoping for more than the occasional holler, which could have been a hundred yards off or more. While the ground had begun to sap his body heat, lying next to the kid didn't help. Where the guy's jeans were flush against his spider suit, no heat seemed to pass between them. If anything, Mark felt colder next to him. The kid probably was sick, but wouldn't that make him hotter? He turned to find that the kid was still staring at him; maybe he'd never stopped.

'What…what are you staring at?' was all Mark could muster.

Muffled behind the mask, the kid only giggled again.

Mark's heart began to beat faster, and his hands were suddenly freezing. He balled them up and tucked them under his thighs. 'You…you're from the Eastview Arms, right?' he asked the kid. 'From the apartments?'

More giggles, the only other hint of what lay beneath that mask were dark eyes Mark could barely make out. Just the flickers of white around the black irises. But then they moved and seemed to roll to the other side of Mark.

Mark turned and thought he was going crazy. Another weird clown. But different. This one was a girl. Same blue jeans, but the wearer was smaller and shorter, and the yarn attached to her mask formed long pigtails, though one of them dangled as if ready to detach at any moment. Like the other kid, she pointed, and—unprompted—lay down next to Mark.

Again, he tried to ignore a growing anxiety. Yes, some other kids had joined them, but he'd have noticed *two* clowns. Both might as well have been wearing the same costume they were so close. Like—

'Twins,' Mark squeaked.

In answer, the boy slapped a hand over the crook of Mark's elbow, fast as a striking snake. Mark tried to jerk it away, not only because he'd been startled but because the fingers were beyond cold against his thin costume. They seemed to radiate a gelid sensation that spread over Mark's flesh like water soaking into fabric. He meant to beat at the kid with his left, but another frigid vice of flesh clamped around his elbow. Smaller, but no less chilling. And while the boy continued to giggle, punctuated by that awful, croupy cough, the girl remained silent.

Mark inhaled a whiff of that boy's breath as the kid hacked again, and the smell nearly caused him to vomit. The Eastview Arms kids had once discovered a maggot-riddled opossum at the bus stop, its mouth agape, as if killed in the middle of a primal scream. Hunter

78

had talked Tony into poking it with a stick, which didn't so much move it as open its hollowed-out stomach, suffusing the air with the burnt-plastic wreak of death and decay.

The kid's breath held the same terrible tang, so intense that Mark whipped his head around to face the girl instead. Her mask was cracked along the skull and down by the chin, revealing a hint of rotting teeth long void of lips. Where the boy's breathing spoke of illness, her rapid panting suggested predation and raw anger. As Mark stared into those milky eyes reflecting the sparse moonlight, her grip tightened and the cold overtaking him spread that much faster.

His own breath grew shallow and staccato, but he couldn't shout, not a whisper. His body no longer cared about the game; it didn't even care about his fear. It only wanted out, to bolt to the safety of that lighted path. Hell, to move at all, to generate enough heat to avoid falling under.

But no; he couldn't get up, no matter his muscles' desire. And couldn't break that awful stare as the girl and her twin brother pulled him down and down into the darkness they'd shared for so many years.

Then his chin struck something unyielding up by his shoulder. The siren! The real metal siren that man had given only to Mark, as if prescient of its necessity. With all Mark had left in him, as if pulling the last bits of warmth from his core to fuel that tiny motion, he leaned down, placed the siren between his lips, and blew.

At first, hardly a sound, and even that ended the boy's giggles and caused both twins to double down on their iron grips. Despite his numb limbs, Mark groaned in agony at their squeezing. But he blew again and again, the sound growing in his panic.

'I f-f-found you,' whispered someone behind the girl's back. It was Tony, cutting a meager silhouette against the high grass. He was shivering so badly it looked like a dance, bare feet covered in freezing mud by now.

Mark moaned a warning, but Tony dove down and wedged in next to the girl. 'I kn-knew I'd find you. You shouldn't have b-blown your...'

Then the girl spun on him. Hands flying off of Mark and hooking into Tony's small frame. Like a wrestler maneuvering for a pin, the boy hopped to Tony's far side.

Mark's muscles discovered they were free from those frosty tethers, and burst into action, pulling him from the sardine can and bolting back the way he'd come. Mark blew on the siren in a long whine, seeing stars by the time he took in another breath, only to repeat the call.

'Ollie ollie…oxen free,' he gasped. 'Game…over. Come…come here.'

Soon the others surrounded him, Hunter forcing a guffaw at his cowardice and Erin shushing the bully to listen. Mark told them that some other kids were hurting Tony, holding him down. That they had to find him and save him.

And yet…

\#

'I knew we'd never find them,' Mark told his wife, a thousand miles and two decades from that awful night. He clutched his throat again and took another sip of his tea, though it had gone tepid a while ago.

'All three, I mean. We found Tony. *Just* him. The official cause of death was hypothermia. They said he'd been out too long in the wet and cold, that laying there like that had done him in. That he'd…fallen asleep and not woken up.'

He rose and poured the dregs of his tea into the sink, fresh tears plunking against the metal basin, as well. 'But it was the twins. They'd wanted me, but they'd settled for him.' He walked to the keyring by the front door, pulled off his set, and returned to his wife. 'You asked me about my keychain on our first date.' He held up the metal siren and the attached keys jangling beneath. 'I told you then, you might not like the answer.'

The October Shadows
Hannah Baxter

Phantasmal faces peered out from the cells of the rolled-up film reels, the silver nitrate nightmare that he'd spent half his life searching for. Duncan couldn't believe his luck when he'd come across the 16mm stock when clearing out the dilapidated old cinema. It had been tucked away in a dusty box in the rat-overrun projection booth. It was a shiny strip of bygone Tinseltown, reeled inside a dented factory-sealed film canister. It wrapped around him and refused to let go. A label was pasted to the side of it, one that had almost been scratched off. But the words that were written were clear as day: *The October Shadows, 1922.*

Duncan's throat seized shut. His gloved hands trembled around the discovery. It wasn't second or third generation, like most silent films survived in. This was the archetype, in all its uncensored glory. He had the holy grail of cinema in his hands, something no one had laid eyes on for over ninety years.

Duncan always loved horror. As a child, he'd been spellbound by the monochrome mystique of the old horror films from the early twentieth century. He'd been introduced to them by his father, a fellow connoisseur, whose own youth they'd brightened with their gallons of chocolate syrup blood and unconvincing monster makeup. They possessed a macabre charm which had ended up turning into a lifelong obsession for him.

Halloween was his favourite holiday, not just to eat his own body weight in chocolate, but a chance to binge all the classics under the cover of darkness—*House on Haunted Hill, Creature from the Black Lagoon, Frankenstein, Dracula, and King Kong*. By the end of the night, his eyes would ache from overstimulation, a dazed, sugar-smeared smile plastered across his lips. It was through this that he was first introduced to Wendelin Müller. Wendelin Müller had started off studying acting. His photograph scared Duncan just as much as his filmography. He was a miserly, bald man with a downturned grimace and crumpled boxer's nose, crushed by flying shrapnel during the First World War. His long, wrinkled fingers were folded in front of his funeral black suit, as if trying to hide something.

He'd sailed to the fabled Hollywood in search of fame, finding work at Fox Studios as a director. There, he'd made a name for himself by infusing atmospheric German Expressionism with lively Art Deco to create a truly unique aesthetic. He'd butted heads with the studio executives, who'd wanted to dial down the 'monstrous elements' of his films.

Still, Müller had ending up producing three films for them-*Fragments in Gloom, A Shadowed City* and *Canvas of Madness*. All had won favour with critics and the box office. Müller's third flick was one of a few that had genuinely disturbed Duncan. The scene of the mad artist slashing at his canvas with enough force to tear the material was burned into his brain. But it had been his fourth film, *The October Shadows* that had made him notorious.

The film had its first and only screening on 31st October, 1922 in Müller's native Munich. The result had been an unrestrained riot. Patrons had slashed seats and cracked open the skulls of those sitting next to them. Some cinemagoers ended up permanently institutionalized. All known copies had been destroyed. The alleged contents of the film became even more horrific with each avid retelling of the tale. There were unexplained deaths, demonic cults. It was said the ghostly activity that had plagued the production of the film imprinted onto every single frame.

He couldn't believe such a precious piece of filmmaking history had been hidden here all this time. That was until he remembered that reels of Carol Theodore Dryer's 1928 epic—*The Passion of Joan of Arc*—thought to have been destroyed in a fire, which was discovered in a Norwegian psychiatric hospital in the eighties. Deleted footage from *Event Horizon* was found stuffed down a salt mine in Transylvania. Stranger things had happened.

A sane person would have put the film canister down and walked away. But there it remained in Duncan's crushing hold. Maybe his mother had been right when she'd lectured him on the deleterious effect of horror films. He just had to see what was inside.

'Duncan!' Ray's voice made the dust motes jump. 'What's taking so long?'

Duncan's panicked breath clammed the inside of his respiratory mask, as if he'd just swallowed bathwater. He tucked his treasure under his scrub-covered arm.

'Coming!' he called.

There was no way he could relinquish it back to the shadows. Duncan was determined to bring whatever was contained within it to light.

Ellen furrowed her brows as he set up the camera. Her raven pixie cut framed her machete-sharp angular face. She crossed her arms, wrinkling the zombie on the front of her t-shirt, an eyeball dangling down its cheek.

'You just found it there?' she asked.

Duncan was hunched over the projector. It was a recent acquisition from their film studies professor, Mr Platt, after Duncan breathlessly explained the circumstances. Platt always appreciated his enthusiasm for his classes. Even in Duncan's near mania, he noticed how the older man backed away, Oxfords squeaking against the fresh waxed floors. He'd probably only gave him the projector to get him out of the classroom.

'I can't believe it either. Back then, no one gave a damn about preserving movies. The studios just wanted to turn a profit. Of course, there was also silver nitrate being highly flammable. Fifty thousand reels were—'

Ellen massaged her temples.

'—honey, I love hearing about your film facts, but I've got a raging migraine. The kind you get when you write over four thousand words in one night about the role of symbolism in Medieval architecture.'

'Yikes.'

'Yeah,' she huffed, 'if I ever see anything Romanesque again, I think I'll have a stroke. But at least I don't have to worry about Dr Bowen breathing down my neck about the extension anymore.'

Duncan squinted through the dimmed room to make sure the function lever was in the stop position, Ellen divebombed a quick kiss on the stubbly skin under his earlobe.

'Well, I'm going out. Try not to burn down the apartment. I don't think Brent would like that.'

Duncan rolled his eyes as he stabbed the trailing power cord into the wall outlet.

'He doesn't like anything I do,' he huffed.

Ellen's purple lips crinkled upwards into a smile, shark piercings twinkling in the faint light. They were almost as bright as her bottle green eyes. Duncan's heart burned like a positive print melted by a bulb.

'Well, he never did have any taste,' she muttered.

Of all the rare Blu-Ray releases and tapes that he'd squirreled away, none were as precious as Ellen. Their fates had entwined when the bus they took to their respective classes broke down. Duncan was scrolling though his phone while dangling from the ring handle when her elbow mashed into his face, breaking his nose. He'd been too focused on her shirt to listen to her frantic apologies.

'Hey, is that *The Cabinet of Doctor Caligari*?' he'd asked, blood flowing from both his nostrils.

Ellen stared at disbelief in him for almost two minutes. Then, she burst into laughter as she pinched his nostrils.

Ellen lived and breathed horror. Underneath her crisp buttoned blouses were slasher movie sleeve tattoos. Anyone unfortunate enough to mistake Freddy Krueger for Jason Voorhees in her earshot would be subjected to a blistering rant.

Duncan was shocked to discover that until then she'd only celebrated it in secret. Ellen came from a constraining conservative home. She and her siblings weren't allowed to watch anything with magic for fear of inviting the devil. University gave her both the freedom and the courage to watch all the movies she'd coveted glimpses of at the video store. Halloween had become Ellen's midnight moment in the spotlight. People still talked about costume from last year, a blood-soaked bride carrying about her own severed head. Duncan couldn't wait to see what she had in store. This year, she wouldn't be the only one making a splash.

He scraped up a chair as the film started. Duncan had never grown past those Samhain screenings of his youth. The only thing missing was a large bowl of popcorn. The promises to himself of notifying the Film Preservation Board about his discovery evaporated from his mind. He just had to see it for himself.

The hastily added German title cards flickered in like a candle in a howling gale. Duncan barely had time to read them before it transitioned into a long-range exterior shot of a Gothic mansion. The many leaded bay windows glowed eerie in the dark, like the reflective eyes of a predator.

Müller never skimped on setting. Some critics accused him of prioritizing it over plot and characters. Duncan disagreed. It was a dark, brooding curtain cast over the unconvincing vaudevillian set pieces of past productions. He utilized it in a way that Duncan had never seen in any other film past or present. They were almost tailored to the characters. The long winding hallways represented the unravelling psyches of his doomed protagonists as they tried to find their way back to sanity. Stairs became Sisyphean torture instruments, enhanced by the claustrophobic cinematography. A simple empty nursery became a haunting mediation on merciless mortality.

It was followed by a brightly lit interior shot of a roaring twenties gala, one that Jay Gatsby would have been proud of. A feather-headed flapper in a black sleeveless sequined gown and a suited man were entwined in a scandalous French tango. People stomped their feet, bobbing their heads as if their necks were broken. A hollow-eyed jack o'lantern with unnervingly human teeth carved into its inverted triangle mouth burned in the background.

In the tundra of his own confusion, fragments of the film's plot emerged in Duncan's mind like a distant mirage. Something about a séance gone wrong at a party in an isolated mansion. It seemed like standard fare for a horror film of that time. Duncan, however, knew better. Wendelin Müller could take the barest bones plot and outfit in the tattered ashen cowl of Death itself. He was a true horror auteur.

A glamorous woman descended the magnificent marble staircase. The wild revelry stopped. The partygoers gaped up at her with reverential awe, like she was a goddess descended from Mount Olympus. Her face was as full and pale as a new moon, framed by raven hair crimped into finger waves. Sooty eyeshadow was smeared below her dark eyes, giving her an intense glare. The printed intertitles popped up again, putting silent words into a female extra's flapping mouth—*Die Gräfin ist hier!* (The countess is here!)

Duncan scraped through his rusted repository of the German language. He didn't know what was being said, but he knew it was important. It slammed into him like an express train through a glass fishbowl. *Gräfin.* Countess. His mouth plummeted open, joining the slack-jawed shoal onscreen.

The October Shadows had faded from pop cultural memory. But the Countess' too-wide hypnotic eyes and pallid, almost vampiric beauty, given life by Evelyn Sinclair, was embedded in pop culture. Through just snippets and stills, she had become a screen icon. Countess Berg had inspired other films, video games, anime and comics, whether intentional or not. A gothic rock band, that rattled through Ellen's wireless earbuds during study sessions, appropriated her face for their iconic album cover.

The closest Müller came to explaining the character was an interview he gave with a Swedish magazine right before his death in 1952. It was one of three he'd ever given and the only one that Duncan could dig up on *The October Shadows*. She'd tormented his dreams for many sleepless months. The only way to exorcise her from his imagination had been through writing the script, which he'd done in three days. He and the actress who'd played her had never recovered. Evelyn Sinclair died in a California mental asylum two years after the disastrous premiere. Her episodes were the worst around Halloween, where she would scream about people climbing inside her. It only added to the film's cursed reputation.

Despite every attempt to bury Müller's masterpiece as deep as they could, Countess Berg escaped the grave like a chain-rattling spectre. No one could forget her, no matter how much they tried.

Even though she existed on a screen, Duncan squirmed under her withering glare, as if she was reproaching him for daring to lay eyes on her.

Countess Berg led her inebriated flock around a lion-legged octagonal oak centre table. A spirit talking board was already laid out, planchette pointed up to the smiling sun on the left-hand side. Duncan almost heard the dread-inducing jolt of organ music.

Müller obsessed over the occult before his near-death experience in No Man's Land. His mother had escaped famine-ravaged Ireland aboard a claustrophobic coffin ship. She'd met Müller's father, a butcher and had seven children with him. Only four survived past childhood. When Müller was still a child, she'd told him of hearing the banshee's mournful wail, watching emaciated men gnaw on their neighbour's shinbones. They'd been the dark palette with which Müller painted his nightmarish masterpieces with. Death was his life.

Countess Berg sat centre. Her lemon juice-patted face glowed in the circle of candles erected around it. Her bow lips opened like she about to shoot a fatal arrow. *Gibt es in dieser Walpurgisnacht Geister bei uns?* (Are they any ghosts with us on this Halloween?)

The planchette shot up towards the first letter of spelling out 'yes' that Duncan saw it. Then, the countess' face changed. Her eyes went black, as if her irises spilled over like two bleeding egg yolks. They sharpened into anguine ones, gouging out a piece of Duncan's soul. Her glossy black bob became as lustreless as a bale of hay. Rotting sores oozed down her wrinkled cheeks. The countess' nose beaked over her chin like a bone tumour.

The spectacular show of special effects went unnoticed by the core cast of the film. There wasn't even an eyebrow raised. The countess snapped back to her usual gothic glamour like a rubber band. As he watched on, more distortions disrupted regular scenes. Faces elongated grotesquely, fingers webbed into claws and shadows' movements mismatched with their daylit counterparts. Humans became horrors.

Duncan was mystified. Müller was well-known for his stylization, but this was something else. It defied all the rules of cinema.

'What are you watching?'

Duncan had been so engrossed in the inexplicable occurrences onscreen that he'd failed to notice Brent's return. His face was even paler under the achromatic film playing, brown hair gelled into a high pompadour. The strap of a conical tennis bag was slung over his well-muscled shoulder. Brent averted his eyes like he had just looked at Medusa.

'Damn it, Davies!' he snapped, 'How many times? Watch your horror movies in your own room!'

Duncan glanced back to the still-playing film. It was pre-Hays Code. Aside from the strange faces, there wasn't anything objectionable. Brent would have had a heart attack if he'd walked in earlier.

'You're treating it like a snuff film.'

Brent gave a disgusted shudder.

'Why can't you be like regular guys and just watch- '

'I have a girlfriend, Brent.'

Brent scowled at the screen. He jostled up his bag, a racquet poking out.

'With the stuff you're into, I'm surprised,' he muttered.

Brent clomped up the stairs, petulantly slamming the door. Duncan didn't bring up Brett's shortcomings as a roommate- leaving his dishes unwashed in the communal sink, stumbling home at three in the morning and walking into private screenings of lost films.

He refocused on the film with a sickened fascination. The Golden Age of cinema had surprisingly sophisticated special effects. Tricks of perspective intensified scenes. An actor dangling for dear life was really a few feet off the ground. Matte paintings made whole new worlds. Pepper's ghost, a Victorian effect where an offscreen object was projected via a series of mirrors was still used. But the effects in Müller's film were decades beyond that.

It must have been the result of the hand-held crank camera used to film it. Maybe hair or dirt on the lens or some other reasonable explanation for such horrific imagery. But it didn't account for how the art design was untouched. It was only the actors who were affected.

Countess Berg's eyes rolled back into her head. She leaned back; jaw unhinged to the point of dislocation. Not even the rough assistance of two burly guests could move her from the baroque green velvet tapestry chair. The planchette spun wildly in all directions, like a compass needle in a magnetic storm.

She levitated, her long, ethereal white gown draping over her ankles like a bedsheet ghost. The countess floated over the stunned crowd with her alarms aloft. Duncan was impressed by how smooth it was. No matter how much he scrutinized the scene, he couldn't see any wires.

There was an uncomfortable close-up cut on her milky-eyed face, her mouth twisting with silent maledictions. Her possessed face was replaced by another intertitle.

Those who were never born seek entrance through living flesh, it read in German.

A chill coursed down Duncan's spine like icy rainwater down a broken gutter pipe. Countess Berg's body contorted like plasticine, limbs defying gravity.

There was a cross-cutting montage of various people screaming in terror. A few raced towards the heavy arching oak doors, wrenching at the heavy brass knockers. One by one, they were possessed. The spirits slipped through their skins like a worm eating inside apple. Their faces deformed again, in a way that made the previous instances look downright pleasant. Bile scalded the back of Duncan's throat.

Like Death high on his pale horse, the possessed countess reigned overall. She glided towards a terrified woman cowering in the corner of the ballroom, half-hidden in shadow. The terror on the actress' face as the countess approached was too real. It was as if she was looking into the face of insanity itself. Duncan pulled down the Still Picture Clutch lever.

Countess Berg's agonizing crawl slowed to a still frame. It failed to lift Duncan's unease. The darkened image harshened her transformed features, making her look like a charcoal drawing brought to terrible life. It was as if at any moment she would crawl out of the screen and lunge at him. He studied her with fearful fascination, heart hammering away in his chest.

The rumours were true. It was Müller's magnum opus. Duncan wished he'd never rediscovered it. He understood now why the audience had rioted over it. There was a gut-wrenching realness to the supernatural violence.

He'd botched his second chance to destroy it. Duncan lay staring at the ceiling while Ellen snoozed on his chest. The canister lay buried under a pile of clothes in his drawer The temptation to watch it again jabbed Duncan awake like the sharp stick. He wanted to know how Müller had achieved such imagery. Since everyone involved in the production of the film was dead for decades, it was all up to Duncan.

The film reels were heavy as lead in Duncan's clammy hands as he loaded them into the projector. He relived the horrors all as it waited for it to wind through the projector through the projector before attaching the loose end of the supply reel. Duncan wondered how Müller and the editors had endured the film dailies to create a coherent narrative. Positioning down the rewind lever, he contemplated letting the film be ripped apart, rarity be damned. But that splinter of rationality was plucked out by curiosity.

Rewinding the film, he pushed up the lever back up. The grinding motor shuddered to a halt. Removing both reels from the arms, Duncan pushed the buttons. The replays offered no insight into Müller's mastery. The anomalies appearing on the negatives obliterated Duncan's reasonable explanations. Rather than drive him away, it made him more determined. There was an answer buried in the reels. Duncan dug deep, like a resurrection man pilfering a corpse from a graveyard.

Countess Berg's eerie face was imprinted on the inside of his eyelids. Her eyes, black as a moonless night, stared intent at him like a lioness spying a grazing antelope. Evelyn Sinclair may have played the role, but the countess was her own being.

He'd stayed awake for almost three consecutive nights trying to figure it out.

'Duncan?'

The projector's shut off. Vision blurred to the point of blindness; Duncan shuffled around. He'd slept in that same seat for days in case he missed a vital detail. Ellen stood there; her teeth clenched.

'Where the hell have you been?' she demanded, 'Duncan, I've been calling you over and over! We've all been worried sick! And this is where I find you? Unbelievable!'

She tore open the curtains. Duncan's body seized up in the outpouring of daylight. Outside, students had erected orange banners and hung plastic skeletons across campus. How long had he been in there?

His unchanged clothes hung off his frame, hair congealed with grease. His round face was gaunt, sleepless eyes sunken so far into his sockets that he resembled a corpse. Ellen's anger cooled to concern.

'Duncan? Duncan, my God, how long have you been here?'

His own name was another language. Ellen patted his jutting cheekbones, desperate for an answer.

'Please, talk to me. When was the last time you ate?'

When he looked back to her, he only saw the countess' sinister image. Duncan yelped. He fell out of the chair, head striking the hard wooden floor.

He came round in the hospital the hospital, an IV drip needled into his wrist. Ellen almost killed him with a crushing bearhug. It was a good thing that she'd found him when he did, the doctors said. With how he was pushing his body, if it had been just a day longer, he would have died.

Duncan fell backwards onto the pillow. How had his life coming to this? He cursed the day he'd ever noticed the sheen of the reels out of the corner of his eye. Worse, he'd put his loved ones through an emotional ringer. When Brent checked in on him, he'd hovered around Duncan's bedside like a nervous bird. To Duncan's shock, he'd slid over a spare racket.

'You could come along when you're better,' he mumbled, 'it's better than sitting in a musty old room. I'll teach you a killer backhand.'

Duncan waited for a punchline that never came. Hell had frozen over.

He never knew how strong a hold the film had on him until he'd woken up gasping for air. Seeing their tender concern, Duncan had almost been overcome with the truth. But it had been jammed inside his constricted throat like a fishbone. It wasn't just them thinking he was crazy. Duncan knew they'd insisted on watching it and the horrible cycle would restart anew. Over his dead body would they see it.

There was something in that film, trying to escape from the silvery spools. For decades, it had lain dormant until Duncan had brought it back. Duncan still no idea what Wendelin Müller had done, whether it was intentional or by accident. But he knew he had to destroy it.

As soon as Duncan recovered enough to walk, he did it. He'd gone out without telling anyone where he was going, a baseball cap pulled over his eyes. Duncan flinched at every incidental brush of those he passed by. He'd been afraid that the battered film would somehow infect them. Duncan would not have wished the contents of the canister onto his worst enemy.

The urban bustle faded away, replaced by the lonely scrape of his shoed soles against the ninety-foot concrete girder bridge. A turn of the century creation, it guided the influx of traffic across the main highway over the endless rush of the river. Cars roared past, their heavy tyres soaking him to the bone.

Duncan glanced over the reinforced steel edge at the considerable drop below. The boisterous rapids had claimed three workers during its original construction. Duncan didn't want to be another victim. Pulling the antique canister out, Duncan scowled down at the half-faded name, one that had come to define his nightmares. Without a word, he let it drop.

Before it was swallowed up by the foamy waters a woman's haunting screech echoed up. It was so piercing that Duncan had almost fell over trying to see who had fallen in. But there was no one. He was consoled by the fantasy of film buried buried in silt and curling pondweed. It would never hurt anyone again. Satisfied, Duncan returned to the real world.

Finding normalcy again took some time. Pins and needles sizzled through his calves from one hundred and twenty hours of sitting still. He'd been swamped with all the assignments he'd missed while holed up in there. To keep his job, he'd gotten down on his hands and knees and begged Ray's forgiveness.

Ellen was the one thing that had kept him sane. She'd re-organized her day to make regular check-ins for him, bringing him drinks and snacks and even recommended a therapist.

By the time Halloween rolled around, Duncan had recovered. But he couldn't even look at a grinning jack o'lantern, let alone watch another horror film. But he was willing to tolerate brief discomfort to ensure the happiness of those around him.

True to form, Ellen had outdone herself. She flounced into the apartment as a broken-faced porcelain doll. She wore a ringleted wig and a baby doll dress she'd shredded with scissors. A skeleton brooch was pinned to the lace front. She batted her oversized fake eyelashes at Duncan, twirling about a fake bloodstained knife.

'So, what horrors do you have in store for us tonight?' she chirped.

Duncan swallowed. Since they'd started dating, a bizarre competition had developed between them. They'd would go out of their way to find the most stomaching, churning uproarious horror films. Ellen's pick from last year, a Japanese body horror, sent five people running upstairs to worship the porcelain god.

Duncan had spent months trying to outdo her. This time, he'd gone for something softer. It was a family movie about witches from the mid-nineties, one that was assigned childhood viewing for every millennial. He hoped that the others wouldn't mock him too much.

'You mean aside from student debt?' he shot back.

Duncan's confidence climbed as she laughed. Just one night, he told himself. He could handle it. Ellen settled in beside him on the couch, a bowl of popcorn sizzling on her lap. The relief in her eyes was palpable, one reflected onto Duncan's expression.

Not even five minutes into it, an unwelcome noise intruded onto their Halloween festivities. It was low but buzzing, like a disturbed nest of hornets. Duncan's body turned to stone.

The film projector stocked in the back had juddered into flickering light. Duncan didn't remember putting a reel into it, or even plugging it in. Long-dead actors flew about on the walls, jazz-age ghosts. The countess' eldritch beauty filled the room, like the flaming head from *The Wizard of Oz*, dark lips pursed with triumph.

Rushing over to the errant movie projector, his blood turned to ice when he saw the familiar chicken scratch on its side. It was one that should have been dampened beyond recognition by the rapids he'd tossed it into.

No one else followed. The infamous summoning scene had placed them under its unbreakable spell. Duncan attempted to wrestle the film tape out. But it was as unmovable as a mountain.

Even in the dusk, he saw it. Brett's nose receded into a skeletal snout. Another girl's ivory veneers rotted into misaligned tombstones. The film distortions spread like a virus through the captive audience. As the collapsing line of dominoes careered towards them, Duncan stumbled back to Ellen.

'We have to get out of here!' he blurted.

He tried to tug her out by the collar to safety when she turned around. Ellen's face twisted into Countess Berg's manic grin. Her eyes darkened into two tarpits oozing black tears, body overflowing with maleficence. Ellen's fingers clenched into knobbed claws, varicose veins spreading up her arms like cracks under pressure.

Duncan could only watch her transformation with sinking realization. It reminded him of the Struss effect, named for cinematographer Karl Strauss. It was where exaggerated makeup invisible in one shade was revealed through a filtered light, simulating facial transformation. Unlike all the other times Duncan had seen it, there was nothing faked about this.

Ellen's new corpse-black fingers stroked his cheek with sickening affection.

'Thank you,' she gargled, 'for finding me.'

Despairing tears singed the corners of Duncan's eyes. Attention. That was the lifeblood that it gorged itself on. After lying dormant for centuries, his obsession had given it enough to restore it to full strength. How many others had it snagged over the decades in its film strips, like an octopus' tentacles?

He'd watched so many horror films to know better that the reel couldn't be destroyed that easily. The force within it couldn't be tamed by mortal means. Wendelin Müller had opened the lid of Pandora's box and died before he could close it. What hope did he have? Duncan didn't have time to contemplate what a fool he'd been when the end lunged at him. Unlike the doomed protagonists, there was no merciful cut to credits for Duncan. There was only a fresh bloom of pain as the bones in his face cracked apart and the darkness flooded his brain, obliterating all he'd ever been.

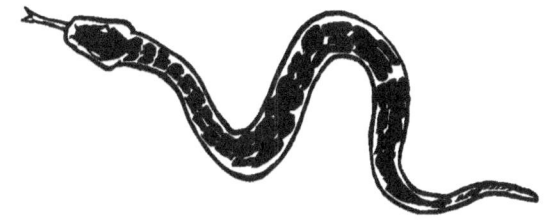

The Black Van
Tom Coombe

When Halloween comes, the older kids warn the younger ones about The Black Van.

The Black Van doesn't need headlights. The Black Van can drive on the sidewalk. Valerie McGrath's brother saw inside the Black Van, and that's why he has that patch of white hair. The Black Van's driver is a pervert, a crack dealer, a devil worshiper who takes kids down to hell.

'If you see it, keep walking,' the older kids say. 'And no matter what happens, never, ever, talk to the driver. Dont answer his questions, dont even look at him.'

Jeremy's mother's Halloween warning is more pedestrian. She doesn't mention The Black Van, because adults don't know about The Black Van.

'Look both ways,' she says as her son heads out the door. 'And don't go to any houses that don't have their porch lights on.'

It is Oct. 31, 1989, Jeremy Weikel's last year for trick or treating.

'Will you be warm enough in just that jacket?'

'It's *fine*, Mom,' he says, regretting his tone. After all, she'd just spent an hour perfecting his Joker makeup, his father scoffing at her efforts.

'Don't get too used to wearing lipstick,' Gary Weikel had muttered from the doorway.

Jeremy's father is in the kitchen now, drinking with his friends, simian chuckles drifting out every few minutes.

'Are you meeting Adam at his house?' Kathy Weikel asks.

'That's the plan,' Jeremy says, donning his purple hat. It's not quite the one Jack Nicholson wore in the movie, but close enough.

'Be safe,' Kathy says. She kisses his cheek, a sadness in her eyes he cannot place.

Jeremy heads out into the night, shivering in his grandfather's wine-colored sports coat, burning leaves filling his nostrils. He weaves his way through flocks of smaller children, a head taller than any of them. Most kids his age were out last night, Mischief Night, throwing handfuls of dried corn at metal storm doors, bathing cars in soap and eggs and toilet paper. Jeremy wants nothing to do with "mischiefing", not that he's ever been welcome among the rough boys who make it a yearly tradition.

Jeremy prefers his own traditions, him and Adam descending on their neighborhood's close-packed houses and filling their bags with bite-sized Three Musketeers and little packets of Skittles, maybe even some root beer barrels or butterscotches to sneak into class the next day. Their sacks full, they'd watch a movie in Adam's basement. Maybe *Roger Rabbit*, maybe *Aliens*.

It would be a great night, he thinks, rounding the corner to Adam's house...only...why wasn't his friend in costume yet? And who was this other boy with him?

'I called your house, but you'd already left,' Adam says. 'I changed my mind about my costume.'

The other boy, taller and a bit older than either of them, smirks. He wears a battered denim jacket outfitted with band pins. Megadeath. Slayer. Anthrax. Adam wears a similar jacket, fresh from the rack.

'You should see your face, dude,' the new boy says to Jeremy.

'Knock it off, Nick,' Adam says, then to Jeremy: 'Look, we can still have fun. I just think we're a little old for trick-or-treating.'

Jeremy's throat goes tight and dry.

'OK...what do you want to do instead?' he asks, hoping it wouldn't involve Nick.

That hope vanishes as Adam and Nick give each other a secretive smile.

'Tests of Courage,' they say in gleeful unison.

'What does that mean?' asks Jeremy.

'We just do, you know, dares,' says Adam. 'Like, last week, Nick dared me to drive my dad's car when my parents were asleep.'

'WHAT?'

'Just around the block,' Adam says. 'It wasn't a big deal.'

'But if you want to hang with us, you need to pass our test,' Nick adds.

'What test?' Jeremy wants nothing to do with this new kid or his scary games.

Nick motions them closer, the boys huddling around the steps like they're plotting an invasion.

'There's this piece-of-crap house up on the High Road,' says Nick. 'It looks like it's ready to fall apart. I went up there with my brother and his friends a few years ago. We knocked on the door on Halloween. There was this old lady in a hospital bed, right in the living room, screaming like a baby. We got out of there and just lost it.'

'Yeah, it sounds scary,' Jeremy says.

'It wasn't scary,' Nick says, making the last word a slur. 'It was hilarious.'

Adam laughs in agreement. Jeremy can't see the joke.

'Here's your dare—Go back to the house. The old lady has a bunch of little Jesus statues by her bed. Grab one, and you're cool.'

'That's stealing,' Jeremy says.

'That's stealing,' Nick mocks, giving Jeremy's voice a lisp.

'She won't even notice it's gone,' Adam says.

Jeremy's stomach roils as he weighs Nick's dare against simply going home. He pictures himself trudging through the night alone, weaving through crowds of happy trick-or-treaters, his sack empty, then rushing past his mom and crying into his pillow. All that is left to do is agree and follow Nick and Adam to the High Road.

#

The High Road—real name Monahan Avenue, though no one called it that—was one of two main roads running east-west through Rainsville, dividing the community into three sections.

Most travelers passing through followed Route 34, which cut a straight line through the center of town. Positioned on a hill overlooking Rainsville, the High Road was trickier, a winding, dimly-lit stretch with nowhere to walk. It was a dangerous proposition for kids who wanted to go trick-or-treating on the north side of town.

'Cars coming around those curves won't have time to stop. It's not worth it,' Jeremy's mom told him. 'There are plenty of houses in the main part of town.'

Jeremy offers her a silent apology as the boys approach the intersection where Third Street met The High Road.

'It's the one with the porchlight.' Nick points to a collection of three ramshackle wood-framed homes. Two appear abandoned, windows boarded, mail and newspaper piled on their porches. The third is just as shabby and saggy, but lights burn its windows. Getting to it would be tricky, with Jeremy walking half a block in the dark along the side of the road.

Jeremy swallows and sets off. He knows you are supposed to walk against traffic on roads like these, but that's impossible on the High Road, where the eastbound lane has no shoulder at all, just a guardrail protecting cars against a twenty-foot drop.

He pushes through the weeds in front of the first house, trying not to think of the things—rats, snakes—that might wait in the overgrown brush. *It's fall*, Jeremy tries to convince himself. *They're underground, hibernating*. He passes the first house and stumbles on a rock hidden in the weeds, steadying himself on the sodden railing of the second home.

'Caaaaaaaaarrrrrr!'

Nick's voice, gleeful. Yellowish headlights glare at Jeremy, a great grumbling engine announcing that this wasn't a car but a truck. He picks up his steps, panic blooming in his chest, no longer caring what he might step on. He is still on the shoulder, but so close to the asphalt that any vehicle that passed by would clip him. The weeds hamper his steps, as though he's wading through a snow drift. The snarl of the truck grows closer. It will be on him in seconds.

Jeremy moves left, out of the weeds and onto the asphalt, which lets him sprint the rest of the way as the pickup rounds the corner. The truck's tires scream as Jeremy runs back onto the side of the road, coming to rest on the mossy steps of the house.

'Outta the street, fat-ass!' bellows the driver, a red-faced man with white hair. Axl Rose wails along with him, telling everyone they are in the jungle.

Jeremy gets to his feet, quaking, tears stinging his eyes. The white-haired man glares at him for another ten seconds before speeding into the night. Nick hoots in the distance, Adam offering up a few half-hearted 'C'mon's.

You're almost there, says a small voice inside Jeremy's head. *Go inside, grab a statue, and you're done.* Another voice, one closer to his mother's, responds: *You don't need to do this. Go to the door, pretend to turn the knob, and tell them it was locked.*

Jeremy approaches the door, decaying wood complaining with each step. His hopes fizzle as the door swings open with his touch, directly into the living room. Lamps burn in every corner, turning the room supermarket-bright. Even more overpowering is the smell, a thick cocktail of cigarettes, hairspray, urine, cooking grease, and the kerosene heater in the center of the room.

The woman Nick described lies hunched against a mountain of pillows, mummified in bedding. Her eyes are cat-green, ageless lakes surrounded by the sunken landscape of her weathered face. Those eyes meet Jeremy's, and he braces himself for the scream. Instead, the woman laughs, a reedy AH-HEE-HEE-HEE.

'Daddy got me a clown for my birthday!' she says.

Jeremy scans the living room for the statues. The room has been rearranged since Nick's visit. Her collection of figurines waits in the dining room, a cluttered room with mail, magazines, and unwashed clothes.

'Are you a circus clown or a magic trick clown?'

She'd assembled an army of ceramic figurines. Not Jesus statues, like Nick had said. There were frogs and sheep and roosters, and things Jeremy can't classify. A robed man with an owl's head. An ancient king on a white throne. Jeremy palms one of the roosters and starts for the door.

'Well, what kind of clown are you?' the old woman wails.

'I'm not a clown. It's just my Halloween costume.'

Her mouth becomes a circle.

'Halloween? Nobody told me it was Halloween! DADDY. It's HAALLLOWEEEEEN.'

The last word comes out in a jumble of sobs. Heavy footsteps thundered from upstairs. Jeremy creeps backwards to the porch, placating hands out to the weeping woman.

'Hey, hey. It's OK. It's...early. You can still...'

Still what? The older voice in his head says. *She's not going trick or treating. She's confused. Get out of here.*

Jeremy bolts as the footsteps overhead grow louder, thick boots pounding old wood. He rounds the porch and sprints back through the weeds, Nick guffawing as he comes.

'Hurry up, Joker! Batman's coming! Boom-baba! Boom-baba!'

Even in his panic, it is the smirk on Adam's face that slices open Jeremy's heart. The three of them turn the corner, out of the view of the house on the high road. Jeremy fishes the ceramic rooster from his pocket and hands it over.

'I said a Jesus statue,' Nick says, inspecting Jeremy's offering.

'There were no Jesus statues,' Jeremy says.

'Well, that changes things.' Nick's mouth forms a hyena smile. 'I don't think...'

The growl of an engine cuts him off, headlights burning in a carport behind the house. The boys look at each other and Nick's cockiness evaporates like water on a griddle.

'Go. Go!' he tells Adam, pushing his friend across Third Street, heading east away from the house.

Jeremy tries to follow, and Nick says, 'Uh uh... We need to split up. Besides, you'll slow us down.'

He and Adam dash into the night before Jeremy can respond. Headlights bathe Third Street as the vehicle rounds the corner. An Econoline van, shiny and oil-slick black.

#

With her husband at the fire hall, Kathy Weikel invites her cousin Michelle over for a glass of wine. They aren't quite friends, but the house is too silent.

'Jeremy's still trick-or-treating, huh?' Michelle asks, sipping merlot in the glow of the TV. On screen, the *Wonder Years* kid is playing football with his friends.

'For maybe another twenty minutes. He's always been good about not breaking curfew.'

'No,' says Michelle. 'I mean, he's still going trick-or-treating? Isn't he in eighth grade?'

'He's in sixth, and he says this is his last year.'

They drink in silence, Michelle opening a miniature Milky Way. They're technically for trick-or-treaters but few kids have rung the doorbell this year.

'I hope so,' Michelle says. 'This town isn't kind to children on Halloween. And let's face it. Jeremy is weak. Remember that dodgeball game?'

Her cousin's words are a rock to Kathy's sternum.

'You don't know him. You see him maybe twice a year at family functions.'

'OK, OK, go easy,' Michelle says. 'Open some more wine.'

'There is no more.'

This is a lie, but Kathy wants her cousin to leave.

#

Jeremy ducks into a side street before the van can cross the High Road. He crouches by someone's front stoop, shivering, bowels turning to water. It's garbage night, and the homeowner has thrown out three trash bags soaked in a fermented reek, but Jeremy doesn't dare move from his hiding spot.

He is not scared of the legend of the Black Van, recognizing it as something big kids used to frighten smaller ones, the way the fourth graders used to warn the first graders about "scary" Mrs. Dolan, the kindest teacher he ever had.

What scares him is rule-breaking, and sneaking into someone's house, stealing a little knick-knack, is the worst thing he's done in his twelve years. It's a road that leads to police visiting the house, his mother crying, his father's face, purple and screaming. His father's fist, clutching his belt.

Jeremy counts to 100 before emerging from his hiding place. Third Street is clear, but he remains in this dim alley. This is Pierce Street, he thinks, three streets from where he lives. He can follow it home unobserved.

Unobserved by cars, that is. After two blocks, he encounters a group of leather-jacketed teens, a fog of beer trailing them. Jeremy stares straight ahead, careful not to make eye contact, but draws their attention all the same, as he always does with boys like these.

'You fucking CLOWN!' one of the teens says, slamming a catcher's mitt fist into Jeremy's arm. The kid has a mop of black hair and the ghost of a mustache. His buggy, bloodshot eyes dare Jeremy to respond, but Jeremy walks on, his eyes welling.

The next two blocks pass without incident, not even a barking dog to mark Jeremy's passing. He is ten blocks from home when a voice cuts through the night.

'We didn't take anything, so fuck off!'

Nick, Jeremy thinks, a few streets away.

'That's a fucking BABY story, Adam. He's just a guy. Probably a pervert. Probably a molester. My dad knows like twenty cops, so—'

Nick never finishes his rant. His words become a wail, rising in pitch like a soprano rehearsing. 'Ahhhhhhhhh-EYYYYYYYYYEEEE-ahhhhh-EEEEEEEEEEEEEEEEEEEE! Aaaaaaaaadaaaaaam. AAAAAADAAMMMMM!'

And now comes the barking, every dog in every backyard for six blocks howling in response to the scream. Jeremy finds the strength to jog, the barking fading as he goes. After three more blocks, he works up the nerve to cut over to Creswell Street, where he and Adam live.

The porchlight burns at Adam's house, though the street is empty of other kids in costume, even with an hour left for trick-or-treating. Adam sits on the sofa, face lit blue by the TV. He's watching *The Great Pumpkin* and clutching the well-worn stuffed bear Jeremy knows he keeps in his closet.

Any relief Jeremy feels upon seeing his friend at home fades when their gazes meet. Adam's eyes have gone as wide as a cartoon character's. He shakes his head no at Jeremy three times, then turns to the TV, his face an abandoned house.

They met on the first day of first grade, the only two boys with brown bag lunches. Everyone else brought their sandwiches in colorful plastic and metal lunch boxes, *He-Man* and *Transformers* guarding their PB&Js.

A sense of loss and terror fills Jeremy's throat, heavier than anything he's ever felt before. It won't be until decades later, when he has his own children, that he feels anything like this again. His only thought now is simple, and not adult: I want my mom. He starts for home, and is two blocks from his house when The Black Van pulls up beside him. Its engine gurgles like a witch's cauldron, putrid black exhaust tainting the crisp fall air.

Up and down the street, porch lights wink out.

The driver is a golem with wheat-colored heavy metal hair, his piggy eyes nearly close enough to touch. His voice is a fork scraping a plate.

'Little boy…tell me your name.'

A sound comes from the van, bumping and a muffled voice. Jeremy keeps walking, his pace casual, casting a sidelong glance at the van. The driver grins, showing teeth placed in his mouth at random, thick brown molars up front and jagged fangs in the back.

'Little boy…tell me your name.'

He stretches his smile crocodile-wide. Jeremy walks on, certain there are other people in the van, the thumping growing more desperate. He's a block from home.

'Little boy…tell me your name. Let me see your clown make-up. You were in my house tonight, weren't you?'

More demanding now. Jeremy pauses next to a house, considers ascending the porch. Maybe if the driver thinks this is his house, the Black Van will move on.

'Is that your home, little boy?' the driver croons. 'Think hard.'

Jeremy moves on, each house taking a lifetime to pass.

'Good call, little clown boy,' says the driver. 'Now tell me your name. You're not in any trouble. Just look at me. Tell me you were in my house tonight, and I'll let your friend go.'

Six more houses until home. Jeremy doesn't dare run, doesn't dare turn his head, or talk to the driver. *Do those things*, he thinks, *and you'll never get home.*

'Boy, tell me your name,' the driver says, the litany growing angrier. Inside the van, the thumping picks up, joined by a pleading voice robbed of all bravado.

'Little boy, tell me your name! Little boy! Tell me your name! BOY! Tell me your name!'

Three houses…the van drifts closer.

Two houses…the driver hangs a meaty arm out his window.

One house away…a sweaty, sour-milk reek spews from inside the van, and those thumping noises are louder than ever…and…he is climbing his steps on watery knees. His mother has left the porch light burning.

'Looks like you're home,' the driver says. 'One more chance to save your friend. Become the school hero.'

Jeremy sees himself entering the van, rescuing Nick from the driver's clutches. The ultimate Test of Courage. Interviewed by the police, then the news. His father shaking his hand. *You're becoming a man, my boy.*

The older voice speaks in his head once more, snuffing out these thoughts. *If you go near that van, you will never be seen again.*

The giant smiles and his teeth have rearranged themselves again, the spaces between them an inch apart. He opens his mouth python-wide and the Black Van's side door slides open with it, releasing milky, sewery stink. The interior of the van is a wet pink mouth, blanketed with abscesses, leading to a bottomless throat. From inside this impossible space erupts the deafening buzz of a thousand wasp nests at war with each other.

No not real this is not no it is not real oh no oh mommy.

Yet Jeremy does not talk, does not take the driver's invitation. After a few minutes or a few weeks, the driver closes its mouth and the van's mouth closes with it.

'Very good, little boy. Wise little boy. Don't let me see you out here anymore.'

The driver rolls up his window and the Black Van rumbles into the night, its greasy exhaust invading Jeremy's nostrils. He'll never eat candy again.

His mom waits in the kitchen, a mug of tea cupped in her hands. She stares at Jeremy long enough for him to ask her if everything is OK.

'You saw the Black Van, didn't you?' she says. 'Saw it and he let you go.'

'Mom?'

Kathy Weikel walks toward Jeremy, taller than his mom since last year. She stands on tiptoes to kiss his forehead.

'It was a black Impala when I was a girl. My brother James saw it.'

His Uncle Jimmy, a lawyer down in Washington, D.C.

104

'But no matter,' Jeremy's mother continues. 'Things are going to get better for us. Nothing can hurt you now.'

'Mom, there was a kid tonight, Nick…and I think…'

'We will never talk about it again,' Kathy says.

She tells Jeremy he can stay up and watch TV, but he declines. In bed, he stares at the ceiling, listening to his father's phlegmy snoring and thinking about his mother's words. He is still awake when the bells begin, calling worshippers to church for All Saints Day.

That Time of Year
Daniel Fox

Sometimes you couldn't shake loneliness no matter how hard you try.

Samantha Button was a lonely little girl if ever there was one. She was mouse quiet, and had a hellish time connecting with the other kids at school.

The real point of pain though, that was at home. Her folks weren't cruel, just *busy*. Always *busy*. Dad with his sales figures (he was a computer parts salesman), Mom with working up the info sheet on the next house she was putting on the market (real estate). Samantha would sit between them on the couch watching TV and feel all the warmth of a winter night wafting from the busy parent on either side of her.

Maybe you don't remember, but when you're all of nine years old and you're gagging for attention, bad behaviour pops up as an option without you even really thinking about it.

Samantha discovered in class one Monday in mid-September that if she mocked Mrs. Wells' croaky voice it made the other children around her snigger and laugh, and holy hell wasn't that just the best feeling ever? She did it so much that she got caught and sent to the principal's office.

And brother, that was even better. Because her dad had to get called out of work to come get her and he talked to her about why she had misbehaved all the way home. And then both of her parents talked to her about it all through dinner, right up until bed time.

They were finally paying her some attention.

It was easily the happiest Samantha had felt in a dog's age. It became like a drug.

She started acting up more and more. Causing fights. Swearing in front of adults. Ruining other kids' art projects. She became a real mean motor-scooter in the space of maybe a month.

She didn't like this new Samantha, this new version of herself she had crafted out of wickedness. But it felt to her that this new Samantha was necessary if she was to feel anything other than sorrow in this world, and wasn't *that* a sad thing to feel at all of nine years of age?

By the middle of October her parents were afraid to leave her alone for more than a minute at a time because she'd cut up one of her dad's work shirts or kick all the flowers out of her mom's garden out back. One or the other of her folks were on her like glue every single hour out of school and Samantha was so happy she could just about cry.

#

The Handsome Man showed up at the front door of the house on the second Saturday of October. Samantha opened the door to this tall blond man with a great big smile plastered on his perfect face. He was excited to meet Samantha, and asked to speak to her mother, saying they were old friends.

Mom was already there, in the hallway leading to the kitchen, looking at the Handsome Man with this big shocked look on her pretty face. Samantha had no idea if her mother was happy to see this guy, or angry, or scared, but she got the vibe that something weird was going on. She didn't want to leave her mom alone with this man, but she got sent upstairs to her room while the adults moved into the living room.

Being in her bad girl phase, she ignored the order to go into her

107

bedroom and close the door. She sat herself down at the top of the stairs and tried to listen in, but the adults kept their voices low. She didn't hear a single clear thing until the Handsome Man was leaving. He was at the front door, giving Mom a big hug, and finally said something Samantha could hear clearly, even if she didn't understand the word.

She didn't feel comfortable asking her mom for clarification. So later, after Dad had come home from his bowling league, Samantha got him alone in the garage and asked him, 'What does "Samhain" mean?'

#

Dad didn't know.

So, the following Monday Samantha took herself down to the school library. After the librarian checked to make sure she wasn't carrying scissors or a flamethrower, he let her pull down a big fat dictionary that weighed almost as much as she did. She thumped it down on top of a table and flipped pages until she got to the letter *S*.

The definition of Samhain was short and sweet: *A festival held by ancient Celtic people, occurring on or around November 1, to mark the beginning of the winter season. Halloween traces its roots to Samhain, but is of a fixed date and reflects Christian and commercial customs.*

So now she knew what the word meant.

But she still didn't know why some handsome stranger had whispered it to her mother.

#

Speaking of Mom, she was a bag of useless all that week. She wandered around the house, forgetting about doing up her real estate fliers, this far-off look on her face. All the attention that Samantha had earned by becoming a little terror evaporated in the face of Mom's absentmindedness. Mom got so bad that even Dad, busy as he was with his sales, noticed that she wasn't her usual energetic self.

'How are you?' he'd say.

'Fine,' she'd reply.

108

'Are you feeling okay?'

'Fine,' she'd say again.

'If you're feeling under the weather, you should take some time off.'

'I'm right as rain,' she'd mumble, and then stand there in the kitchen, looking off into space.

After four days of this, Samantha pulled on her dad's sleeve when they were alone. 'I think I know what's wrong with Mom,' she whispered. There wasn't really any need to keep her voice low, Mom's mind was somewhere out in the atmosphere, but this felt like a situation where being sneaky was mandatory.

She told him about the visit from the Handsome Man. Dad thanked her for the information, then assured her that some man was not going to change Mom that much. He was sure that Mom was just tired after working so hard without a break for so long. Everything would be fine after Mom just had herself a little rest.

#

Two weeks before Halloween, the Handsome Man returned. Dad was out again, and once again Samantha was sent upstairs while the Handsome Man and Mom had themselves another little chat in the living room.

This time, Samantha crept down the stairs, lifting and placing her feet with a cat's care, little ears radar-sharp, attuned to the frequency of adult whispers.

She paused just beside the entrance to the living room and heard:

'....finally time...'

'...asking a lot...'

'...greater good...'

'...the others died for this...'

'...what decision is there to make?'

And then the Handsome Man was there, stepping in front of her, scaring her so bad that she nearly jumped up straight through the ceiling.

He knelt down, pulling up his business suit pant legs so they wouldn't stretch, and took her small hands in his own. 'You have no idea how special you are, do you?' he said. He smoothed down her hair, then gave her a hug. When he stood, he was wiping tears from his eyes. He said good-bye and went out the door.

For the first time in her life, Samantha actually wanted to take a bath and scrub her skin until it screamed.

#

For the third time, Samantha drew her Dad aside, this time while Mom was in the shower. Once again, Dad acted like the Handsome Man simply didn't matter.

Samantha understood something about her father—he was afraid. She was sure he did believe that the good-looking man was coming to their house. He knew the Handsome Man was having hushed conversations with the mother of his child. But Dad was pretending that it didn't matter to him. This pretending was a force field, keeping out the idea that his wife was doing something behind his back. And the more Samantha tried to pop that bubble with news of the Handsome Man, the more frightened Dad became, until he was angry.

And wasn't *that* a thing to learn—then when adults got angry, sometimes it was really just a mask to hide their fear.

#

There was something the Handsome Man had said during his last visit that stuck in Samantha's little head. Something like 'the others died for this.' It bounced around in her noodle for a full school day, pinball-style, and she all but ran from the classroom when the day's final bell did its thing.

The way the Handsome Man had said "the others died for this"—didn't that sound like he meant a bunch of people all died at once? It surely did to Samantha. If that was something local that had happened, it had to have been in the newspapers. Samantha was sure that the school library wouldn't have information on something like that, so she bee-lined it to the local public library.

Before that day in October, 1986, when Samantha had gone to the public library she had always made a right turn into the children's section with its tables painted with ladybugs and star-ships. But this day, she took a left out of the cool entrance area and made her way into the adult section with its serious-looking tall shelves of books and its no-nonsense metal-framed chairs.

She knew from school how to work a card catalogue. The cards ruffled past her fingertips, sending up the scent of old yellowed paper. But where to look? Under what letter? Which subject? *Death?* That would take in all of human history. *The town?* The town was old, its roots going far further back than when the Europeans came ashore. She tried "Samhain" and pulled out books about Celtic history. They talked of Roman times bleeding into the now, but they said nothing about her mother or the Handsome Man.

The librarian, a round-bellied man with the fluorescent lights bouncing off the top of his bald head, came across the spectacle of a nine-year-old girl frowning down at books with an adult-sized scowl. He hunkered down beside her and asked if he could be of assistance.

'I'm looking for a story from history,' said Samantha.

'You've come to the right place,' said the librarian, his smile creasing his round red cheeks. 'We're drowning in history here. We're in an ocean of it. Can you narrow it down?'

'I think it's something that happened here in town.'

'That's better. Now we're down to the size of a great lake.'

Samantha figured her mother's age. 'I think it must have happened in the last thirty-five years.'

'The lake grows smaller. Now we can swim across it if we're in good shape.'

'I think more than one person died.'

'Oh dear, how sad. But that does turn our lake into a pond, though perhaps the far side is clouded in fog.'

'There would have been young people there. Maybe even children.'

'The fog grows thin.'

'And survivors. At least two survivors. One a pretty girl or young woman with grey eyes like mine. And a young man who looked like a movie star.'

'Did I say a pond? Why, on second look, it's little more than a big puddle.'

'And maybe, just maybe, it happened around Samhain. Or Halloween.'

111

The librarian's round cheeks lost their creases. 'Ah,' he said as he stood, smoothing out his pant legs.

'You know what I mean, don't you?'

'I suppose there are many of us that do. Adults, I mean. Ones who were alive back then.'

'Do you have anything I can read? Books? Old newspapers?'

The librarian looked around, his eyes fixing for brief moments on the other adults in the room. 'That is a grim subject, young lady. A story that perhaps you'd prefer to avoid.'

'But what if that story didn't avoid me?'

#

The newspapers from the incident had long ago degraded to yellowed bits and pieces. So the librarian introduced Samantha to the joys of one of the library's two microfiche readers. Finished with his tutorial he stood back, looking like a man with a warning all primed and ready to fire, but he held it behind his teeth, because he seemed to understand the depths of Samantha's determination.

Samantha turned the handle. Pages of the town's local paper, once printed in fresh ink twenty years ago, whirred by in black and greenish-white. A new issue every Monday. Images blipped like sunlight dapples on a lake-top.

She found the October issues of 1966.

Here, a notice of the school's new gymnasium being opened. There, a sale on ice skates for the coming winter season.

Monday, October 17, 1966.

The front page was a full-page spread of a burnt farmhouse, blackened beams cracked like broken teeth, the roof collapsed in, an old-fashioned fire engine parked off to the right. The headline in large black letters: TRAGEDY AT ESTHER LAKE.

The long-and-short of it came to this:

A number of adults, teens, and children of families from the area had gathered together in a barn owned by Ammon Bulwer-Talbot near Esther Lake for a party to celebrate the end of the harvest season. The barn hadn't joined the electric age, so the affair had been lit with kerosene lanterns. A lantern had accidentally been kicked over, and the barn, mainly used for storing hay, had gone up

112

with gusto. The reporter had written that all of the funerals had been of the closed-casket variety, which Samantha took to mean that people had been burned so bad it would have made people puke if the caskets had been open to see their bodies.

The story continued on page five. She zipped down microfiche pages and got hit in the face with a picture of her mother, fifteen years old, face stained with tear-streaked soot, being handed a blanket by a twenty-something young man with the good looks of a movie star. The picture was titled, *The Only Survivors*.

#

Samantha jotted the information down, her pencil scratching along nearly fast enough to set her notebook on fire.

She took the information home. She showed it to Dad.

He sat in the garage, on the bumper of the station wagon, taking her notes seriously. Taking *her* seriously. Paying attention to *her*. In a way, it was one of the best moments she had experienced in months. Maybe even years.

He finished reading. The hand holding the torn notebook papers came down, rested on his leg.

'What do you think?' said Samantha.

'I think... I'm thinking too many things. It's likely none of them are accurate. I can really only think of one way to figure this whole thing out, and that's to ask your mom. So come on. Let's wash our hands, set the table, and have a nice little family chat.'

Those were maybe the sweetest words Samantha had ever heard. Her father had *listened* to her. He *believed*. For a girl that had been lonely for a long time, this was the feeling of someone drowning in the ocean hearing the sound of a life ring land in the water within easy reach.

They entered the house and washed their hands and Samantha set the table while Dad mashed potatoes and Mom pulled a ham out of the oven.

They sat down. They ate ham and potatoes. They drank water with ice cubes tinkling in their glasses.

Somewhere in the midst of all this domestic bliss Dad brought up what Samantha had learned about the tragedy from Mom's past. He asked who the Handsome Man was. He asked why Mom had never talked about being part of the local famous tragedy. When Mom stayed quiet, her face tilted down so it was hidden by her hair, Dad had a hunch and asked if it had really been a dance out there in old Ammon Bulwer-Talbot's barn, or if something else had been going on out there.

Mom raised her head and asked who wanted ice cream. She stood, took her plate into the kitchen.

Dad and daughter exchanged a worried look over the remains of the ham.

Mom returned and plunged the carving knife into the side of her husband's neck. As he gurgled and shook and his face went white, she turned the knife so the blade was facing out, and then pressed forward, so it emerged from the skin at the front of Dad's throat like a fish emerging from dark waters. A waterfall of red followed the blade's progress, spilling down onto Dad's sky-blue button-down shirt, drenching him so that the material clung to his slim body.

The unreality of this violence crashed down on Samantha's nervous system. She had no experience of this sort of thing. No reference points. No muscle memories. Her entire being didn't know what to do with this red brutality. So, it shut down.

She just sat there like an idiot thing, her wide leaking eyes taking in the spectacle of her father thrashing, gurgling, as he drowned in his own blood. Mother smoothed down his hair with a gentle hand, the one not holding the knife, making soothing noises and telling him, 'It's for the best. It's for the best.'

In his very last moment, Dad's eyes locked on Samantha. He tried to get up, reached for her, then collapsed back in his chair. And then Samantha no longer had a father.

Mom turned her head and looked over the table at her daughter. Considering she was holding a long carving knife that was dripping with the life's blood of her father, Samantha didn't really care for that look, and the most basic parts of her brain finally got it together and insisted that she get away from this bad scene just as fast as her feet could fly.

She was too slow.

Mom darted around the table, athlete-quick, and grabbed her by the wrist. She dragged her over to the table in the living room and held Samantha fast as she dialed and then spoke into the phone. 'I've started early. Now. It must be now.' And then, 'We'll met you there.'

#

In the long-storied history of awkward car rides, the one Samantha shared with her mother that night had to rank in the top ten of all time.

Neither of them said anything. Mom drove. Samantha, her hands tied behind her back with her own jump-rope, huddled in the passenger seat. The silence between them was gross and dripping with the murder of Samantha's father. Finally, after maybe twenty minutes of driving, Mom turned her head slightly and said, 'It's all for the best.'

Seeing as that was pretty much the same thing she had told Dad after cutting open his throat, it failed in a stupendous fashion to make Samantha feel any better.

Not long after that, Mom took a turn onto an unpaved road. Gravel pinged on the underside of the car, crunched under the tires. Samantha peeked out the bottom of the passenger-side window and saw a corn field run riot, long untended, the stalks bending under the weight of unharvested corn cobs that brushed along the side of the car. Twenty minutes later, Mom slowed, peering at the corn on the right until she could pick out a lane that barely existed anymore.

The station wagon bucked its way through sink-holes. The lane wasn't so much a lane as it was a slight space between the corn stalks. Overripe cobs banged off the windshield.

They emerged from the corn at an old wide two-story house. There were no lights. The yard grass was almost as tall as Samantha. The porch steps sagged at a crazy angle. Samantha could see where the front windows were broken because of how the moon's light stopped reflecting beyond the glass' sharp edges.

Mom didn't stop at the ragged end of the drive. She kept the station wagon crawling forward through the long grass that grew alongside the house, following a lane of crushed blades just wide enough to accommodate them.

Then they were at the barn. The one from the old newspaper

photographs. It was little more than the short stone walls that made up its base.

Another car sat nearby, the one that had made the crushed pathway through the long grass. It was a sporty thing, a convertible, orange in the light of the line of kerosene lanterns that sat along the uneven top of the low stone walls. The Handsome Man stood nearby, bouncing up and down like a kid waiting for Christmas, looking out of place in his sharp-looking business suit.

He clapped his hands with glee as he hurried over to open the station wagon's doors for them. 'Ladies! You are most welcome.'

Mom followed him to the remains of the barn, her head hanging low. He took her chin in his fingers and tilted her head up. 'It's for the best.'

'It's for the best,' Mom repeated.

Samantha understood then that this was something they had been saying to each other all their lives. It was something they had likely been taught when they were children, even younger than Samantha, for surely what was going on now was an old thing, even an ancient thing, kept alive as a deep dark secret here in this new world when their ancestors had landed on the east coast of the continent.

The Handsome Man turned back to Samantha and untied her hands.

He led her to the nearest stone wall so they could look over it. 'Do you know what you're looking at?'

A breeze came through, flicking burnt-orange leaves at them. Samantha shook hair away from her face and looked into the interior of the remains of the barn. Once, twenty years ago, this building had stood tall and proud with the lake rippling just off to the left. Two dozen, three dozen people had gathered to do something she was sure was just awful. Something dark and wrong. Something that had to be hidden from the rest of the town.

Now, there were only those low stone walls. Here and there the weathered stump of a vertical wooden post poked out of the stone. Other than that, the long grasses had claimed the interior of the barn's outline.

'I guess your mother never explained,' said the Handsome Man. 'There is a place that is both very far from here, and yet right on top of us at the same time. In this place, there are beings, wonderful

116

entities that are stronger and wiser than us. They have a vision of how our world could be and they want to share it with us, but it's so very difficult for them to get to us. It's not a matter of distance, but of barriers. There is a barrier between here and there, one that the wisest and best amongst us can see through sometimes. It drives some people crazy, but for others, it's like looking at angels. Old man Bulwer-Talbot was one of those people. The man who had owned this farm. He inherited the sight from his grandmother. The barrier, it's ice on a lake. But instead of getting thin in spring, it gets thin at a different part of the year.'

'Samhain,' whispered Samantha.

'Yes! That's right! It's thin now, honey. Thin as it ever gets. Boy, I can practically see through it myself, and I never did have the sight without Ammon's help. Your mom though, she can see it.' He looked at Mom again. 'Can't you?'

Mom turned. Her grey eyes, so like Samantha's own, travelled over the twisting grasses contained inside the stone walls. 'Yes. I can see.'

'Are they there?'

'They're there,' said Mom.

'Are they beautiful?'

'They're eager. Reaching for us.'

Samantha turned her own eyes down. The grasses were still there, but now it looked like they were seaweed, or plants in a fast-moving creek, bending and swaying with the push of invisible water. Underneath that water, there was... something. Things. Living things. Twisted things. Hungry things. Worm things. The Handsome Man called them 'beautiful.' His definition of 'beautiful' did not line up with her own. What little she could see of them was so ugly that it made her nauseous to look at them. And they surely did not look wise. They looked crazy. Insane. Dribbling madness. She turned her eyes away.

The Handsome Man sat on the stone wall and took Samantha's hands in his own. 'The thing is, we can't break through the ice with anything like an axe or a hammer. It takes something else. It takes a sacrifice. Something that is deeply loved.' He leaned forward and peered at her. 'You. That's why your mother had you, kiddo. You were born to help the world be reborn in their image. The last time

117

we tried this, the selected mother couldn't go through with it and kicked up a fuss and knocked over some lanterns, and, well... It was awful. Just awful. But that mother wasn't as strong as yours. This time, we'll do it right.' He held onto her hands as he tried to pull away. 'Don't be scared. It's going to be over so fast you won't even notice it. And then this mean old world will get torn apart and put back together into something so much better.'

The Handsome Man wrapped one of his hands around Samantha's thin wrists. The other hand lifted, palm up, to Samantha's mother. It was an invitation to redo the ritual that had been destroyed when they were young.

'It's for the best,' he said.

'It's for the best,' Mom replied.

She then snatched up one of those kerosene lanterns and busted it up the side of his handsome head.

Samantha jerked her hands back and fell on her keister. The smell of kerosene became strong as it splashed over the Handsome Man's head and shoulders. His perfectly pomaded hair, which had more or less been defying the wind, became a torch.

He screamed. He slapped at his head with his hands.

Samantha's mother lunged forward and pushed him over the wall. His feet went up and over, and then he disappeared into the long grass inside of the barn's old low walls.

Samantha got up. She didn't want to see the Handsome Man on fire, but boy howdy did she feel *drawn* to witness the spectacle.

The fire didn't kill him. *They* did. The things on the other side of the barrier.

The Handsome Man staggered around, calling for Mom, blindly reaching out his hands for her. He went in the wrong direction. And as he fumbled around, he came undone. A puppet with its joints snipped apart. Blood gushed as his left arm just fell off at the shoulder. The front of his belly slid out the bottom of his shirt, followed by his intestines. His right leg sheared off from his groin, hanging loose in the leg of his pants which quickly turned wet and red.

The final threads were pulled, and the Handsome Man, his head still on fire, fell apart, his bits and pieces pattering down into the grass.

Samantha looked up at her mother. Tears glistened on her face, yellow in the light of the remaining kerosene lamps. She looked back, expecting the ground to erupt in a geyser, or the sky itself to rip in two like velvet being pulled into pieces.

But nothing happened.

'Did you love him?'

'I loved him,' said Mom. 'I always did.'

'But nothing happened.'

'I guess I didn't love him enough.'

'Will you give me to them?'

'No. I love *you* too much.'

'I love you too.'

With that, Samantha took five steps back, then charged forward, throwing her full weight against her mother's lower back. Mom screamed as she flipped over the wall. She screamed even more as the beings on the other side of the barrier took her apart. Samantha thought the Handsome Man had lied about the deaths that the beings caused were over in a moment, because Mom had time to scream a lot before she finally fell apart.

The ground shook. The grass outlined by the low stone walls fell away, like it was dropped down a well. Instead of a cave down there, there were *stars*. And something blocking out more and more of those stars as it came hurtling up with a sound of triumph to greet her.

The world she had grown up in was such a lonely place. She couldn't wait to see this brand new one.

Vengeance of Halloween
Kevin M. Folliard

They found Holland Slate gutted in front of his former place of business. His entrails splayed like octopus arms onto the pavement. His eyes gaped at autumn clouds. A bloody butcher knife lay by slack fingers.

It was a nightmare for everyone who loved Holland, but for the new VoH—Vengeance of Halloween—superstore, it was good for business.

Don't be late, shop Slate!

That had been the slogan for the now late Holland Slate's Discount Furniture Depot. Slate's store had liquidated earlier that summer, and in Holland's words, turned into 'one of those soulless Halloween joints.'

Since July, Vengeance of Halloween had been slapping neon banners over the label-scarred exteriors of failed businesses.

Holland drowned his sorrows at my pub, kitty-corner from the strip mall where Vengeance of Halloween claimed his turf.

'It's not Starbucks,' I'd told Holland, the night before he allegedly offed himself. 'These seasonal joints open and shut, August to early November.'

'Not this place,' he whispered. 'They don't rent. They buy. God only knows what they plan to do after November.'

'Turn into Christmas stores?'

'Then what, Curtis? Seasonal stores rent dead retail space. They're not supposed to buy up the property.' Holland's beer sloshed. 'They have five locations in our town. Five! They're oversaturated. They've got some sick agenda.'

'You're always looking for conspiracies.' I squeezed his shoulder. 'Take care of yourself. Listen, I wasn't gonna say anything, but the small business association took up a collection.'

'I don't need charity, Curtis! I need you to listen!' Holland knocked my arm away. His glass slid over the bar and broke. He hung his head. 'Sorry.'

'It's all right.'

He sniffled into his sleeve. 'Back in April these bloodsuckers approached me to buy me out. I told them they'd have to kill me to take my dad's store. You know what they said?'

I shook my head.

'They said; "Fine."'

'Suits,' I spat out the word. 'They prey on—'

'No, no,' Holland slurred. 'Listen, man! Faruch Salem who owned the Pita Hut. Nobody's seen him since these monsters bought his restaurant from the bank. I'm telling you, these guys *make* it happen.'

'Times are tough. Everyone's struggling.' I shook my head. 'Must be nice to have no conscience. To be a worker bee for an evil real estate corporation with more money than God.'

'They're worse than that, Curtis. Much, much worse. It's hard to explain.' He sobbed, then collapsed.

It was bad for business, but I let him sleep there right on the bar until closing time. My heart broke for the guy. The furniture store had been in his family for three generations.

I'd driven my friend home that night, seen him to his bed. He was low, but the man loved his daughter and his grandson. He had savings. He had a backup plan. He wanted more than anything to get his store back or start a new one.

He definitely did *not* want to kill himself. And even if he had gotten that low, there was no way he would have made it a gruesome spectacle.

Holland Slate had been murdered.

After Holland's services, Vengeance of Halloween's business seemed to skyrocket, specifically at the location where Holland had met his end. Every macabre sicko in the tri-county area made pilgrimage to that store. From my bar across the street, you could see the line wind down the block on October afternoons.

I told my day manager to mind the shop and paid VoH a visit. Chills danced down my spine as I crossed the parking spot where Holland's body had been found. The concrete was still stained pink.

I pushed through the doors, and spooky organ music chimed. Blacklight reactive paint splattered dark walls. Scarecrow thin identical twin cashiers manned the front counter. They simultaneously closed their cash drawers and flashed double stink eyes before serving another pair of customers.

Gaudy wigs and skimpy outfits lined the walls and endcaps, along with racks of plastic weapons, daggers, swords, axes, sickles, and phony barbed baseball bats. Silvery sci-fi getups, laser guns, cowboy gear, and raunchy *everything* spanned the space where once Holland had created elegant living room displays.

Shelves of specialty candy formed the maze-like impulse buy corral to my left. In the center of the store—where Holland once hosted a pleasant customer service desk—there now stood a crusty gray stage with a cardboard pillar and phony brick façade. Three gaudy animatronic characters formed a macabre tableau.

An Amazonian animatronic towered front and center, her face stitched with dark threads. A shock of swirling white jutted up her beehive hairdo. She had icy blue skin, rusty neck-bolts, and in one bulging arm, held a Styrofoam barbell. The sign above her read 'Francine the Franken-Frauline.'

To the right of the Herculean woman, 'The Mad, Mad Doctor Mummy' clutched an oversized power drill between cobweb-caked claws. He wore a lab coat and an Egyptian headpiece with a doctor's light, which gleamed over a skeleton in a dental chair.

To Francine's left, a lizard man with scuba gear and a long fishing spear had simply been labeled 'Jacques.' His scales shimmered, and his bulging yellow eyes glowed to life as a teen walked past him. '*Sacre bleu*! Jacques shall gut you like ze little fishy!' His webbed claws scraped air as he erupted in snorting laughter.

The startled girl shrieked and laughed. Her friends started to test out the motion sensors on the other two dummies.

Francine shouted in a thick German accent. 'I vill bench press your tombstone!'

'It's time for your check up!' Doctor Mummy's voice came out scratchy as broken glass. His phony drill erupted in a high-pitched *Zzzzzzzzzzzzzzzzzzzzzz!*

Much as I hated to admit, it was a fun store. Packed with kids. Cash flowing to the counter.

Then I spotted shelves of specialty lollipops, molded like a wretched man, clutching his stomach. Gummy worms spilled out in place of intestines. I picked one up, took a close look. The label read 'The Sad, Sorry, Salesman Sucker.'

The molded red face, with its puffy nose and sunken eyes, looked *exactly* like Holland Slate.

My blood broiled. Cases of this candy in dozens of flavors spanned the shelves next to the animatronics.

I took a closer look at a novelty tombstone which read: *Here lies that old guy that got gutted.* T-shirts sported the slogan: *Spill your guts at VoH*, with graphic imagery of bloody intestines embroidered on the stomach.

I shouted. 'What the hell is this?'

The din of shoppers quieted. The twin cashiers smirked in my direction. Spooky sound effects filled the silence.

'Salutations,' came a reedy voice. I turned to see a thin man in a black tuxedo with a high widow's peak and dark feathery hair. 'I'm Mr. Lucard, the day manager. How may I help you?'

I clutched the gummy worm sucker so hard it broke. 'You don't think these are in poor taste, Mr. Lucard?'

He smiled. 'On the contrary, they're bursting with a variety of taste. Bloody Berry, Cantaloupe Crypt, Lemon Lime Leeches—'

I squeezed my fist. Reared back. The manager quieted. It took every ounce of willpower not to punch Lucard in the jaw, but I thought of Holland. I thought of the legal repercussions.

It would make me feel better, but it wouldn't make this right.

'You're openly profiting off a man's death,' I said.

'What man would that be?' Lucard stared blankly.

'Holland Slate, the man who owned this store. The man who died outside those doors.'

'Ah,' Lucard softened. 'Good sir, I understand you must be grieved. Please know that Vengeance of Halloween and its parent company Samhain LLC express full condolences regarding that unfortunate business. However, I assure you, we have not altered our products in response.'

'Bullshit!'

'This candy had been in production since earlier this year. It took months of product testing and market research to develop.'

'Your company anticipated that *salesman* suicides would be big this year?'

'I don't appreciate your accusations, but I admire your imagination.' He gave a canned-sounding chuckle. 'Before his incident, your friend visited our store and harassed the customers on a number of occasions in late September. He may have seen these items and used them as...twisted inspiration.'

'That's not the kind of man Holland is.'

Lucard grinned. 'Was.'

Then I *did* hit him. His face felt hard as plastic.

He crumpled like a ragdoll against a display of seasonal glassware. Orange shot glasses shattered. A line of ketchup-red blood dribbled from his nose.

Twin cashiers approached. A muscular teen hovered nearby, unsure who to help.

'It's all right, everyone!' Lucard stiffly got to his feet. 'This gentleman was about to show himself out.' Then he lowered his voice, 'In which case, there would be no charges.'

I scowled and snatched another salesman sucker off the rack. 'I'm reporting this to the Better Business Bureau.' Then I left.

#

Later that night, the usual barflies lingered until close. I still couldn't shake the image of Holland, gutted in the parking lot. Couldn't stop my skin from crawling. Those sickos were cashing in—and worse, kids seemed drawn by the store's grisly allure.

After my employees mopped up and went home, I lingered in dim bar light and stared at the candy sculpture of my dead friend.

Who was I kidding? There was nothing illegal about it. All I could do was try to turn the community against the store. And it was too late for that to matter. Already, Vengeance of Halloween was rolling in October profit. By November, they'd be selling Christmas crap.

I pocketed the Salesman Sucker, locked up shop, and headed to my car.

A gold sickle of moon arched over the strip-mall across the intersection. VoH's orange 'closed' sign glowed in dark windows. I approached my car.

A gravelly voice whispered; '*Pardonez-moi, monsieur.*'

I spied a dark shape with a wide face, silhouetted by street lamps. A muscular tail swished behind the figure and thumped a pick-up truck. In one hand it clutched a long, sharp object. The other hand scratched the glass windowpane. 'My engine is stalled, do you have ze jumper cables?' The stranger gave a high, snorting laugh.

I hit the panic alarm on my car and reached for the door just as someone grabbed me from the side. My feet lifted off pavement. Air rushed, vertigo swirled, and I slammed against the hood of my car. The alarm blared. Bright spots speckled my vision.

I struggled to sit upright. An enormous woman—Francine the Franken-Frauline—towered over me. Her decayed, stitched-up face flashed in blinking headlights.

The lizard man Jacques thumped over my car, somersaulted, and jammed his fishing spear straight through the hood. I flinched. The horn squelched to a halt. He had skewered my car's electrical system and landed nimbly on huge webbed feet. His scales glimmered in moonlight, and my heart jolted.

These did not look like animatronics *or* costumes.

Jacques yanked the spear free and waggled it within inches of my eyes. 'Such noise is not appreciated, non?'

The loud *Zzzzzzzzzzzzzzzzzzzzzz!* of Doctor Mummy's drill sounded to my right. I cowered against my windshield. Francine snatched me by the collar and yanked me forward. 'Ve vould like to have a frank and open diskussion with you, Mister Barman.'

'You people are crazy!'

The woman smacked me.

'We are not ze people!' Jacques scoffed.

'You're monsters.' I spat blood.

125

'Correct.' Doctor Mummy snarled. 'We've come to bargain, barman.'

I scanned the mostly empty lot. The night was dead, save red and green traffic lights. My bar was always the last business to close. Maybe someone had heard the alarm. I had to buy time. 'You want money? My soul? I—'

'Your retail space,' Francine thundered. 'Samhain LLC demands it.'

'Why? Your ridiculous company already has three seasonal businesses in this town, and one of them is *right* across the street.' I gestured toward the VoH store.

The mummy snatched my right hand and slammed it against the hood of the car. I reached out with my left to stop him, only for Francine to pin it in place.

The mummy's drill inched toward my palm. *Zzzzzzzzzzzzzzzzzzzz!*

'*Mon Dieu!* He wants to play ze hardball!' Jacques chuckled.

'Stop!'

The drill died out. The Mummy's decrepit jaw stretched into a grin.

'I'm open to selling, but...' I panted, 'I need...a sales pitch.'

The trio of monsters exchanged puzzled glances. My head throbbed.

'I want to understand exactly why this transaction benefits the community. I'm head of the small business association, and there could be questions.'

Francine rubbed her square jaw. 'He vants a presentation.'

I nodded. 'A detailed one.'

'It is a formality, Herr Barman, you must understand, because you vill sell or die, like your friend the lollipop.'

I swallowed hard. 'Okay. Let me call my attorney and have him set up a time.'

Doctor Mummy produced a blood-splattered doctor's bag and opened it. 'Your attorney is unavailable.' He hoisted the blood-soaked toothless head of a bald mustached man with a distinctive mole on his right cheek.

'Jesus!' My stomach turned. I vomited in the direction of Jacques. I had only glimpsed the head, but it was unmistakably my lawyer Jim Angus.

Within seconds, Jacques was slurping up my vomit with a long, pink tongue. I turned away to retch again. Gasped. 'Why?'

'Our organization is not fond of red tape,' Doctor Mummy explained. 'Part of our business model is to sever out the middlemen.'

'Ve deal with stakeholders directly.'

Francine started dragging me, and glass scraped my legs. Doctor Mummy and Jacques marched behind us. I jerked and squirmed, at first, but then the Mummy started revving his drill, and I went slack.

As we cut on a diagonal across the intersection, my heart leapt at the sight of headlights down the road. This late, after all the bars were closed it could only mean two things: riff-raff or...

Blue and red mars lights sparked to life, and a police siren cut the night. The three monsters halted and faced the approaching squad car. Franken-Frauline jerked me into a sitting position and squeezed my neck.

The officers exited their vehicles, weapons drawn. 'Freeze! Hands in the air.'

Doctor Mummy slowly raised both arms. In an instant, a snakes of yellow wrapping coiled out and bridged the space between the monsters and the officers. Both officers arms were bound, yanked skyward. Shots echoed. Doctor Mummy conducted the wrappings with his fingers, jerked the pistols into each officer's face. Meanwhile Jacques twirled his fishing spear and stalked forward.

'No!' I said. 'Stop!'

The lizard swiped his weapon. I squeezed my eyes shut. Heard the sound of blood splattering road, and I instantly knew who had gutted my friend Holland Slate.

I screamed louder. Francine yanked me into a chokehold. I struggled for breath. My feet kicked, but the woman's legs were as strong as steel poles. 'You vil be silent,' she commanded. 'Or I vil break you neck. Ve have other vays of achieving our goals.'

I stopped struggling, and she relaxed her grip.

Doctor Mummy reached into the squad car for the police radio. 'Everything's okay on this end,' he said, in perfectly human-sounding imitation. 'Moving on.'

Static echoed, and the Mummy dropped the radio.

'Clean this up,' Francine said. 'Dispose of the vehicle. Then meet us back at VoH.'

The monstrous woman slung me over her shoulders like a sack of potatoes. My head swirled with vertigo. The Mummy's drill echoed, and the sharp slice of moon danced above the neon orange Vengeance of Halloween sign.

Within moments, we were inside the darkened store. Francine hurled me onto the gray stage where the three monsters had previously stood on display as animatronics. All I saw now was a dummy dressed like the store manager, Lucard, and the two sickly scarecrows, wearing VoH cashier polos.

I struggled onto my knees as my captor leapt onto the stage. She lifted the mannequin of Lucard and licked its cheek. 'These enchantments serve us vell during daylight hours. You didn't really think a human could run a store as successfully as VoH, did you, barman?'

'Well,' I wheezed. 'With the right timing, inventory, and rollout, anyone can—'

She kicked me in the gut, and I doubled over.

'It takes a monster to take the business of Halloween to the next level. In fact, it takes scores of us. VoH is more than a store. It is an experience. A lifestyle. A culture. Ruthlessness transcends every market.'

'Please,' I wheezed. 'Don't kill me.'

The woman smiled. 'I see you understand our business model.'

'No, I don't! I don't understand why people have to die—why my friend had to die—for Halloween!'

She scowled. 'Halloween is not a holiday. It is a lifestyle. A culture. A—'

'You said that already,' I snapped, surging with bitter adrenaline. I got to my feet. 'But Halloween is fake. Halloween ends!'

'Not this year.' She strutted across the gray stage, kicking aside one of the twin scarecrows. She pulled a cord down, and produced a PowerPoint clicker from inside her Frankenstein jacket. A projection lit up the screen with the title card 'VoH Business Model.' Then she rapidly clicked through a number of slides and landed on one labeled: *Performance: Year Over Year*, showing stacks of pumpkins in a colorful bar graph.

'The Coalition of Monsters that formed Samhain LLC is not

satisfied by these seasonal spikes.' She clicked forward to show a graph of 'Projected Growth' in which the pumpkins piled up more and more for the next decade. 'Ve have developed a strategy called Eternal October. Complete socio-economic takeover by Halloween. Far too long has our presence been artificially sequestered in the markets, and it's time ve had justice. Hence...' She gestured to me.

'Vengeance of Halloween,' I rasped.

Francine clapped. 'Very good!'

'But this doesn't make sense. It would be total saturation. People don't need this many stores for costumes and decorations and—' I tossed the candy from my pocket '—*sick* lollipops.'

'Ignorant barman.' She produced a contract from her vest and tossed it at my feet. I stooped down and perused the documents, which included a plan for "Witches' Brewery".

'It's not just costumes and treats ve're after. Ve vant *everything*. A tavern can be Halloween. Grocery stores can sell Halloween food. Furniture stores can sell Halloween furniture. It's all branding. And vhen you own the culture, you own the market, and you own the souls. It's already happening. It cannot be stopped.'

I glanced around the darkened store. In pale moonlight, I saw the hulking forms of Jacques and Doctor Mummy lumbering toward the doors through the empty parking lot. But I noticed something else too. Gleaming yellow rays reflecting off rows of merchandise.

I glanced back down at the dummy of the store owner. 'You—uh—monsters. That's the correct term?' I asked.

She crossed her arms. 'That's *our* vord. Ve're taking it back. You may refer to us as entrepreneurs.'

'You're nocturnal entrepreneurs, correct? These dummies run the store in the day, and by night, you live. Like werewolves, awakened by moonlight, right?'

'Very clever, barman. Ve depend on familiars like Mr. Lucard. But soon our curse vill be all powerful. Eternal night,' she boasted.

'Good business plan.' My heart surged. 'Are you trying to corner the market for mon—people like you?'

'Humans are all monsters seeking nocturnal birth. You vill all crave our products. The youth are easiest to vin over, but in time, Samhain LLC vill go global.'

I was starting to see the store more clearly. Where once there had been plastic spiders, now there were grotesque creatures wriggling on the walls. Where once gummy worms had spilled from the suckers, now they literally wriggled, crinkling the plastic. And where once there had been dull plastic prop weapons, there were now shelves and buckets filled with deadly metal weaponry.

'What's the timeline for your global expansion?' I pretended to flip through the proposal for the Witches' Brew Bar. 'You know I think this is a good concept, and I might know a few more colleagues who would be interested in selling.'

She arched her eyebrows in suspicion.

'Really,' I said. 'Just uh,' I hobbled off the stage toward the props. 'Let me get a pen.'

Severed hands—no longer props, reached at me with bloody fingertips. I eyed daggers, swords, sickles, and sabers, all transformed sharp as a hooked moon. *I'm not fast enough, not good enough with any of these weapons to overtake them.*

The front door opened, and Doctor Mummy and Jacques flanked the exits, arms crossed. The mummy revved his drill.

My eyes landed on the rusted edge of a chainsaw prop.

Francine cleared her throat. 'Pens are by the counter, barman. No tricks.'

The image played out of myself, woozy from being roughed up, trying to lug a heavy chainsaw and keep them at bay. Bad idea.

Then I caught a gleaming silver Space Ranger costume hanging across the warehouse. 'I'm just tired,' I said. 'It's late.' I proceeded to the counter and grabbed a pen. Then I signed every line. 'You can't beat big business. Just stave it off for a few decades, I suppose.'

'Bring it here, barman.' Francine beckoned with one hand.

I played up my wooziness, veered right—near the rack of space ranger accessories—and snatched a toy ray gun off the wall. I aimed, pulled the trigger.

At first, only the blaring noise of the phony toy gun sounded, but when the woman's eyes widened, I squeezed the trigger tighter, A blue glow emitted from the tip of the gun, and I released it.

A blinding flash of energy blasted across the room. The Franken-Frauline exploded into fiery chunks of flesh. The cardboard backing, still attached the ray gun caught fire, and I dropped it in surprise.

'Stop him!' Francine's flaming head demanded, tenuously attached to pieces of her charred torso. Her severed arms crawled in desperation. I tossed the paperwork into the air, stomped the flaming cardboard, reached down and yanked the ray gun free from the packaging.

Doctor Mummy was already upon me. *Zzzzzzzzzzzzzzzzzzzzzz!* I tucked and rolled behind the display, squeezed the trigger, charged up another shot.

'Time for your check-up,' the doctor snarled. Putrid wrappings snaked around the display stand, wriggled for my wrists. I released the energy blast, and it exploded between us, shoving me against the wall. Fiery wooden shrapnel lay everywhere amid burning pieces of Sci-Fi costumery. Doctor Mummy lay trapped under the toppled display, his bandages burned. He gave a ghoulish wail.

I charged another shot, searched frantically for the lizard man, but he was nowhere in sight.

Just run, I thought. The door was unguarded.

Or was it?

I glanced up at the ceiling. Jacques clung to the rafters with his claws. His tongue dribbling. 'Nice try!' I blasted up.

He skittered aside, but the neon blue blast sent him flying behind the counter. His severed, charred tail thumped the floor. I darted for the door, leapt over the smoldering appendage, and pushed into the chill October night. I only made it a few feet when something grabbed my ankle and dragged me to the ground. My ray gun cracked against the curb.

Jacques' fiery torso crawled over me. His tail stump smoldered. His legs were twisted, broken, and flickering with blue flame. I reached for the ray gun and squeezed the trigger, but only a tiny battery-operated light flashed. Whatever magic was keeping the props real was stronger *inside* the store.

I kicked and backed away.

The creature snarled, hissed, and cursed in French. His rubber scuba suit gave off a horrible burning stench as it melted into his scales.

Lizard spittle poured over me. I punched his jaw. Jacques snapped and gnashed my fist. I cried in agony, kneed him in the gut. He clawed my stomach, and I felt blood spilling down my sides. I stared up at the orange sign, glowing in moonlight, and realized I was dying in the exact same spot as Holland.

I was too weak to fight back.

But the lizard man was slowing down. He slumped over me. His eyes went wet and wide. I smelled his burning flesh. He was expiring, but he was far too heavy for me to move.

And I was losing blood.

My head swam.

At least I had put up a good fight.

Those monsters thought they could change the rules, but that didn't mean there wasn't any competition left.

I snickered and drifted in and out of consciousness.

I gave those blood-suckers a run for their money, Holland, I thought.

#

I awoke to the steady beeps of medical equipment. A white room came into focus. My hand was wrapped in a splint where Jacques had bitten me. I tried to sit up, but the raw pain in my abdomen stopped me. With my good hand, I reached down and felt straps of gauze covering my midsection, where Jacques had attempted to gut me. *Like ze little fishy*, his voice seared in my mind, and I shuddered.

'Take it easy. Lie down. You've been out a long time. A nurse hovered over me. 'Can you tell me your name?'

I answered her questions as she came into focus. A homely woman in white scrubs.

'How long have I been out?'

'Months. It was touch and go for a while.'

'What day is it?

'October first.'

I stared for a moment. 'I've been out for a year?'

'Just a couple months.' She smiled, showing teeth yellow as parchment. 'I'll get you some food.'

I pulled my sheets down. My hospital gown was covered in jack o'lantern print. I glanced up on the wall and saw; *Samhain Mummorial Hospital: Room 666.*

I leapt out of bed, then clutched my abs in agony. The calendar on the wall read October. I hobbled over and flipped to the next page. October. October. Every month was October!

On staggering legs, I fumbled for the window. Across the street stood business after business of Halloween merchants.

Creepy Café.

The Hardware St'Horror.

Chupacabra's Chimichangas.

My head swam. The papers. I had signed them. Left them strewn on the floor before I attempted to escape.

'Get back in bed!' The nurse reappeared, shoving a tray of candy corn, suckers, and chocolate bars in my face. 'Have something to eat, honey bunch.'

I knocked the tray to the floor. Tried to get around her, but my guts blazed like fire.

She put her hands on her hips. Shook her head. 'Doctor! Please assist with this patient.'

From the hallway, a shrill noise echoed...

Zzzzzzzzzzzzzzzzzzzzzzz!

Where the World is Thin
Arthur Goodhill

It is a strange thing to say you have seen death, no matter how it has presented itself to you. For some, it may be a bright light with sounding trumpets and euphoric pulses coursing through the body. For others, the flashing of memories both good and bad, recalling a lifetime recounted in the briefest of moments, drawing painful consequence or benevolent gratitude from its summations. In my case, that brief encounter has lingered with me in my dreams, until now. There have been many accounts and speculations surrounding Death, along with vast amounts of fiction and myth, some describing cloaked skeletal figures that carry scythes, while others mentioning only vague feelings and presences never truly formed into the physical. I have no right to cast doubt upon any account, only stitch together a conclusion from what strange and haunting memories still reside in my mind. There is not just one lonesome reaper that stalks those due to depart, but countless haunting wardens of death, across the span of countless lands that menacingly tend to their allotted flock. In old Irish folklore, there is a dying wisdom surrounding places where strange things happen, where the barriers between that of our own world and the next are weakened. These are known as 'thin places'. Let me say this, as I look out my cottage window, the loose straws of thatch scraping against the silhouette of that desolate mountain, I believe the barren marshes of Slieve Bloom to be the among the thinnest.

There are always questions that surround those unknown facets of existence, life after death. The journey there and the ultimate destination. But for the most part, these only facilitate a morbid curiosity, and any claims to know the particulars are often proved false, either by ignorance or outright deceit. There are no signs of life outside, and selfish as it may seem, what I would give for a stranger to call. For someone to unwittingly enter and trade places with me, for it seems that tonight I have assumed the burden of knowing whatever morbid truth lies beyond the land of the living. For what it's worth, this account which I tell I unreservedly believe to be true. And now, on the night of Oíche Shamhna, that which I have spent twenty years hiding from has found me again.

#

It was the winter of 1962, with a record cold having crept into the country, leaving the grass white tipped with frost and the roads dangerously veneered in ice. The damp hung in the air but never made it to full precipitation, having little to no rain. I had just returned home from Boston due to complications arising from a late night brawl and subsequent irregularities with my immigration paperwork. Suffering with a traveller's unrest, my bags still lay packed in the family home in County Laois, in preparation for any awaiting adventure. The cottage itself was small but well-tended, with a turf fire where hearty meals simmered in cast iron pots that hung from the crane. The cottage lay in the shadow of the mountain, and every evening was cut short as the sun set behind the looming slopes.

Towards the end of October, two separate hikers disappeared in a particular section of marshy plain in the mountainous region close by, and so the council sought out the help of local volunteers. Together, some from the village and myself formed an impromptu search party, and began doing our part searching for the missing persons. A strange detail regarding one of the missing persons was the account from a friend that was travelling with them. They swore they were no more than ten or fifteen feet ahead of the vanished wanderer when they noticed the squelch of their own footsteps were no longer echoed by their companions, and turned to see nothing but the endless fog that had enveloped the land. Day after day, we trudged through the barren acres that stretched along the Laois/Offally border in search of the waylaid travellers, but without luck. The walks were quiet, with broad lines between us, some poking sticks in the ground and some small chattering between others. Their names escape me now, but we did call out for them in those first few days, shouting into the bitter wilderness, until we didn't anymore. After the fourth day, there was no chatter, no diligent poking of clay, only silent walking through the mountains. The only gain from the futile search was identifying a very specific stretch that this friend claimed was where the disappearance occurred. Having spent the best part of two weeks combing the area, the authorities in charge concluded that while the past disappearances were to be mourned, future ones could be mitigated by way of some basic infrastructure.

#

In this particular section, there is a stretch of a little less than five miles running from north-east to south-west. While the altitude is high enough to tighten breath, the terrain itself is flat, and covered with clumped formations of liverwort and gorse that beds between the marshy grass. Its colour is a mixture of lifeless browns and blacks, with those parts not swallowed by the joyless growths faintly showing green in small pockets, as if slowly drowning beneath the marshy surface. This blanket of uneven growth makes traversal through the area a far more laborious effort than one might think, requiring large lunging steps and carefully calculated footfalls in case ones ankle might turn against the mounded tufts. To add to the difficulty, that winter, the aforementioned fog had covered the entire area, leaving visibility close to impossible beyond thirty or forty meters. Along this route were small sticks stuck into the ground, protruding upwards like swords left behind in battle, placed by countless wanderers in hopes to mark their course or possibly aid those behind, but the result was a concatenation of orderless pikes that rose up from the earth without intention or pattern. If you have done any share of hikes or treks you will surely know of the gentle reassurance one feels when discovering evidence of those who came before, having in the finding a clue of being on the right track, a validation of your journey. But here it was not the same. These vestigial

markers showed only the desperate attempts of so many who came before to clamber hopelessly through the bog, and in their colossal quantity, spread vast and without order, it showed only a cold assurance of despair.

Close to the halfway point in this forsaken marsh, lies a small and unusually round lake. Nowadays it has a much more inviting moniker; Clear Lake, but back then I knew it only as 'the drop'. A natural phenomenon, some have speculated that it is a turlough, although turloughs are notable for their draining and filling throughout the seasons, while this lake has persisted for many years without falter. Others have said that it is the result of a meteorite making the mountain its explosive resting place in years long since past. Regardless of its cause or origin, there wasn't the time nor resources to dive the water, and the witness had claimed that the occurrence took place at an area at least one hundred metres west of the watery landmark. But being a halfway point of sorts, it was along this section that we erected three wooden posts dug deep into the earth, from each hanging a small lantern. One to the North-east, one to the southwest, and one in the centre, beside the drop. On the southern slope, a small cabin was erected that held a bed and a north facing window that could view out onto the marshy plain. The cabin was no more than thirty square feet in size, with a bed that spanned length to length, enough for an average sized man to sleep. At the culmination of the work, we gathered at the newly built cabin, and the local authority asked who would volunteer for the role. None spoke, and while I was eager to take on the role, the hesitancy of the others brewed doubts in me. But after a few moments of silence, I raised my hand and was hastily briefed and lauded by the local councilman, no doubt pleased to be done with the affair. As the group disbanded and headed back to their homes down the mountain, many of them looked at me strangely as they passed, as if sharing in their silence some collective sorrow. It wasn't in that instance that those observations were made, but upon reflection much later. Had I only picked up on those subtle hints then, what harrowing terror I might have avoided. But I didn't, and anything to occupy my time since coming home was welcome. It was to this cabin that I would bring my food and supplies, promising to stay and light the lanterns, until that fog had lifted.

#

My preparations were short, and along with some dried meats and well wrapped potatoes, my journey up the mountain for my post was uneventful. The wind came across the crest of its stretching silhouette gently, but carried in it a horrible cold. With the aid of a felled birch, I had a walking stick to assist the ascent and it wasn't long until I was inside the makeshift cabin, unpacking my bedding and finding suitable storage for food and other items on the one erected shelf to the side of the small space. On that southern slope, the north facing window was exceptionally small, leaving the interior in almost complete darkness throughout the day, save for one extra lantern and a large box of thick white candles in a wooden crate left by the local authorities. There was also a small makeshift stove made from an aluminium can and a grate that had been cut to shape down towards its base. On the side of the candle box in large letters spelled out '10 Hours Burning'. By the time I was settled in, what little light there was had already diminished, leaving the first round to be complete.

Carrying my own lantern up the remaining crest, just before the marsh levelled into the barren moor, the thick fog spilled across the edge and fell downwards with slivers that broke off and dissipated in faint strips, like gnarled fingers warding off visitors. On the marsh itself, those sporadic pikes lay prickled about, only their tops visible in the lingering fog, like desperate drowning arms that clutched for air. A uniformed oblong gap in their otherwise dense dispersal lay in the centre of the bog, pointing me towards the drop. Having served a guiding purpose after all, it wasn't long before my lunging treks brought me around to the far side of the water where the post had been laid. I lit one of the white candles off of my own lantern, then placed it inside, turning around to make way for the next post that lay about a hundred and fifty meters north-east. After it was lit, I made my way back past the drop and lit the third and final post before heading back to the cabin. Even with the newly lit guides, the fog was thick and unforgiving, and attempting to head from the south-west post directly to the cabin proved more difficult than I anticipated, so I opted to return to the drop and retrace my steps from there. This worked well, and not long after I was approaching the same crest that dipped down to my temporary home. When I turned to look back at my work, seeing three faintly

flickering lights where before there was nothing, brought me some small pride, and could have sworn I saw the faintest of shapes and shadows moving in the mist, guided now through the dark by my hand.

During that winter, atop the bleak mountain, the term *first light* was an expression of time, alone. True, it became brighter at dawn, but only just. The bulging, dark greys of clouds that blanketed the lifeless sky showed hints of a burning sun behind their stretching expanse, but never permitted any of its light through. The fog remained. Thick and persistent as ever, and at dawn I rose to re-ignite the guiding lanterns. At that hour, there should have been some burning left from the night before, but looking out the cabin window showed that they had expired at least an hour before their expected time. Still, I went about my rounds all the same, seeing each had died a little before the end of their life, having in them an inch or two worth of wax left to burn.

This time, after finishing the south-eastern post, I felt confident about the shortcut across to the cabin, and hastily made my way back. Before getting beyond the turn of the slope, a shadow much like the ones that seemed to appear the previous evening, caught the corner of my eye. I turned, but all I could glimpse was a dark silhouette moving hastily away from the water and disappearing into the enveloping mist. Much to my dismay, this lonesome wanderer— whoever it was—had extinguished the candle by the drop before departing.

I'll admit that in that moment, the only emotion I felt was anger. The malice of some careless hiker to extinguish an aid at a time when most needed filled me with rage, and I started off for the drop, my lantern in hand ready to catch those who had undone my work.

At the water's edge, there was no sign of anyone, and even if they were close, the fog was an unbeatable cloak. Shouting expletives into the surrounding nothing proved worthless, and the dampening of sound from that seeping mist dulled any echo, with each outburst ending abruptly in a flat and eerie silence.

It was only after opening the lantern's small hinged door that my anger was replaced with confusion. The extinguished candle had not smouldered and smoked as would normally happen when blown out, but its wick was frosted white at the top, as if pinched into darkness by hands of ice.

With the door closed and faced again with the barren marsh, that same unnatural silence took on a very different feeling. The acres and acres of reclusive nothing that only the day before seemed like a pilgrimage in need of aid, now seemed an infested and unwelcoming territory, and one that I volunteered to wander.

Across the glass-like water of the drop there began a shimmering ripple, which in and of itself is not unusual, only that this lake is without aquatic life. Panicked rationales followed; maybe a surreptitious bird that swooped at the pool for a quick meal, or a lingering water flea sailing across its surface. But the ripple was far too big for that of a water flea or any other insect, and no birds fly above that mountain. Distant caws and tweets that so often punctuate even the more barren parts of Ireland were absent there. Only that same unnerving silence remained as the gentle ripples died away and the water came to rest. There was something out there, watching. Somewhere in the bleak surrounds lay hungry eyes that leered longingly in my direction.

I left immediately around the water's edge and didn't care to look back at whether or not the candles remained lit, but hastily returned to my cabin and lit the stove.

#

Later that night, the lanterns were lit swiftly and without incident. The initial lure of adventure and purpose had now turned purely perfunctory in the bleak uneasiness that crept about, and sleep was intermittent and restless. The following morning I woke to hasty wet steps and belligerent shouts outside the cabin. As I got dressed, an aggressive rapping started on the door, and the angry councilman from that first search party, with five or six locals standing behind him greeted me when I opened it.

He pointed to the unlit lanterns, shouting all sorts of expletives and accusations. I threw on my shoes and jacket to show what I knew to be the anomaly. Leading them to the lantern at the drop, upon opening it, it showed the same strange manner of extinguishment.

The council man grunted but ceased his accusations, informing me that they had new reports of a missing person from just the previous evening, having not arrived at the camp at the lower side of the mountain. Their last known contact was with a day hiker who met them on the far side of the marsh.

After assuring the council man and accompanying mob of my diligence, they reluctantly made their way down the steep slope to civilisation, with one exception. Inside the cabin was one of the older men that had come, warming his hands against the dying cinders of the stove.

'I'm glad you're alright, young fella,' he said as I entered, closing the door behind me.

He only looked at me briefly as he spoke, like a great deal of worry had been lifted from him when he saw me. The cabin was washed in a dull unyielding grey from the small window. It spilled in at an angle, coldly lighting one side of the small space, but where he sat lay in darkness, only the smouldering embers casting a faint red light on his face. I threw a few sticks on the stove and put the small kettle on top, offering tea.

'No thanks, I won't be long. But have a seat there now. There's a few things we've to chat about.'

He wore a navy blazer with a crusty looking farmers cap on and a thick woollen jumper that had an off white shirt collar creeping up at either side of his neck. With a nervous curiosity, I obliged and sat quietly on the bed beside him as his thick workman's hands stretched and rubbed together against the growing flame.

'Did ya know that Halloween is an Irish tradition?' he began. 'Oíche Shamhna, it's called. But there's a bit more to it than trick or treating. The Morrigan, Banshees, fairies and all sorts of Irish legends have been reported on Halloween. People hearing screams

141

in the distance. Lights in the sky in the dead of night, and others of a more human sort, dancing around fires in celebration.'

The flame needed no help, and he pulled his hands away, resting them on his lap and staring into the crackling wood within the stove.

'I've heard it said that the reason these things happen, is because on Oíche Samhna, or Halloween, the space between our own world becomes sort of fuzzy, ya see? Everywhere has a sort of blending together, this world and the next I mean. And some spots, some spots hold a connection of their own to the other world. In some spots, that other place is always more close than far away, if ya catch my meaning.'

He paused, his eyes moving my direction, but never fully meeting my own, before re-focusing on the fire.

'Do you know why we call it the drop?' he asked. 'Some say it's just a drop 'o water up there on the mountain. Simple enough explanation, I suppose. But, it's actually a mistranslation from the Gaeilge. *An Titim* is the word, and it means *the fall*. Nothing to do with how many ankles have snapped in that marshy bog either. We were told, all of us when we were younger, that lake goes somewhere else.'

He turned to me then, his eyes dead set on mine, and whatever calmness was there before was replaced now with a stern and unmistakable seriousness.

'Not you nor I, nor that twit of a councilman are going to stop whatever thing haunts the fog. You be sure of that. So light your candles if you like and say your prayers. But best get off the mountain, young lad. As soon as you can.'

He stared at me for a moment, until the whistle of the kettle began. Then his eyes softened and he groaned as he stood up. When he opened the door, the dull light spilled in, painting his black hunched silhouette against the unending grey of the sky. He stopped and turned towards me, looking like he might speak again. But whatever it might have been, he thought better of it, and left.

What followed was a natural cadence of thoughts. First was considering with the harrowing confirmation that I was not alone at my post on Slieve Bloom, but was kept company by something else that stalked the sequestered mountain marsh. Following this came rationalisations and the dangerous arrogance of youth that assures us we know better. Just a demented old man, I told myself. Too stuck in the myths and legends that have conveniently slipped into obscurity with the passage of time. Even still, I knew that if I didn't light the candles on my next round, they wouldn't be lit again. What was required was to act in defiance of the superstitions laid at my feet, and see out my appointed task.

The rest of the day was spent waiting in the tiny cabin, cautiously looking out the small window to see the faint floating orbs still lit through the dense fog. My nerve was fragile, and the worried waiting for a premature extinguishment only built up the idea of the task ahead. As the dull sky grew darker and darker, eventually night closed in. Stepping out of the cabin and onto the marsh, the lanterns remained flickering in the distance, with my own once again in hand. Before leaving I left some extra wood on the stove, so as to have its own glowing light as a guide for my return. One round to prove him wrong was all it would take.

Across the mulching and muddy bog, that same stillness gripped the air. The distant surrounds held black shapes against the darkening sky as land and firmament blended together in nightfall. My own lantern showed the molasses-like fog that hung around just above my knees, begrudgingly floating around my legs as I went. In the shadowy distance there was nothing only the faint lights of those lanterns, still flickering gently, waiting for revival. Nothing out of the ordinary happened at the drop, nor to the north eastern lantern, and not the south western.

On my return, I was unable to see the glow of the cabins stove in the window, so once more I returned to the water's edge opposite the first lantern to get my bearings. But before turning my back to the water, there was a noise. Like before, a small ripple in the water. Looking into the glass-like pond, that first lantern that I had lit was reflected perfectly in the gently pulsating waves that's stillness was now disturbed. It was as if the one above the drop lay in reality, untouched and unimportant, and its reflection that wobbled in the now rippling surface lay beyond this place, somewhere else.

Standing on the water's edge, there was no evidence of what had made the break in the bobbing surface, but yet it was impossible to leave. Then, that circular aura of light that surrounded that reflected image in the drop, wobbling and rippling, had something appear at its base. From the bottom of the inverted post, beginning at the far shore where reflection met reality and through those undulating waves came a darkness that began to swallow the image, creeping further towards me. The water became more disturbed, steadily pulsating with the once small waves growing and growing, until the reflection was swallowed, and the mirrored image that once lay in the water, was gone.

Bringing my eyes up from the dark waters, the surface too was swallowed in this new dark, with the lantern that only moments ago lay freshly lit and flickering, now absent. It was only when the squeak of the lantern's hinge met my ears, followed by the sharp hiss of an extinguished wick, that I knew this was not some shapeless abyss that had grown out of nothing, but a thing more terrifying than words can account for.

Standing at the far edge of the water, between me and the now extinguished lantern, was that which had rose up from those terrible depths. Fear gripped me, and whatever movement I might have wished or hoped to do was at the mercy of my own petrification. The light I held still burned brightly by my side, and a quiet tear rolled down my face as whatever this thing was, turned around, and languidly glided across the water.

Shrouded in a dark cloak, the pale and hairless face held a crazed and wide bloodshot stare as it approached, with bags under its eyes as if it hadn't known sleep for an age. When it reached me, hunched and all as it was, it floated on that watery shore standing at least a foot above my own head. I held my breadth as it outstretched a gnarled and wrinkled hand that reached towards my lantern, unhinged its small opening and pinched into nothing the flame that lay within. The tear that lay streaked down my face froze against my skin, and in that endless dark, the stark whites of those crazed eyes met my own. Behind it, there were multiple splashes in the water, but I could not look away from that thing that stood before me, and it was only when the faint lights left and right that had been gently glowing in the distance suddenly died, that the shadowy figure disappeared.

#

I do not know when or how I came down the mountain, only that at some point in the night, my parents took me in, offering food that I refused to eat and tea I let go cold in front of me. I found out much later that after my third week of silence, commitment to St. Fintan's asylum for the insane had been arranged, but was withheld after my coming around not long after. Reclusiveness followed, a condition whose shackles still bind me to this day. It pains me to say that my own parents died before their time, not being able to bear the stress and heartache of their only son's sharp withdrawal from normal living. The older man who tried to warn me visited for a time, bringing me my messages, and often staying to chat. He told me that following Halloween is another old tradition, called Samhain. The first of November marking the last of the harvest and the shift from light to dark. There were other stories too, which I try to remember fondly, but in truth, when he passed a few years back, I was glad of it. It wasn't his fault, but every time he came, it only served as a reminder of his warning that I had paid no heed.

I never spoke to anyone about my time on the mountain, only internally tormenting myself instead with theories and speculations on what had happened. There was a time when I had nearly convinced myself it was all an abhorrent hallucination. A miasma of fanciful events conjured up in my mind as a way to stifle the excruciating isolation of home. But as I sit here staring out at that mountain, the sun long set and

creeping dark reminds me of that fear so deep it cannot be conjured up unaided. No, none of us are equipped with thoughts so menacingly debilitating alone, they have to come from somewhere else. Why I escaped that night and so many others perished was never clear to me, until now. My lantern is still lit to my side, with boxes of candles strewn about the room so it may never go out. I write these final words in hope that it will serve those who find it, and lend credence to those tales we so often dispel as myth. There is a chill in the room now, and while my sight is failing, in the doorway to the hall I can still make out the whites of bloodshot eyes that glare with intense familiarity. Up on that mountain, in that sickening fog that swallowed so many, my survival was only a consequence of my own unreadiness. Half-grown, unfinished. But as the hour draws closer to midnight on the night of Oíche Shamhna,

145

the last of the harvest is upon me, and the slowly wilting candle by my side that flickers into nothing, tells me I am ripe.

Whispers
Martin Livings

'Gemma!' Ed hollered as he climbed the stairs of their cozy suburban home. 'Come on, kiddo! Time to go!' The lights weren't working, the power outage lasting the whole afternoon thus far, an annoyance any time of the year but especially today. It was no huge surprise, though; the oil crisis had been going on for months now, and occasional blackouts had become almost normal. Though the phones didn't normally go out as well, so that was a whole new wrinkle. *Interesting times*, he mused. *Bring on the eighties, I say.*

'One minute,' his daughter yelled back from behind her closed bedroom door. Then he heard a sound that had seemed so damn endearing last July when Gemma's ninth birthday had come around, but which he was now utterly sick of. The harsh squawk of a walkie-talkie. She spoke again, in a more hushed tone. He couldn't make out the words.

He opened the door to her room, poked his head in. She was sitting cross-legged on the windowsill, the pane raised and the long antenna of the radio sticking out into the chill fall air. Ed looked past her, out of the window; the sky, entirely covered by rolling waves of clouds, was beginning to show the first hints of sunset orange. 'We're late,' he reminded her, pointing at the Felix the Cat clock on the wall above her aggressively-pink bed. 'All the good treats'll be taken.'

Gemma tried to look nonchalant at that prospect, but failed. Everyone knew that Mrs Anderson on Cedar Avenue gave out full-size candy bars, but she only ever bought one big pack of them, so they were always snapped up pretty fast. She pressed the talk button on the walkie-talkie. 'See you on Jackson Street soon, Kit! Over and out!'

That horrible crackly screech again, then a distorted voice. Gemma's best friend, Kit. 'Over and out!' Then blessed silence as she turned the handset off with one last loud crunch of static. She put the walkie-talkie down on her bed and stood up, straightening her Luke Skywalker costume, basically just one of Ed's white shirts that was way too big on her, with a thick leather belt, jeans and boots. She'd been wearing the same costume, more or less, for three consecutive Halloweens now, ever since the movie had come out in that crazy summer of '77. Every year Alice, her mother, suggested that perhaps she'd like to go as Princess Leia this time around, just for a change. And every year, her answer was the same. *But mo-o-om, Luke is the hero!*

She quickly grabbed her 'lightsaber', a length of wooden doweling that Ed had painted light blue for her, then ran to him in her doorway. When she reached him, she gestured for him to crouch, then quickly whispered in his ear.

'I don't like going to Kit's house. It smells funny.'

He bit back a laugh at this, just nodded with exaggerated seriousness. Ed had read books about parenthood before they'd had Gemma, and many of them mentioned the special connection between daddy and daughter, but he'd never imagined it could be like this. Gemma trusted him completely. Their ritual of sharing whispered secrets was a long and cherished one. *I just hope it survives puberty*, he mused.

'Come on, Luke,' he chuckled, ruffling her shoulder-length blonde hair. 'Let's hit the road. Grab a flashlight.'

Gemma bristled at the suggestion. 'I can't carry a flashlight, dad,' she insisted. 'I need both hands for my lightsaber.' She demonstrated, swinging it around dramatically, making the noises with her mouth.

Of course you do, Ed thought; he was already tired, and trick-or-treating hadn't even started. 'Fine,' he sighed. 'I'll be your shining beacon. Your guiding light.'

'Yeah! Obi Wan to my Luke!' Gemma replied with a grin.

'Obi Wan? Didn't he die?'

She rolled her eyes. 'No, dad,' she groaned, 'he just became more powerful than you can possibly imagine. He's one with the Force.'

Ed wondered if his daughter's obsession with that ridiculous movie would ever end. Probably not, he realized, especially since they'd announced a sequel coming out in a year or two. *Gee, I can't wait,* he thought sarcastically.

They walked down the stairs together into the hallway. 'Alice, babe,' Ed called over his shoulder as he and Gemma headed to the front door, 'are you sure you won't come along?' He already knew the answer, but he always asked. Another tradition.

'No, it's okay, hon,' Alice replied, sticking her head out of the spare room where she did her mind-boggling array of crafts, usually three or four projects at a time as a rule. 'Halloween is daddy-daughter time. I'm gonna finish up my owl, then bring the laundry in. Looks like rain.'

'It's looked like rain all day,' Ed pointed out. 'These clouds are weird.'

'Ooooooh,' Alice intoned in a deep voice, waggling her fingers. 'Halloween! Spoooooooky!'

Ed sighed. 'Nobody takes me seriously in this house.'

'That's because you're silly, dad,' Gemma laughed.

He shrugged. 'Guilty as charged, I guess.'

He took his daughter's free hand in his, squeezed it tightly, and they headed out the front door, waving goodbye to Alice as they went.

The neighborhood wasn't exactly abuzz with activity; this was a fairly small suburb, a good twenty miles out of the big city, though you could just see its tall buildings in the distance. *Close enough for its conveniences, far enough away to avoid its problems,* Ed mused. *Perfection.* Directly across the street, he saw George Stein in his wheelchair on his porch, overflowing bucket of candy at the ready for the oncoming hungry hordes. Next to him, his fat old Dalmatian Baxter was looking up and down the road, excitedly awaiting all the kids who were, presumably in his simple doggy brain, all only visiting to pay attention to him. George smiled and waved at them, and he and Gemma waved back as they headed down the street. They'd swing by on the way back for some leftover Ho Hos and a slobbery cuddle with Baxter, like always.

He looked around and saw groups of kids, some with hapless parents in tow, others all on their own, all wending their ways from house to house, porch to porch. There was a wide array of costumes on display, though he spotted at least half a dozen Supermen, thanks to the hit movie of last Christmas. And a goodly number of Princess Leias and Darth Vaders as well, of course, among the more traditional vampires and witches and Frankensteins. All heartwarmingly wholesome, in Ed's eyes.

He and Gemma made their way from one house to another with practiced efficiency, collecting decidedly unhealthy amounts of candy as they went, while, both nearby and in the distance, they could hear the usual squeals and happy cries of kids going about their trick-or-treating business as noisily as they possibly could. Adults on their front porches handed out bars and lollipops to Gemma, told her how cute she was as little Luke, even when she waved her lightsaber menacingly in their directions. *Especially* when she did, in fact; the more serious she was, the more they laughed and clapped. Ed had his flashlight on, but they didn't really need it; between the jack o'lanterns dotted around and the colors in the sky, there was plenty of light to see.

This made Ed frown for a moment. He looked up at the sky, still illuminated with color, though the sun should have well and truly set by then. The clouds had faded a little, shifted away from their usual dusk shades and hues into a color that made somehow Ed uncomfortable. It looked weirdly ultraviolet and infrared at the same time, like someone had taken the spectrum and bent it back on itself, and it kind of hurt his eyes to look at it. But at the same time he had a hard time looking away.

150

'Dad?' Gemma asked by his side, and he tore his eyes from the sky, looked at his daughter. She was gazing across the street, a frown lining her tiny brow.

'What is it, pumpkin?' he asked.

'Who are they?' She pointed.

He followed her gesture, looked over at a small group of boys there. They weren't in costumes, just their normal clothes, jeans and sweaters, but they were all hunched over, and were moving around erratically, their hands almost touching the sidewalk. Ed and Gemma watched them for a moment or two.

'Just kids, I guess,' Ed said in the end, aware that he was stating the obvious. 'Probably tricking rather than treating. You know the type.'

Gemma nodded, her face serious. She knew bullies, alright.

'Let's just hang back, see what they do,' he said to her quietly, taking her hand again.

She didn't respond, just held onto his hand tightly.

One of the boys loped over to another child, a younger boy dressed in the classic Dracula outfit, complete with cape, puffy shirt, white face and slicked back dark hair. The kid looked a bit alarmed but didn't move away as the older boy sidled up and grabbed his shoulder, putting his face close to his ear. Ed could just make out the older boy's lips moving, as he whispered something. The younger boy listened, his eyes growing wide. Then the hunched boy released him and moved on, headed towards a small group of adorable tiny girls dressed as fairies.

The little Dracula just stood there for a moment, face blank. Then he slowly bent over, crouching the same as the other boy, and moved away down the street, disappearing into the gloom.

Ed thought for a moment, then laughed. 'It's some kind of game,' he told Gemma, relieved. 'Like tag.'

'Are you sure?' Gemma didn't sound convinced, as she watched the first boy whisper something to the girls he'd approached. They hunched over as well, and went in separate directions.

'Of course I'm sure,' Ed told her, with all the certainty that only a father comforting his child could muster. 'It's Halloween. It's the season for tricks.'

'I prefer treats,' she grumbled. She looked up at him, eyes troubled. 'Can we go home please?'

Ed was taken aback. Gemma's stamina on Halloween was legendary, usually wearing him out entirely by the end. 'You sure?' he asked. 'We haven't even reached Mrs Anderson yet. She probably still has some 3 Musketeers. And what about Kit?'

She shook her head, still watching the slouching kids. There were more of them now.

'Okay, let's go,' he said. They turned to head back, but stopped in their tracks.

Ahead of them, on the sidewalk, a mother and daughter Ed didn't recognize were walking towards them. The girl was in a Minnie Mouse costume, with a red polka dot dress and mouse ears. The mom was walking ahead, her expression that all-too-familiar parental mix of annoyance and exhaustion. The little girl was dragging her feet, looking through her treat bag at the booty she'd plundered so far. And, behind her, two boys, both in soldier's fatigues, were catching up, each bent over almost in two. Ed saw the kids lips moving as they approached the girl, but couldn't hear the words they spoke. One stopped and raised his head up to whisper in the girl's ear. The other continued up behind the weary mother.

Ed opened his mouth to say something, anything. A warning, perhaps, though he didn't know exactly why, just that all of his instincts were screaming at him. But instead he just stood there, mouth agape, as the boy sprang forward and tackled the woman from behind, the two of them collapsing to the pavement under his weight. He watched, horrified, frozen, as the boy grabbed the woman by the hair and slammed her face against the sidewalk with a sickening crunch. She shrieked, just once, then was silent, but the boy didn't stop. He pounded her head against the ground, again, and again, and again. Blood sprayed across the concrete with each blow.

Gemma screamed then, no words, just sheer terror, and that broke whatever trance Ed was in. He gasped loudly, releasing a breath he didn't even know he'd been holding in. Gemma's shriek also caught the attention of the boy, who looked up at them, fingers still clasping the woman's bloodied hair. His eyes shone in the beam of Ed's

152

flashlight, bright and silvered, like the eyes of a cat. Behind him, the other boy and the little girl also approached, hunched over and scrambling on the sidewalk, their eyes also aglow.

'Run!' Ed yelled to Gemma. He turned and yanked her hand, dragging her away from the grisly sight. She cried out a little, in pain and surprise, but followed as fast as she could manage. Behind them, Ed heard an awful sound, fast shuffling footsteps in an unnatural rhythm. They ran, barely aware that they were running away from their house, not towards it. It didn't seem to matter in that moment.

Ed glanced around the street as they ran. Here and there, he saw kids in the same huddled up postures, scuttling along the road, through yards and over fences. Just a few, at first, but more and more as they went. And, on the ground, he saw bodies, larger bodies. Adult bodies. Each one bloody and still, like the poor woman they'd left behind.

The thought of her hit Ed like a punch to the chest—took his breath away. The sight of her head hitting the pavement over and over filled his mind, but he pushed away the vision, pushed away the absolute terror he was feeling, and forced himself to just keep running. He had to protect Gemma, that was the main thing. Had to keep her away from those...those *monsters*. That was his duty as a father. His mission.

No, more than that. It was his *purpose*.

They took a hard left down Cedar Avenue, Ed hauling Gemma around the corner as they sprinted away from...*them*. Behind them, he heard the children's arrhythmic footsteps continue up the street, not following them. He relaxed, albeit only slightly, and as they continued to run, Ed looked to the left, where Mrs Anderson's house sat, usually as appealing as a candy cottage in a dark forest. But Mrs Anderson was nowhere to be seen, her famous treats scattered on the porch and down the front steps. There was dark liquid spilled there too, looking black in the fading light, with just a shimmer of pink from the strangely-lit sky above them. He could still hear screams and cries in the distance, like every Halloween, but they didn't sound like happy children anymore, oh no. They were deeper, and darker. The horrified cries of the grown-ups of the neighborhood. Those caught outdoors cornered by whatever these things were, whatever they'd become.

But what about those still indoors? What about Alice?

Ed took another left, this time onto Jackson. He tried to look everywhere at once as they ran, alert to any of the scuttling kids with the glowing eyes. He was scared for himself, but even more scared for Gemma. If they got to her... if they whispered in her ear...

Something crashed into Ed on his left side, and he stumbled and fell, releasing Gemma's hand as he tumbled. He rolled on the pavement, and looked up to see a teenage girl hunched down almost to the ground. She was dressed as a witch, her red hair tumbling down from beneath her tall black conical hat. Her eyes were wild, glimmering pink in the reflected light of the sky above them, and her lips were moving, forming words he couldn't hear. She charged him with terrifying speed, like a jungle cat striking. He watched, frozen, as she came at him, almost close enough to hear her words. Almost...

There was a blue flash, and blood spurted from the girl's temple as she spun around and collapsed to the sidewalk in a limp pile. Ed looked over and saw Gemma standing there, her painted doweling rod clasped resolutely in her hands. The end of it was wet and dark.

'Come on, Dad!' she barked. 'Get up!'

Ed scrambled to his feet, trying not to look at the child lying near him, a growing pool of blood around her head. She didn't seem like a monster, not anymore, just a kid. She could have been Gemma in just a few years. He felt bile rising in the back of his throat, but swallowed it back down. Took his daughter's hand in his, so small, so fragile. Looked at her with new eyes.

'Come on!' she urged, and ran, pulling him this time. He followed dutifully, and they reached a house he recognized, the Millers. They were an elderly couple, retired. He'd been a doctor, and she was a teacher. The reason he knew all this, knew them, was that their house backed onto Ed and Alice's. And, on one side of both houses, there was a narrow alley that joined their streets, barely wide enough for a bicycle to get through. The kids used it all the time, for good and...not so good. Gemma urged Ed into the alley, and it suddenly went dark, properly dark, that weird unnerving glow of the sky finally blocked by overhanging oaks and sycamores from the yards on both sides. The ground was rough but worn, a thousand small feet having beaten a path through the weeds and gravel over the years. Ed shone his flashlight ahead of them as they ran.

Then Gemma skidded to a halt, just a few yards from the end of the alley, and Ed pulled up behind her. They stood for a moment, looking down the passageway.

There, blocking the other end, were three little boys, all in tattered zombie outfits. Ed knew who they were right away; the Richardson triplets from down the street. The boys were always together, always dressed pretty much the same. They were a couple of years younger than Gemma, just started school in the fall. They were good kids.

They *were* good kids. Not now, though. Not good. Not kids.

All three of the boys were hunched over, and had their backs turned to Ed and Gemma, focused intently on something on the ground in front of them. One by one, taking turns as they always did, the Richardson kids lunged forward, and each time there was an awful sound, a wet crunch that made Ed's skin crawl.

He looked around, glanced to his right, and realized their house was right there, just a few feet from the fence. Ed gestured to Gemma to stay quiet, then pointed. She looked, frowned for a moment, then nodded. He stood by the fence, crouched, and laced his fingers together, and she placed one foot in the stirrup he'd made with his hands, reaching up with one hand towards the top of the fence, the other hand still determinedly holding her makeshift lightsaber.

As quietly as he could, Ed heaved his daughter up onto the fence. She grasped at it with her free hand, and swung her other leg over the wooden palings. They creaked under her weight; the sound seemed impossibly loud in the silence of the alley, and Ed flinched, looked back to the Richardson triplets. They didn't seem to have noticed, though, still preoccupied with whatever the hell it was they were doing. Gemma leaned over to lower herself to the ground on the other side of the fence, but hesitated.

Ed looked up, and immediately saw the problem. She needed her other hand to steady herself. Before he could say anything, suggest anything, Gemma quickly dropped the blue doweling rod. It fell end-first into their yard on the far side of the fence, and the ground there was mercifully soft. There was no noise, at least for a moment or two.

155

Then, inexorably, it fell back against the fence with a loud crack.

As one, the three Richardson boys turned and stared at Ed, faces painted bright green, their eyes suddenly luminous in the beam of his flashlight. Each of them held a stick in one hand, broken roughly, the ends sharp and jagged and covered with dark liquid. And, behind them on the sidewalk, Ed could make out a shape, a hairy lump that wasn't moving, wasn't breathing. He saw the spots on its body in the eerie light of the sky, and, aghast, knew immediately what it was. What *he* was.

Baxter, the dalmatian from across the street. That harmless old goofball of a dog that everyone loved. That had never hurt anyone, bothered anyone. The boys...these *things*...had just been stabbing the poor thing with their sticks, over and over again.

But now they'd found something more interesting to grab their attention. Something much more exciting than a dead dog.

I can take them, Ed thought for a brief moment, furious and disgusted, as the three kids approached, all bent over like old men with osteoporosis. *They're just little kids, and I'm a grown man. Even three to one, I can take them. They're just little goddamn kids.*

Except no, they weren't, not anymore. He knew that, deep down in his soul. And he also knew, in a moment of terrible clarity, that he *couldn't* take them, not even if he got past a lifetime of instincts that prevented him from harming a child. He knew he would fail, would fall. Would die. Because these boys weren't children. They weren't *human.*

And he still had a duty. A mission. A purpose.

Without further hesitation, he turned from the boys and clambered up the fence with one hand, vaulting all the way over it in one smooth motion. *Mr Wilson, my gym teacher, would have been so proud,* he thought vaguely. He landed hard on both his feet in the dirt between the fence and his house, though, the impact making his shins ache. *Maybe not that proud.* Behind him, he could hear the scratching and clawing of the Richardson triplets on the other side of the wood, mercifully too small to make it over the fence. Gemma stood there waiting for him, lightsaber in hand, her pale face streaked with tears.

'I'm so sorry!' she sobbed. 'I didn't know it would hit the fence.'

'It's okay, kiddo,' he told her. 'But we have to move, get inside. Find mom.'

She sniffled, nodded, wiped the tears away with her free hand. Then, together, they ran to the front of the house. Ed tried not to look across the street, couldn't bear to, but still somehow saw George's wheelchair on its side at the bottom of his front steps. One wheel was turning. There was no sign of George.

The front door was closed but not locked, which filled Ed with a mixture of relief and dread. They ran inside, and he slammed and locked the door behind them, then turned to Gemma. 'Go upstairs to your room,' he commanded. 'Lock the door. Don't open it to anyone but me or mom. Okay?'

She nodded, then turned and ran up the stairs to her room.

'Alice?' he called into the darkened house. 'Alice? Are you here?'

There was no answer. He hurried down the corridor with his flashlight, checked her craft room, but she wasn't there, just the piece she'd been working on, the black shiny eyes of the macrame owl flashing in the beam of light. Like the eyes of the kids. Of the not-kids.

He thought back, remembered her words before they left. *I'm gonna finish up my project, then bring the laundry in. Looks like rain.'*

No, no rain. Something much, much worse.

Frantic, Ed headed for the back door, which was also closed. He opened it and looked out into the yard, which was only dimly lit by the glowing clouds above. He shone his flashlight around.

'Alice? Babe? Are you…?'

He stopped, breath caught in his throat. There, by the clothesline, was laundry scattered on the ground. Some of it looked dirty, stained. One pile was bigger than the rest, and it took Ed long seconds to understand what he was seeing.

Then he saw a pale hand, palm up, covered in blood, and knew it was his wife. Or what remained of her.

From behind the pile…the body, he corrected himself, his wife's body, his *wife's dead body*…a pale face rose up, eyes aglow. And another. The two kids' faces were stained black with Alice's blood,

157

and they looked at Ed with a hunger he'd never seen, never even imagined.

Without a sound, but their mouths still moving as if they were speaking, they charged towards him, leaping over the fallen mound that was once the woman he loved, the mother of his child.

Ed stumbled back inside and slammed the back door, locking it as securely as he could. He leaned on it for a long moment, eyes closed, trying not to break down completely. *Alice...Jesus Christ, Alice...*

He'd have stayed there for ever, but his fractured thoughts returned to Gemma. His mission, his purpose. He forced himself away from the door, away from Alice, Alice who was gone, not even hearing the tiny fists beating on it from outside.

Then another sound, muffled, this time from upstairs.

The loud crackle of a walkie-talkie.

Oh God, no, please no, he prayed, and ran for the stairs. He climbed them two at a time, ignoring the exhaustion he was feeling, the agony in his legs, in his chest. It all disappeared into a blurry distance, irrelevant, overwhelmed by this new absolute dread. He ran to Gemma's room. 'Gemma, no!' he screamed, trying to open the door, but she'd locked it, just as he'd told her to. 'Turn it off!'

'Kit?' he heard Gemma ask through the door. 'Kit? Is that you?'

He took two steps back and charged the door, shouldering it open, the frame ripping away from the wall in a shower of dust and splinters. He staggered into her room, off-balance, and saw her standing there by her window, her back to him. In one hand she still held her lightsaber, her stupid goddamn piece of wood painted blue. The other held the walkie-talkie to her ear, the antenna stuck outside.

'Gemma?' he said, his voice breaking. 'Pumpkin? Are you alright?'

Slowly, she lowered the radio from her ear, putting it down on her bed. Then she turned to face him.

Her eyes glowed in the flashlight's beam, and his entire world shattered.

'No!' he screamed, and turned to run, but she was on him in an instant, lashing out with the wooden rod. It caught him across the back of his head, and he fell forward, onto the top of the staircase.

Another blow landed on the small of his back, and he tumbled down the stairs. He felt something in his left shoulder crack and tear as he fell, the pain filling his head with ringing alarm bells. He hit the foot of the stairs hard, and all the strength went out of him, all at once, as if he was some kind of electric doohickey and someone had pulled the plug on him. Or maybe it was a blackout. His left arm stuck out at an unnatural angle, bent like a gnarled branch.

He tried hard to catch his breath but failed, something inside his chest scraping against his lung. All he could do was lie there and watch, gasping, as his daughter approached him, stalked him, hunted him, descending the stairs on all fours. She slowly climbed onto his chest, sending new searing lightning bolts of pain through him, then she leaned forward and gently put her soft lips to his ear, as she had so many times before.

And she *whispered*.

The words, those damned words he had never managed to hear before, weren't English, weren't any language intended for a human tongue. And yet, somehow, somehow, he understood them. No, more than understood. He *became* them, and they him, as if his flesh and bone and mind and soul was nothing more than a parchment, waiting for the words to be written upon. They permeated his very existence, filled him to overflowing.

And, finally, yes, he *understood*.

'Oh,' he breathed, filled with sudden wonder and joy. 'Oh, I...'

Then Gemma's teeth found Ed's throat, and bit, and ripped, and bit, and ripped, and bit, and ripped. Through his skin and flesh and ligament. Through his windpipe and esophagus. Through his aorta, sending blood spraying across the hallway carpet, so much blood, so *much*. Bit, and ripped, and bit, and ripped, until there was nothing left to bite and rip, nothing but bone, bone that was too hard to break with her soft baby teeth. Then, and only then, did she stop and survey her work, taking in the carnage she'd wrought. Like it was a piece of art, a museum exhibit. Father, deceased, in scarlet.

Something outside captured her attention, drew her from her father's dead body, a beatific smile still frozen on his cooling lips. She sloughed off him and, hunched over, scuttled to the front door. Opened it, and loped outside, where the other children were gathered.

159

She joined them, in their dozens and dozens, as they made their crooked way together down the street, a crowd, a pack. They were called, irresistibly, towards the jagged silhouette of the metropolis in the distance, still and black without power, softly lit by the impossible colors in the sky.

They were called, and they would come. To spread the word.

Candy Train
Em Starr

The train to the western suburbs smelled like new cologne and old cigarettes. It reminded Gary of his ex-wife's Cosmopolitan collection; gloss magazines with fragrance strips burning in a backyard incinerator, along with her make-up and clothes. Cosmo would have described it as a smoky oud scent with base notes of chewing gum and sebum; subtle and lingering, yet strong enough for him to be grateful when the auto-doors parted.

Gary was just grateful it didn't smell like sugar.

The last of the trick-or-treaters had disembarked at Footscray Station, taking their saccharine stench with them. Candy sacks gaping. Parents following like loyal dogs. He'd made sure to openly scowl at the procession of witches and ghosts as they departed. Considered tripping up a pot-bellied parent who looked like Pam's new husband. Exercised restraint, as per the current court order.

Gary disliked public transport at the best of times, but Halloween was especially excruciating. The stink of emulsified cocoa, the sugar crumbed seats and sticky handrails. Too many fucking kids. The anniversary of his divorce. Soon as he got home, he would lock the door and turn off the porch light, and when the candy-seekers came

161

knocking, he'd scream through the peephole and make them cry. Twelve stops to go. Next stop, Seddon. He wondered if Sleeping Betty's bungee-spit would drop before then.

Sleeping Betty was the woman sitting across from him. She'd been shut-eyed and hang-mouthed since Flinders Street Station, a single string of drool suspended from her bottom lip; whenever the train jolted, she'd startle and suck it back between her teeth, then down, down, down it would come again. It helped Gary pass the time, watching that spittle unfurl and retract like a cane toad's tongue. He pretended she was a Halloween installation in someone's front yard, zapping children as they came through the gate and storing them inside her papier-mâché gut. Trick or—*zap!* Happy Hallo—*zap!*

At the far end of the carriage, a tired mum sat with two children in school uniforms. The kids had been Halloween-excited for most of the trip, yipping about their costumes, the treats they might yield, but now that it was dark, they were wide-eyed and whispering, hands cupped against the window to see what waited outside. Their mother was watching reels on her cell phone, volume up too high. Gary doubted she heard the driver, when his voice crackled over the speakers: *Seddon Station, Seddon Station.*

The train pulled up at the platform and Sleeping Betty woke. She wiped her chin and gathered her tote bag, fishing inside it for a melted candy bar. She peeled back the foil and took a bite. Saw Gary staring and wished him a Happy Samhain through chocolate chompers. He looked away. Tapped at his cell phone as if he'd been messaging Pam for the last twenty minutes, as if his number wasn't blocked, as if the court order didn't forbid him from reaching out to tell her he missed her, loved her, forgave her—that he'd kill that fucking prick husband of hers if he ever ran into him.

He scrolled through old photographs, faux-happy holiday snapshots that spanned more than a decade. Her, like a model on the cover of Cosmopolitan, convincing smile for someone who claimed she was never in love. Then it was on to the new batch, pictures downloaded from her sister's social media account. Halloween at her (their) house. Wine-sipping and pumpkin-carving; obnoxiously orange, oversized pumpkins, nothing like the butternuts she used to roast with potatoes every Sunday. Kitchen fully renovated. Pumpkin skin and seeds all over his mother's antique dining table. He was still scrolling when Betty disembarked. Still cursing pictures of Pam in her cat-woman costume, clown-husband beside her, wedding ring shining on his greasepaint finger. He didn't notice the passenger that slipped through the auto-doors. Didn't smell him until he was sitting beside him—burnt maple and roadkill, with base notes of nope! nope! nope!

I'm dreaming, thought Gary, *lulled to sleep by the train's click clack rhythms, stuck in some lucid All Hallow's nightmare*—then he saw the image in the window. A willowy, waxy, weasel-faced man. He caught Gary's eye in the reflection, waved at him with fingers, too long.

'Trick or treatsies?' he asked, voice like vapor.

Gary had been on this line enough times to know when to avert his eyes. The stranger scuttled closer, and dear fucking god, his breath! It was deathly cold against Gary's cheek, sticky like molasses.

'Tricksies or treat?' he asked again.

Gary turned to confront the stranger. His eyes were white jelly with rheum in the corners, knees at odd angles, teeth all askew. Lips mouthing lullabies on mute. *Trick or treat or trick or treat or trick or treat or trick or treat or...*

'Trick,' Gary said, words uttered before he could stop.

The stranger held up a finger—*wait!*—and felt inside his pocket. Gary tried to look away, but his gaze was fixed on those too-long phalanges; he watched them writhe inside the stranger's jacket like snakes, saw his eyes widen when he found something of interest. He held up his prize, a human eyeball, soft and filmy grey. Popped it between his crooked canines and chewed it like a boiled lolly.

This can't be real. It can't be. I must be dreaming, napping and dreaming.

But it was as real as Gary's hands on Pam's throat. Dark as a hallway. Dark as a locked room. Dark as the end of a train line. He extended a bony finger to Gary's brow. Traced around the socket like a surgeon marking an incision line. Nails dirty and pointed. Gary wondered what it would feel like if the stranger took his eyeballs, then and there—*pop!* and *pop!*—hollowed his skull for candles and propped it on Pam's doorstep to invite in the werewolves and ghouls.

'Tricksies or treatsies?' the man asked again. He looked to the end of the carriage. Saw the wide-eyed children with their faces to the window. Waggled his finger—*tsssk, tsssk, tsssk*—and slipped from the seat to the floor. He left Gary with both eyes intact. Skipped down the empty car toward the family. Trick or treat or trick or treat or trick or treat or...

The mother looked up from her phone, confused, half-smiling. Realisation dawned. Then, horror. 'You can't be here,' she said. 'I've got a court order.' She ran to shield the children.

Not like this, thought Gary. *It's not supposed to be like this. We haven't even got to the end of the line yet. Twelve stops to go. Twelve stops until I put on my mask, and knock on their door, and slip inside her (our) house, and lock the door behind me...*

The stranger taunted Pam and the children, skipping this way and that. Talons extended.

'I've already called the police,' Pam was saying. 'They're on the phone right now. They'll be at Yarraville station by the time we get there.'

Gary turned away as the strange man closed in on his family. Shielded his ears from the screams that sounded like a plague of trick-or-treaters. Like pumpkin-heads in steam. They stunk up the carriage, thick and sickly, the slip-slap-thwack of freshly plucked vitreous lost to the overhead speaker: *Yarraville Station, Yarraville Station.* When the auto-doors opened, he was grateful for the fresh air.

The police were waiting on the platform, as promised. There was a phone call, they said, twisting hands up his spine, slapping on cuffs that pinched at his skin. They pushed his face into concrete and candy wrappers, called him a killer as the westbound train departed—at the far end of the carriage, two children watched, hands cupped to the glass to see better, their mother beside them, scrolling reels on her cell phone. The smell of sugar was sickening.

Toomie's Ghost Story
Epiphany Ferrell

We were sitting around, swapping ghost stories, and Toomie, who's always got a story for every damn thing, didn't have one. At the time, I was kinda mad about it. How could he not have a ghost story? So, I pushed the point.

'Toomie,' I said, 'I bet you got a ghost story. A real one, not this urban legend shit.'

'I don't,' he said, swigging the last of his beer.

I passed him a PBR. Can, there were no more bottles. I'd not seen my old pal Toomie in a good many years. I'd run into him at the Roll N Up when I'd stopped for a six of cold beer to drive around with as I delayed going home. I'd already missed taking my kid trick or treating, so what was the point in hurrying? So here I was at the clubhouse, a little cabin back in the woods, drinking with some of Toomie's friends.

'Come on, Toomie,' I said. 'It's Halloween!'

There were sounds of general support for Toomie to tell a story.

He heaved a sigh and I knew it was a real one, not one for dramatic effect, and something made me feel I wanted to call it back, to ask instead for the story about the time he was day-drunk and propositioned a parking officer. That story never gets old, even if you've heard it seven or eight times.

But Toomie started in on the ghost story.

'I had a friend, let's say his name was Zack. It isn't, but let's say it was.'

Toomie looked at us all as if our agreement on this mattered. We all nodded.

'Zack was an all-right guy. He meant well. His high school sweetheart went and married his best friend when he was working on an oil rig in the Gulf. He got a mechanics job, married a woman whose car he fixed. They had a couple kids. Nice life.'

Ah, so the story could almost be about me, some of the details fit. Toomie did that sometimes. He'd tell a story you could swear was about you and you'd realize later two other guys thought it was about them. He was an odd, old bird.

'Then his boy got sick,' Toomie went on, 'and his wife went and got the kid a dog, supposed to make him feel better. Some hound-dog mix she got from the shelter. The kid got better after a long while, and him and that dog were inseparable. Zack didn't much care for the dog and I guess the feeling was mutual.

'Then Zack's wife got sick. She had the cancer. It was in her bones. Bad deal. She was a long time in the hospital, and they didn't have good insurance. Chemo, drug trials—in the end, none of it worked. She suffered something terrible. Finally, they called in hospice so she could die at home with her family.'

I looked around, trying to see if anyone else looked as uncomfortable as I felt, if they were squirming like the story was about them, if the details were hitting too close to home. I didn't like it. No one wants to be in a ghost story. Especially not one Toomie was telling, with his weird ways of knowing people's secrets.

'Then there was the funeral,' Toomie said. 'Funerals are expensive even when you try to cut corners. And Zack's in-laws, you know, they might have helped out but all they did was criticize. He should have took better care of her, he should have sent her to Mayo, he should have had a better coffin, even. Zack took to drinking maybe a little more than was good for him. Speaking of which, are we out of beer?'

Someone handed him a can. It cracked like a gunshot when he opened it.

'Then one night, after something his mother-in-law said to him pissed him off, he backed out the driveway real fast and he run over his boy's dog.

'Now, he didn't care so much about the dog. It didn't like him, he didn't like it. But he didn't want his boy to know the dog was dead, him having just lost his mom and all. So he put the dog in the back of his truck with the rest of the crap he had rolling around in it, drove to the old bridge, tied a cinder block to the dog with some clothesline, and threw it in the river.

'The boy started looking for the dog right away in the morning, and Zack told the boy the dog run off. I never understood telling a kid that his dog run off when instead it was dead. Makes the kid think the dog would rather be with someone else. It ain't right. But in this case, I guess I can understand how hard it would be to tell the truth.'

The story was making me sweat. I felt like my throat was closing up, and threw back the last of my beers. I wanted Toomie to stop weaving whatever spell he had going with this story.

'Is there a ghost in this story? It's supposed to be a ghost story,' I said. I got a few dirty looks from the other guys; no one interrupts a Toomie story.

In the flicker of the wood stove, with his long beard, wild hair, and dark eyes, Toomie looked like an old wizard. When he glanced at me, my blood went cold and I wished I'd never accepted his invitation, never come to this cabin in the woods, never asked him for no goddamn story.

'Zack's poor boy, he went out looking for that dog, calling its name and looking every place he could think of. He put up flyers and he asked the postman, the police, everybody, to keep an eye out for his Buddy. He was broken-hearted, that kid was. I imagine it was a terrible thing to hear that little boy's thin voice on the cold wind calling for his dog until long after dark. Zack maybe should have told him the truth, but he was in it so far now he didn't see how he could.

'It was at least a week, maybe more, and that boy wouldn't stop calling for his dog to come back from wherever it was. And then the boy went and got sick again. Not the cancer like his mom. He was weak from when he was sick before and all that wandering at night, calling for his dog, he got pneumonia.

'Zack found him one morning, cold and pale in his bed, his clothes all wet like he'd been feverish. But when Zack pulled down the covers—'

'That's enough, Toomie,' I said. He continued like I hadn't spoken.

'—there were muddy paw prints on the sheets and everything smelled of river water.'

'Damn you.' It was indecent of him to go on about me like that. No one could say I didn't try to do right by my boy. I was sorry about that dog, I was. I didn't mean to run it over, I didn't see it back there, it's like it dove under my tires or something. I thought it was the best thing to do for my boy after that, to say the dog was off away somewhere, not another thing dead, and sure as hell not that I run it over.

I'd never seen no muddy paw prints—Toomie made that up and he'd say I was crazy for taking it personally. *It's just a story*, he'd say. *You feeling guilty?* he'd say. My boy didn't have pneumonia, he was wheezy, that was all. Of course he went looking for his dog, goddamn near killed me having to help him put up flyers. But I did! I was out with him, not letting him wander around at night.

How'd Toomie even know about my boy and his dog? Had he seen me dumping it that bright-moon night? Was he spying on me? Maybe it hadn't been coincidence, us meeting at the liquor store, him inviting me out there to that clubhouse. I remembered then some of the stories I'd heard about Toomie, about him learning weird, old secrets when he was a soldier, when he was in the jungle in Vietnam, when he was gone from his platoon for days and they figured him for dead and then he showed up, filthy and emaciated and talking gibberish that seemed always to come true. I'd never believed any of it, not even when the boss warned me never to cross ol'Toomie, that he'd get me back. When had I ever offended him? What could I possibly have done?

My boy, he was home with his grandma and his little sister, and I

168

always done my best by them, by God. I just needed one night away from it all, from all the sadness in my boy's eyes, from the way my girl looks at me like she don't know me, from that old woman's constant blaming and condemning me.

Toomie's eyes glowed by the light of the woodstove fire and his voice took on a sound of gravel and chant, and he looked into the flames as he said, 'The dog come back. He come back because the boy called for him.'

I stood up and the campstool I was sitting on fell over behind me and the other guys were staring at me.

'That dog, he's going to haunt Zack. Zack'll never be rid of him,' Toomie uttered the words like a curse, like something he was going to make happen. Or that he had the power to stop, but wouldn't. Then he looked right at me. 'Have you forgot what night it is, old friend?'

I ground my teeth in rage, and I left the cabin and stomped out to my truck.

And there he was. Just like Toomie said he'd be. Buddy. Standing there, a-shimmering at the edges, that clothesline knotted around his shoulders like a harness and the cinder block behind him. He growled low in his throat, and he took a step forward and I should have heard that cinder block drag on the leaves, but there wasn't a thing to hear. I threw my beer can at him and it went right through and then nothing was there but night.

I cursed myself for being a gullible, ghost-story-believing fool. I had half a mind to storm back into that cabin and rail at the guys for playing a sick joke on me. How dare they, me having lost my wife, and a sad little boy at home.

I drove home like a crazy man, expecting red and blue lights behind me the whole way, but no, they were there in my driveway when I pulled up, and there was my mother-in-law and an ambulance and a stretcher with a covered shape on it.

'You've got beer on your breath,' my mother-in-law said when she saw me, and she raised a hand to slap me and let it drop. 'And you let in that filthy dog!'

I barely heard her. My boy was still, and paler and colder than the moon, lying there on the hospital stretcher. They put him in the back of the ambulance and it drove off, no lights, no sirens, taking my boy to the morgue.

A little girl in a witch's pointy hat clung to my mother-in-law, crying and looking at me with wide eyes, because it was Halloween, and I was supposed to take her trick-or-treating, and she'd been excited to show me her costume and share candy with her sickly brother. Now she was looking at me like I was a monster. The way she clung to her grandma made me feel things I didn't want her to know, so I turned away and didn't watch as they left.

Halloween. A night when anything might happen. A night when the veil is thin. I'd never believed anything about it one or the other. Now I wasn't so sure. I went in the house, and I smelled it right away. River muck. I walked up the stairs like I was going to my execution and maybe I was. There was the dog, lying dead across my son's bed, its ribs showing and the clothesline still knotted. It wasn't like a fresh dead neither. It was like it had been in-the-river-a-week dead.

Toomie. That goddamned wizard. He must have seen me. He must have fished that dog out of the river, that sick son-of-a-bitch, and dropped it on my son's bed for him to find, and oh God, the shock of it must've killed him. *Toomie, you've killed my boy*, and I don't know if I thought that or screamed it. I was murderous driving back to the clubhouse. My truck rattled on the rutted road to get there, headlights bouncing like deranged swamp gas until they swept onto the clubhouse, dark and leaning. There were no other trucks, I was alone. I left my lights on so I could see, ready to barrel in there and grab Toomie by the throat and—

The door creaked open when I pushed it. It was cold inside, the woodstove rusted, a few broken chairs around it, dirt and grime on everything. *I must have the wrong place,* I thought. I will search this whole damn woods to find Toomie, to make him take it back.

I saw my campstool, where I'd been sitting. Six empty cans of Pabst Blue Ribbon, the only things in the room not coated with dust. And a yellowed newspaper rustling in its own breeze there on the floor with a few sticks of dry wood, rattling like something was trying to make me read it. I didn't need to look because somehow I knew, but I looked anyway, and there was a picture of Toomie, much as I saw him just hours ago, with a short obituary that's not much more than two dates, and according to that yellowed paper,

Toomie has been dead for a year exactly, died on October 31, 20--.

And here I am, in a motel on a dark highway, writing all this down so if I'm gone in the morning, my girl will know it's not that I run off, it's that I was took against my will.

That damn hellhound is outside my window, Toomie a dark shadow right next to him. Both of them a-shimmering on the edges. One of them growls, low and menacing. They're waiting for me.

Maybe my boy is, too.

Sweet Tooth
Brian Moreland

'Don't eat the candy yet,' Helen told herself. 'Leave plenty for the trick-or-treaters.'

As if in mischievous rebellion, her left hand snatched a Snickers from the big bowl that she'd just filled in her kitchen with an assortment of packaged candies.

'Put the candy back,' Helen ordered her hand. Her fingers clutched the mini Snickers tighter, refusing to let go. 'For heaven's sake, you're a grown woman,' she said, sounding like her mother. 'Stop behaving like a brat.' After she disobeyed herself again, Helen pulled a rubber band on her wrist as far as it would stretch then snapped it. The familiar pain against her wrist jolted her inner thief. She put the candy back in the bowl, feeling guilty and foolish.

The rubber band trick was her therapist's idea to curb her sugar-eating compulsion. In their last session, Dr. Foster had told her; 'When your inner child tries to make you eat sweets, it's best to punish her the moment she commits the bad act.' He'd given her the thick rubber band and a box of Xanax. 'Until the antidepressant medication helps you get your disorder under control, I advise you to stop bringing candy into your home.'

While sitting on her therapist's couch, Helen had cringed at the suggestion. 'But Friday is Halloween.'

'I suggest you skip it this year.'

'Skip Halloween? But giving out candy is tradition.'

'It's quite easy. Simply turn off the porch light and pretend you're not home.'

Helen had fidgeted with her hands. 'Last year, the neighborhood kids voted my house the best for trick-or-treating. I won a trophy.'

'Then for this year, give them non-edible gifts instead,' Dr. Foster said callously. 'Halloween stickers or trinkets.'

She scoffed. 'The children will say my house is the worst on the block.'

'Your diabetes is only getting worse, Helen. You have to avoid candy altogether. At least, until you gain power over your sweet tooth.'

Like a good little patient, Helen had taken her prescribed meds and resisted buying candy all week. When Friday arrived and she saw people dressed in costumes and masks everywhere she went around town, she began to feel pins and needles under her skin. Her will broke that afternoon while shopping at the grocery store. She'd somehow ended up in the Halloween candy aisle. As she perused the colorful packages, inhaling the sugar in the air, something inside her took over. She'd dropped bag after bag of candy into her basket. After returning home, she'd taken great pleasure in filling up the big glass bowl that was adorned with black cats and jack o'lanterns. She provided only the best treats for the costumed kids who would be visiting her door this evening: miniature Hershey bars, peanut M&M's, Reese's peanut butter cups, packaged candy corn, and her favorite chocolate bars filled with peanuts, nougat, and caramel. The mini-Snickers looked so tempting. It took another rubber band snap to keep her hand from grabbing one.

Using her rational voice, Helen told herself, 'Let the kids have their share. At the end of the night, whatever is left over, you can eat.' She always gave out three pieces to each child. Knowing the approximate number of little trick-or-treaters who came to her house each year, she did the math in her head and calculated there would be between three and six candies left over for her. This promise of a future reward appeased her inner hellion.

At five o'clock that evening, she placed the candy bowl on the table in her foyer and switched on the front porch light. She played spooky organ music through outside speakers. Smiling with anticipation, she waited for the doorbell to ring. Helen had decorated her windows with paper ghosts, skeletons, and witches. The covered front porch was lined with faux spider webs. The black rubber spider hanging above her door never failed to provoke spooked giggles from the children. She hoped to win the neighborhood POA's Best Halloween House contest again this year. Last year's ceramic ghost trophy stood prominently on the foyer table next to the bowl of candy.

She opened the front door and peeked outside. It was twilight with an orange-streaked sky. The October air was crisp with the sounds of wind blowing dry leaves down the street and distant children's laughter. Costumed kids began to visit the houses across the street. Helen closed the door and waited anxiously for ten more minutes. The bowl of candy seemed to call to her. The little girl voice in her head said, *Take some pieces and stash them for later.* Her hand reached into the bowl. 'No!' She snapped the rubber band against her wrist just short of picking up a fistful of candy.

The doorbell rang and Helen's heart surged with delight. She opened the door. Three kids dressed as a pirate, witch, and stormtrooper raised their bags. 'Trick or treat!'

'My what precious costumes! Here you go.' She placed three candies in each of their bags.

'Thank you!' they said together, then hurried off to the next house.

Helen sighed. She envied those children. When she was growing up, her mother never let her go trick-or-treating. *There are too many child snatchers out there,* Mother had said. *Not to mention sickos who hide razorblades in the candy. It's safer to be the candy givers.*

So, every Halloween during her childhood, Helen had helped her mother answer the door and hand out candy to the neighborhood kids. She'd stashed away a few chocolates for herself, but when Mother discovered her daughter's thievery, she punished Helen, making her stand in a corner with a bar of soap in her mouth. *The candy's for the trick-or-treaters, Helen. You can have what's left over, but not until the last trick-or-treater gets theirs.* Mother gave each kid three candies. Helen had counted candies throughout the evening, watching the amount in the bowl dwindle. She'd even caught her mother increasing the handouts to four and five candies per child toward the end of the evening. Some Halloweens, the bowl was empty before Helen got to eat even a single piece of candy. By the time she was an adult and free from her mother's tyranny, Helen had been too old to be going around the neighborhood trick-or-treating. She was unmarried, childless, and nearing forty, so she had no kids of her own to live vicariously through. Regardless, she had happily continued the tradition as a candy giver.

The doorbell rang again.

Her chest filled with excitement. She opened the door and her eyes widened. On her doorstep stood a stocky woman in a white nurse's costume. She loomed a head taller than Helen and was twice her girth. The nurse had stringy brown hair that looked unwashed. A crude, white, oval mask covered her face. Papier mâché had been molded to a large face with a flat nose and hardened into a shell. Red crosses had been painted on the cheeks. There were small, round cutouts for the eyes and nostrils and a wider hole for the mouth. The masked woman grinned, exposing yellow, uneven teeth. She held up a plastic pumpkin bucket and said in a deep voice, 'Trick or treat!'

Helen looked around for any children, but there was only the lone woman on her doorstep. 'Miss, aren't you too old to be trick-or-treating?'

The nurse's big-knuckled hands held out her orange bucket. 'Candy.'

Helen reached for the bowl on the table. In her head, she did quick math, subtracting three more candies from her supply. She pulled her hand away without picking up any candies and faced the costumed woman. 'I'm sorry, but my candy is reserved for the children. Have a good night.' She shut the door on the woman.

Five minutes passed. The doorbell rang again.

On the doorstep stood a little princess and a Harry Potter wizard, and behind them towered the burly nurse in the papier-mâché mask. All three held up their candy buckets. 'Trick or treat!' The woman's hoarse voice practically drowned out the children's.

Masking her annoyance with a smile, Helen dropped candy into the buckets of the princess and wizard. 'Happy Halloween, kiddies!'

She gave the nurse a disapproving eye before shutting the door.

'The gall of that woman asking for candy at her age. She had to be close to thirty. And her atrocious mouth!' She shuddered, recalling the nurse's yellow smile. 'Cavities must be chiseling away at her teeth.'

Helen had wisely avoided hard candies. Her weaknesses were of the chocolate variety. And candy corn, but only on Halloween. Just to make sure she had some left over, she buried a package of candy corn with a few Snickers bars at the bottom of the bowl.

The next half hour she received a steady flow of kids and happily gave them candy. In one group, a quartet of boys and girls were dressed as superheroes with cheap plastic masks. The two mothers who chaperoned them politely waited in the middle of the front walk, while Helen filled their kids' bags with three candies each for a total of twelve. The next group was a crowd of seven kids: a clown, fairy, sheet ghost, and four Ninja Turtles. Just like that, twenty-one more candies vanished from the bowl.

The pins and needles began to prick beneath Helen's skin. Her supply was down to less than twenty pieces and there was still at least a half hour of trick-or-treating yet to go.

Heavy knocks pounded at her door, startling her. When she opened it, the tall masked nurse held up her empty pumpkin bucket. 'Candy!'

It sounded like a demand.

Helen's face burned hot. 'You should be at home handing out candy, not asking for it. Now, go away.'

She slammed the door and deadbolted it. Leaning back against the foyer wall, she placed her hand on her chest. Her heart fluttered like a frightened bird against her sternum. She was shaking all over. She ran into the kitchen, fumbled with her box of Xanax, and took two to calm her nerves.

The sinister organ music had grown annoying, so she turned it off. Back in her foyer, she waited for the next round of children. She listened at the door for the approach of little running feet and giggles. Ten minutes passed...fifteen. Then half an hour, without another group coming to her door. But she still had some candies left to give. Halloween wasn't over yet. Where were the trick-or-treaters? Did that woman in the white mask scare them off?

Helen peered out the living room window. Dusk had blackened to night. A shroud of darkness had fallen over the street. Only a corner lamp offered a haven of visibility. There was no one out there. She paced her foyer. Something was off. The trick-or-treating always lasted until eight o'clock.

She hurried into the den and turned on the TV to check the weather. Perhaps, a thunderstorm was headed this way. She switched through the local network channels, but only found regular evening shows with no weather ticker.

The doorbell rang several times: *ding-dong-ding-dong-ding-dong...*

She ran back to the front door and peered through the peephole. The white papier-mâché face with red crosses appeared warped in the fish-eye lens. The nurse's gruff voice said, 'Candy!'

'I'm all out!' Helen yelled through the door. 'Go try another house!'

A thunderous *whack* shook the door, as if the woman's meaty fist punched the wood.

Don't be so pigheaded! barked Helen's mother's voice. *Give her some candy already!*

'No, she doesn't deserve it,' Helen growled back as if her mother were still with her in the foyer. She felt her inner girl shrink with shame at the brazen backtalk to Mother, but adult Helen felt justified. At this point, her refusal to give candy to a grown woman in a costume wasn't just a matter of principle. Helen was afraid to open the door. She turned off the porch light, hoping the woman would take the hint and leave.

The nurse's voice roared through the door. Her fist knocked again and again, followed by incessant ringing of the doorbell. She then just stood there on the dark porch for a long, nerve-wracking minute as Helen remained quiet and statue still in the foyer.

Finally, the woman's heavy footsteps walked off the porch.

Helen released the breath she'd been holding. That was the final straw. The pestilent woman had completely destroyed the Halloween fun. The kids and parents seemed to have stopped visiting Helen's house anyway. She carried the bowl of leftover candy into her den and set it on the coffee table.

Eighteen candies in colorful wrappers were still piled in the bowl.

Eighteen sugar rushes. Fifteen chocolate delights plus three bags of candy corn bliss. That was the most she had ever had remaining at the end of Halloween night. The little girl inside Helen clapped her hands and squealed with glee.

Mother's disapproving voice said, *You should have given out more to the kids. You eat that much sugar, you'll turn into a roly-poly.*

Dr. Foster's voice chimed in, *If you indulge your sweet tooth, you'll suffer a major setback.*

Helen tuned them out. 'I deserve treats too.' She reached into the bowl, fishing past mini-Hershey bars and yellow M&M bags for the Snickers.

Her hand froze short of grabbing her favorite treat.

On the TV, a cartoon switched to an anchorman reporting breaking news. The words *PUBLIC EMERGENCY* flashed across the screen. Grabbing the remote off the coffee table, she turned up the volume. '...a red-alert warning for the town of Mill Creek. Earlier this evening, Girdy Rathburn, the notorious Doll Face Killer, escaped from the Hollybrook Mental Hospital.' A photograph on the screen showed a wide-faced woman with stringy hair, doughy cheeks, and offset eyes. Helen became rigid with fear as the anchorman reported, 'Before escaping, the mental patient strangled a nurse to death. Girdy Rathburn is believed to be disguised in a nurse's uniform and a white and red, papier-mâché mask she made in art therapy. Girdy is considered extremely dangerous. If you see this woman, do *not* go near her. Call the police immediately. Stay tuned for more on the story on the ten o'clock news. Now, back to our scheduled Halloween program.' The news break cut back to the cartoon.

Helen's whole body trembled. Every inch of her skin prickled. Her mind couldn't fathom that she had possibly stood face to face with a local legend right here on her doorstep. The Doll Face Killer. The disturbed woman responsible for murdering six people at the Rathburn house of horrors. Helen had watched a true crime documentary about the massacre that happened several years ago at an isolated pig farm in the woods, ten miles outside of Mill Creek. The investigative reporter had toured the two-story, clapboard farmhouse, exploring cluttered rooms cram packed with dolls. Blood spatters and crimson streaks had stained the dolls' faces and dresses.

Helen remembered the scene of the teenage girl's bedroom vividly. Pink wallpaper peeling at the edges. A rusted iron bed with a knife-mutilated mattress was covered in goose feathers and dismembered dolls. White dander had floated in the air as the reporter walked into the filthy room. An orange Halloween bucket with a jack o'lantern face sat on a nightstand. The floor had crackled as the reporter's shoes stepped on discarded candy wrappers. Porcelain and papier-mâché masks covered every wall. A hundred hollow-eyed faces stared blankly into the camera as it panned around the room. A closet was stored with an array of oversized cotton dresses of every color. Plus dresses made of velvet and lace. The closet's floor was lined with pairs of large shoes too fancy for a farm girl.

During a gruesome montage of bloody crime scenes, the reporter had narrated, 'Of the six murdered victims, the police found the first woman, Debra Rathburn, on the ground outside with multiple stab wounds in her back and legs. The butchered remains of Willard Rathburn, the pig farmer and Girdy's uncle, were half-eaten inside the barn's pig pen. Four slaughtered bodies had been found in different rooms inside the house.' The reporter had listed off the names of three victims not related to the Rathburn family. 'Those three had the misfortune of visiting the farm the Halloween night that Girdy Rathburn snapped. According to Girdy's testimony, the massacre stemmed from an argument with her mother, Agatha. After trick-or-treating, Agatha refused to let her daughter eat any of her candy, because Girdy had gotten 'fatter than a hog fit for slaughter.''

The reporter had next entered a low-ceilinged room with cubbies stuffed with doll parts. Small, frilly dresses hung above a sewing machine. 'And here, in the dollmaking room, seated on the floor among a blood-stained pile of naked dolls, is where the police found Girdy's mother. Agatha's eyes had been carved out, leaving hollow red pits. Later that night, the police located Girdy walking down a country road, wearing a blood-stained dress and porcelain doll mask.'

Remembering the disturbing images from the show, Helen became terrified by the thought that such a monster was on the loose in Mill Creek. *That couldn't have been Girdy Rathburn at my door.*

179

No, it had to be someone else. Helen's mind kept seeing the nurse's uniform and that white hard-shelled mask with the red crosses on the cheeks.

A loud noise, like the slamming of a gate, sounded from the back yard. The neighbors' dog began barking.

Helen about jumped out of her skin. Her pulse quickened. She muted the TV, listened. In the next yard over, the barking dog was going berserk, snarling at something.

All Helen could see in the back windows was her reflection standing in the den. Feeling exposed, she dimmed the ceiling lights. The only light came from the TV. She moved along the windows, closing curtains. She made sure the sliding-glass door was locked. Her heart thumped wildly as she pressed her face to the glass, trying to see outside. The back yard was pitch black. There wasn't even a sliver of moonlight to help see beyond the glass door.

She turned on the back porch light, illuminating the furnished patio and neglected garden. The light only reached part of the unkempt lawn of tall grass and weeds before tapering off into utter darkness.

The neighbor's dog had gone strangely quiet. From the dark, a hurled brick flew toward the house and smashed the patio light. The black night swallowed the back yard and pressed against the sliding-glass door.

Helen screamed and backed away, bumping into her couch.

The woman's voice called from the dark yard, 'Candy!'

'Go away!' Helen screamed. 'I'm calling the police!'

Outside, a large white blur ran through the blackness across the yard. Near the garage attached to the back of the house, metal screeched.

'She's trying to break in!' Helen searched for her phone. She felt both frazzled by anxiety and an oncoming wooziness as the Xanax kicked in. Her den whirled around her. The carpeted floor tilted this way and that, like a carnival funhouse room. Her legs felt made of rubber as she tried to walk around the couch.

'Where's my phone?' She dug through her purse but it wasn't in there. She remembered plugging the phone into the charging station on the counter beside the fridge. As she entered the kitchen, the back door to the garage swung open.

The burly nurse in the white mask filled the doorframe and held out her pumpkin bucket. 'Trick or treat!'

Screaming, Helen backpedaled, bumped into her dining room table, turned, and ran-stumbled into the foyer. She almost made it to the front door when a large hand snatched a clump of her hair from behind. As Helen was yanked backward by her hair, she grabbed her ghost trophy from the foyer table.

The big woman pulled her into the den, then let go of her hair.

Helen screamed, 'Get out of my house!' She swung the trophy at the intruder's masked head, but the woman caught her forearm, jerked it so hard that Helen felt her upper arm bone pop out of the shoulder's socket. The ceramic ghost statue flew out of her grip, struck the fireplace, and shattered.

Bolts of pain shot through Helen's shoulder. The fight in her gave out. Terror paralyzed her. Looking up, she stared into the blank eyes that peered through the mask's round holes. The yellow-toothed mouth breathed a rancid, fruit sugar stench into Helen's face, like the smell of sunbaked Jolly Ranchers in melted plastic wrappers.

'Girdy, please, don't kill me,' Helen begged.

The escaped mental patient flung her hard to the floor, knocking the wind out of her. While Helen lay beside the coffee table in pain, the woman dumped the entire bowl of Halloween candy into her plastic pumpkin bucket.

My candy! cried the little girl in Helen's mind.

Forget the stupid candy! said Mother. *It's for the trick-or-treaters!*

You should have kept the candy out of your house, said Dr. Foster.

'Shut up, all of you!' Helen screamed aloud. 'Get out of my head!'

Her outburst caused the masked lunatic to snap her head around and gaze down at her. Grunting, the heavy-set woman stepped over her, then sat down on Helen's back, using her as a human sofa. The enormous weight pinned Helen's chest to the carpet. Craning her neck, she watched in horror as the woman dug into her bucket, tore open wrappers, and stuffed the sweets through the mask's mouth hole. She moaned as she smacked loudly. 'Mmm, candy corn... Mmm, Mr. Goodbar... Ooh, Snickers...'

Making herself at home, she picked up the remote, turned up the TV volume, and watched a Halloween cartoon. She chuckled at the antics of the animated characters spooked by noises in a haunted house.

Hurt and helpless beneath the woman's crushing mass, Helen cried a steady stream of tears. Candy wrappers littered the floor around her head. The child inside her counted each sweet treat she wouldn't get to eat. A few of the torn-open wrappers were Snickers.

The woman wiped her chocolate-stained fingers on Helen's hair. Terrified, Helen wet herself. She lay in a warm puddle that soaked her pants and the carpet. Despite the agony of being crushed and sheer terror making her heart pound, she did her best to not utter a sound. The woman sitting atop her continued to greedily cram candies into her mouth and laugh at the cartoon. Every so often, her hand pulled the rubber band on Helen's arm and snapped it painfully against her wrist.

Sometime later, Girdy's nails scraped the bottom of her pumpkin bucket. She set it down on the floor. Her heavy hands pressed Helen down against the carpet as the woman pushed herself up to her knees, straddling Helen's prone body.

Helen braced herself to be strangled like the nurse back at the mental hospital. *This is the moment I die*, she thought with dread. *Murdered in my den at the hands of a deranged psychopath.*

Girdy Rathburn rose to her feet and grabbed her plastic bucket. She tossed an unopened package of Snickers on the carpet near Helen's face.

'Happy Halloween!' the masked woman said. Then, she walked out of the den and left through the front door. Her heavy footfalls clumped down the porch steps, trailing off into the night.

Shaking to her core, suffering from body aches and a dislocated shoulder, Helen remained lying on the floor, shocked to still be alive. The smell of sweets, mingled with the stink of urine and the woman's foul breath, still hung in the air. All the voices in Helen's head had gone strangely silent, as if her mother, her therapist, and her little sweet tooth had walked out of the house with the crazy lady. With what little strength she had left, Helen reached her uninjured arm through the litter of torn-open wrappers, toward the last remaining package of candy, and batted it far away.

Living Creatures
Elle Jones

In the beginning, it wasn't even meant to be a house. Mariah told Lacy and I that we were going to an abandoned chapel, and though I can't be certain, I think she actually believed it. There's no way she'd have wanted to go so bad if she knew it was a house; they were too ordinary for her. You could find abandoned homes slouched on most corners of Jimson Cross, our tiny unincorporated community just below Georgia's fall line. An old church was rarer; it held more novelty. And a chapel would have avoided the other problem with houses, which is, of course, that they are prone to being haunted.

Mariah said she'd heard about the place from a boy who gave her a ride to a Friday night football game. Our high school team was the Jimson Cross Animals—not any specific kind of animal, just a generic, bestial figure. The mascot looked like a cross between a dog and a horse, with a cloven hoof at the end of each leg. On Fridays all the girls wore animal print to show their school spirit, except for Mariah, who wore black. The only 'school spirit' Mariah had was the vodka she bought in the girls' bathroom during study hall, but

183

that didn't stop her from going to the games. It must have been easy for her to coax the building's location out of the boy, to get him to spill about the hole in the barbed-wire fence and give her the key so she wouldn't need to break a window. She said she promised him a kiss in exchange, and whether I believe that or not, I know he'd have given her the key anyway. Mariah had power over people like that. And she was lucky. I doubt anyone would agree with me on that now, but it's true. She was lucky as hell.

#

The first time we visited the house was at the tail end of September. In Georgia that time is too hot to be autumn and too worn out to be summer. It's some other season, with its own yearly symptoms: four-inch spiders spinning yellow webs, ripe wild grapes clouding over with yeast, a world on the brink of death by suffocation. Lacy drove us to the place Mariah said the chapel should be, and the minute I stepped out of her old SUV I was sweating. The car was pulled over on the side of a highway, one of the desolate rural stretches with woods all around, where the road constricts to just two lanes. From there, Mariah led us into the trees, glancing back every so often with an addicting little glint in her eye. We traipsed around in the woods for nearly half an hour before I glimpsed the shine of whitewash through the branches. Then the building began to reveal its shallow-sloped tin roof, its chimney, and we suddenly realized that it had been a house all along.

All things considered, the place wasn't in bad shape. It was two stories done in the style people call 'carpenter gothic', with a big slab of porch jutting off the facade like an underbite. The windows were all intact, except for one or two empty frames on the upper floor. A tangle of kudzu had crawled up the outside wall and spilled through them into the house. The paint was peeling, the wood rotting in places, but the door was sturdy. There was a hole in the fence, just like Mariah said there would be. A shed crouched nearby, much worse-off than the house, with a sunken roof and walls bulging like a rotten pumpkin. Lacy said it looked like a brown recluse bite waiting to happen. Mariah said it looked like a mausoleum.

The lock on the door was crusted over with rust, but Lacy

managed to jam the key in and get it to turn. Stepping over the threshold was like being swallowed by a sepia photo. It wasn't any cooler inside the house, but the heat was different—drier, dustier, like an attic. There was a smell, too, raw wood with a hint of soil. The door opened straight on a flight of stairs and a narrow hallway that led to the rest of the house. It soon became clear why Mariah's boy had thought it was a chapel. The walls were decked almost floor to ceiling in religious art, and between the frames I could see the same mint-green paint that covers the inside of old Baptist churches. Later I heard Mariah say that all the pictures were of angels, but this is one lie of hers I can definitively refute, because I know I saw other things on those walls. Certainly there were angels, both the babyish greeting-card variety and the four-headed burning monstrosities I'd learned about in Sunday school. But there were other creatures, too: icons of dog-headed saints and wood figurines of Jesus that looked like they'd been ripped off of crosses. And when I say the art was religious, I don't just mean it was Christian. I saw a crude drawing of a woman with a lion's head holding two serpents, and even a few childrens' book illustrations of fairies. Mariah received the sight with a kind of glowing wonder. Lacy just seemed glad there hadn't been a squatter waiting inside with a loaded shotgun. As for me, I was finding it strangely difficult to breathe.

Mariah crept along the hallway, deeper into the darkness of the house. She took a lighter from her pocket and held it in front of her, which was stupid, because all of our cell phones had a flashlight function. As we moved through the house, our discoveries grew more and more incomprehensible. In the bathroom all the bare crosses that had been split from their Jesuses were nailed to the wall above a cracked sink and toilet. One vacant room held a pile of roughly carved wooden baby dolls. Mariah wanted to take one home, but when Lacy refused to have it in her car, Mariah didn't get upset. That's one thing about Mariah I feel I have to make clear. Whatever influence she had, she never actually forced us to do anything. We did it all because we wanted to.

At some point we became aware of a faint chemical smell and followed it to the kitchen, where dead flies floated in open jars of vinegar on the counter. Mariah started snooping around in the cabinets. I have no idea what she was looking for, but I guess she found it in the clear plastic tub she pulled out. A cloudy, bleach-smelling liquid sloshed around inside, just enough to submerge the skeleton resting on the bottom. It was small, four-legged, maybe belonging to a possum or a raccoon. Mariah put her face close to the murky surface and took a long sniff, and I swear she was about to reach in and pull the thing out when I heard Lacy snap,

'Don't fucking touch it, oh my God!' Mariah pulled back and looked at her with a mischievous smile, but she gently placed the tub back in the cabinet and closed it.

'Time to go upstairs, I think,' she said.

The stairs were creakier than the rest of the house, and the railing had fallen off in a few places. Still, we made it up to the landing without crashing back down to the first floor. The upper story was smaller than the lower, just a short hallway with a single door at the end. Upstairs the air was warmer and heavier, and that musty smell was stronger. Somehow, I got to the end of the hallway before the other two, and, not wanting to reveal how nervous I really was, I shouldered open the door.

In many ways that room was the most ordinary place in the house. There was an old box TV squatting in the corner, a few wooden chairs, and at first, I didn't see any pictures. The busted windows I had noticed from outside framed a square view of the woods, which looked incredibly appealing just then. I followed the tendrils of kudzu with my eyes as they snaked over the windowsill and around the room, and it was then that I realized the wall next to me had an enormous image gouged right into the plaster. Through the splinters I could make out a seated human figure with deer antlers sprouting from the top of its head. It was flanked by various creatures, most of which were too poorly rendered to recognize. A bird, a snake, something with horns, something that might have been a cat. Beneath the mural lay a pile of VHS tapes, maybe fifty or sixty of them. Mariah was instantly drawn to these, when I finally stepped through the doorway to let the others in. After a brief inspection, though, she sighed and said,

'Damn. They're all broken.' It was true. Every tape was either pulled off of its reel or screwed into a smashed casing. A breeze came through the open window, and with the momentary breath it gave me I asked,

'What do you think the picture means?' Lacy gave it a glance, shrugged, and said,

'It's just some weird graffiti. Clearly we're not the first people to come here.' Then she crossed her arms and a shiver ran through her. 'I'm ready to leave.' I was beyond grateful that it had come from her mouth instead of mine. The two of us started for the door, and we were already halfway down the stairs when I saw Mariah hadn't followed. I called out for her, but the only response was the distant creak of her footsteps. I saw her body flicker briefly in the sliver of doorway that was still visible to me, then she disappeared again, like she was pacing around in there. I called her name a second time, and began to climb back up the staircase, when she finally emerged from the room and skipped down to join me and Lacy. Stepping off the house's porch steps onto soft soil filled me with such relief that I actually giggled. Mariah locked the door behind us and tucked the brass key into her pocket. By then I had started marching away into the woods. I am not a natural leader, but I stayed ahead of the others all the way to Lacy's car.

#

I can't definitively point out when Mariah started acting strangely, because she had always acted strangely for as long as I'd known her. Even today, I cannot say with certainty that what happened had anything to do with the house. Maybe things would have turned out similarly even if we'd never been there, or if we'd stayed away after that first visit. But of course, Mariah never could have stayed away. It was less than a week before she went back, alone.

She told me about her second visit a few days after it happened, when she, Lacy and I were skipping seventh period to hang out at her place. We were in the living room, helping ourselves to her father's beer when she said,

'I have something to show you two.' She kept talking as she reached under an old armchair and pulled out a black object. 'I couldn't stop thinking about those tapes, so I went back to the house, and actually I got a couple of them to play on my parents' VCR.'

I knew she wanted to tell that story, so I asked, 'How? Weren't they smashed?' Mariah flashed a conspiratorial grin.

'Well, I have a ton of these bible story VHS's, you know, fundie shit, but I figured I could take those bible tape reels out of their cases and replace them with the reels from the house.'

'And that worked?' Lacy asked. Mariah shrugged.

'For some of them. Some are too busted up to salvage, or the tape is ripped. I'm gonna go back again with more empty cases so I can fix the rest. You guys should come, too.' Lacy and I glanced at each other.

'Okay,' I agreed. And really, it did seem okay. The house couldn't possibly be as bad the second time around. Mariah pushed some buttons on the TV and slid her tape into the VCR.

'This is the best one,' she said. 'Watch.' Then she pressed PLAY.

The screen was black at first, but soon an image appeared, indistinct and gritty, from which I could discern nothing but shifting light. When the picture cleared up, I recognized the upstairs hallway of the house. Whoever was holding the camera pointed it unsteadily ahead of themselves as they descended the stairs, turned into the hallway, and stopped at a door. I had not, by that point, memorized the layout of the house, but when a hand appeared and opened the door, I saw it was the room with the wooden babies. They were there in the video, arranged in a row along the back wall. There was also a small mattress with white sheets lying unmoored in the middle of the floor. The camera was still for a long time, except for the ambient trembling of its handler. Then there was a cut, almost imperceptible because the new clip was of the same room, from the same angle. The only difference was a vaguely defined form lying under the sheet, covered head to toe. The camera advanced, and I saw the same hand as before reach under the sheet and pull out one of the figure's pale arms. Up close, the body looked like a woman's. The person behind the camera cradled the arm in their hand and began to describe its parts.

'These are the fingers. Um, forefinger, middle, ring, pinkie, thumb. This is the hand.' The voice was masculine but very soft and gentle. 'This is the wrist. Here's the forearm and the bicep. The elbow connects them.' He touched each place as he named them. Was she a corpse? No, I saw her fingers twitch. When the man reached her shoulder, he carefully tucked the arm back under the sheet and

188

moved to the foot of the mattress. He folded the sheet back to expose one of her legs, bare all the way up, and continued his narration. 'This is the ankle. This is the lower leg. The bone is the shin and the muscle is the calf. This is the thigh—'

A sudden burst of static made Lacy and I flinch away from the screen. The video continued, but it was covered with a veil of distortion.

'Ugh, I couldn't fix this part,' Mariah said, 'I'll fast-forward it.' The tape whirred ahead until the image became somewhat clear again. The camera was on the floor, pointed at four people standing with their faces just out of frame. They were each rocking a wooden baby, swaying and humming discordantly. The clip played for a minute or two, long enough that I started to get antsy, then there was another cut. This time the shot was of the kitchen counter. There was a mass of pink and red lying there which looked, to me, like an emaciated skinned chicken, or some kind of embryo. The hand reappeared and spread the thing's limbs.

'This is the spine.' It was the same voice as before. 'This is the rib cage. These are the haunches.' He picked up the head between his thumb and forefinger, and the thing's neck was horrifically soft and pliable, its flesh moving easily in his hands. 'This is the snout. Here are the teeth. Here are the eyes.' The screen went black again. The only sound was the faint squeaking of tape. I could see mine and Lacy's disturbed expressions reflected on the TV.

'Who were those people?' Asked Lacy.

'I don't know,' said Mariah, 'but didn't it seem like they were doing something important?'

#

That night, I dreamt someone was taking my limbs from under my blanket and pointing out their features. Their voice was different from the one on the tape, and their hands felt cold and damp. I couldn't see who it was, because my sheet had been pulled over my face, and no matter how hard I clawed and pushed at it I couldn't throw it off. Finally, moving with an effort that could only be required in dreams, I sat up in bed and wrenched the sheet down. My room was dark and empty; I had woken myself up. I checked my phone and saw that it was two in the morning, and I had a text from Mariah: *u awake?* I replied: *yeah. had a weird dream about that video.* I typed out a brief synopsis of the nightmare. By now she was probably asleep, and I wasn't expecting a reply, but a few moments later my phone buzzed. *next time u have to try harder to see its face.* I stared at the message for a long time, so long that Mariah sent another one. *i have the dreams too. i know they're scary but it's better when u can see their faces.* Even though her messages were cryptic, and she was technically to blame for my unease, talking to Mariah soothed me. She had the dreams, too, and she'd had them for longer; she could guide me through them. *ok thx.* I replied. *gonna try and sleep now.* Just as I lay down, I got one last text from Mariah: *haha good luck.*

#

The three of us returned to the house a week into October. We took Mariah's car; she had offered to drive. I think it was her way of asserting control. The dreams had been keeping me awake at night and clouding up my thoughts, so when I caught the faint smell of rot as we approached the house, I assumed it was my mind playing tricks on me. Then the wind changed directions and it hit me straight in the face, the awful unmistakable stench of a dead animal.

'Oh, God,' Lacy muttered, pulling her shirt over her nose, 'What skunk decided to crawl into these woods and die?'

'It didn't smell like this last time,' Mariah said, her voice tinged with something like excitement. We kept walking, and the smell got stronger until it was almost too much to tolerate. Finally the house came into view, and with it the barbed wire fence, and with the fence the corpse of a deer whose antlers had gotten tangled in the wire. We all stopped and stared at it for a long moment. It must have killed itself thrashing or starved to death. Of course we had all seen a dead deer before, but that didn't make the sight any less disturbing, the way it was hung up on the fence like an impaled body before a medieval warlord's castle. Mariah was the first to move, tentatively stepping towards the animal. Carefully, so as to avoid the barbs, she unwound the wire from the deer's horns. When she was done, its body fell to the ground, and her gaze shifted up to Lacy and I,

190

watching her with shock and a little admiration.

'Can you help me move this?' She asked.

It was slow going, moving the deer's body to the shed. Lacy and I had to hold our breath while we dragged it, then step several feet away every time we needed a gulp of air. I don't know how Mariah managed to stand next to the thing without gagging.

'We should give it a sacrifice,' Mariah said, when it was done. She walked back to the fence and pricked her finger on the barbed wire. 'Just a few drops of blood each.' I watched her in awe. Somehow this seemed like the most loving and selfless action I had ever been given the opportunity to take. Following Mariah's lead, I took a rusty barb and pressed its point deep into the flesh of my thumb. I squeezed the skin tight until a dark bead of blood appeared and ran back to the shed before it could clot. I held my breath and stepped into the damp half-light of the derelict structure. The deer's head was folded back on its shoulder, as if it were sleeping peacefully. I knelt and smeared my blood over the wiry fur on its forehead. The half-decayed face entranced me. Behind its empty eye sockets, I saw a gray mass which I at first thought was the brain, but then I saw the mass squirm and I realized with horror that it was a crowd of maggots. Without thinking, I gasped, and immediately I choked on the thick pungency of the air. I fled the corpse, hacking and retching, eyes watering, tasting rot in my throat. Mariah and Lacy were standing nearby on the house's porch, having already opened the door. Whatever my reservations about the place, I wasted no time in entering and putting its green-painted walls between me and the dead deer.

That visit marked our first offering of blood, as well as Mariah's first mention of her Halloween plans. She told us she was going to perform a ritual, one that would help with the dreams which had been afflicting us all. Over the next few weeks, we went back to the house several times. I couldn't say how many exactly; sleep deprivation made that month a blur, and my dreams of the house both during and after have blended inseparably with reality. Mariah started carrying a knife, first for her own sacrifices, then for me and Lacy as we sought to emulate her. With every visit the smell of rot grew stronger; it seeped into the house. I know Mariah was going on her own, too, to prepare for the ritual, which metamorphosed from a

191

simple spell to ease our nightmares into a grand summoning rite. We were going to bring the angels down to us, Mariah said, we were going to give them a body, and it was only possible if we all had faith. It had to be on All Hallows Eve, she said, because that was their day. I believed her, but now I know it was a lie. Halloween was Mariah's day—hers. Frightening, black-clad—the high priestess of blood. Her power was strongest then.

#

When the thirty-first came, I was so exhausted I felt drugged. All that kept me awake was a sort of nervy, electric anticipation. The sun was beginning to set when Mariah rolled to a stop near the woods. By this time we could better find the house by smell than sight. We had just stepped through the hole in the fence when Mariah announced she had forgotten her knife in the car and would need to go back for it. She gave Lacy the key and a candle she had brought for the ritual, asking her to put it in the upstairs room in the meantime. That's how Lacy and I ended up alone together in the house, without Mariah for the first time. I was feeling lightheaded from the smell, so I sat on the bottom step while Lacy took care of the candle. I heard her creaking up the stairs, heard her cross the short hallway and pull open the door. Then she let out a long, ragged scream like she was watching someone die in front of her. I turned around just in time to see her vomit on the hallway floor, eyes bulging with burst capillaries.

'Lock the door,' She pleaded with a voice like broken glass, 'lock that fucking crazy bitch out.' I was so shocked that I obeyed her immediately. But then, stupidly, I asked,

'How will Mariah get in?' Lacy jerkily made her way down the stairs, a look of dread frozen on her face, muttering to no one.

'She's crazy. She's actually fully insane now. What the hell are we doing? Blood sacrifices? Why? Why did we do that?' I eyed her warily. I didn't like her disparaging all we had accomplished. I might have completely ignored her and unlocked the door again if she hadn't looked me straight in the eyes and confessed, 'I'm scared.'

It was then that we heard footsteps on the front porch outside.

192

Mariah tried the door, and, finding it locked, cheerfully called our names. Lacy and I stood frozen, even when she began to pound against the rotting wood. We heard footsteps again, and then, too late, we saw her face in the window which overlooked the porch, and she saw us and our terrified mutiny. Mariah's face contorted and disappeared from the window, but my eyes remained fixed to the place she had been. The next thing I saw there was Mariah's hand, and the rock grasped inside it shattering the pane of glass.

Lacy took me by the arm and pulled me down the hall to the kitchen. I could hear glass breaking behind us, then Mariah moaning in pain as she climbed through a window frame edged with its shards. As we cowered against the sink, there was the sound of her landing on the floor, then slow, shuffling footsteps. I could not then understand why Lacy was so afraid; in my mind she was the irrational one. But now, knowing what she saw in that upstairs room, I understand that Lacy was probably absolutely certain Mariah was about to kill us. We heard her stumbling footsteps on the stairs, in the second-floor hallway, and then directly above us in the tape room. There the sound stopped, and everything was quiet. Lacy turned to me.

'We need to make a break for it,' she whispered. I started to speak, but she continued, 'This might be our only chance.'

'No,' I said, 'Mariah needs help. She's not going to hurt us.' Lacy's expression was agony. She took my hand.

'Please,' she begged, 'Please come with me.' I shook my head. There were tears in her eyes. 'I have to leave,' she said. 'Please follow me. We have to leave.' I stood rooted to my spot by the sink. She dropped my hand and tried one last time to get through to me. 'Please follow,' she said. Then she ran.

I stood there in the kitchen for a long time. Night had long since fallen, but the moonlight was strong and came through the windows in long bars of white. I was afraid to go upstairs, not of Mariah, but because whatever Lacy saw had shattered her belief, and I didn't know if my faith was strong enough to withstand it. Surely Mariah herself would be a gruesome sight after climbing through the window. It was this last thought, of Mariah possibly in serious danger, and of her self-sacrificial commitment to the ritual, which finally roused me from my frozen stupor. The hallway was dark; I

193

had to feel my way along the wall, my fingers tracing along wood frames and pained Jesus-faces. I ascended the stairs and came to the door. It was closed. I don't know how Mariah knew I was standing there, but I heard her voice call softly,

'Come in, come here, come look.' And, God help me, that request was all it took. I opened the door, and I looked.

In truth I only saw the room for a moment before I turned and ran, but that fleeting glance seared itself deeper into my memory than a longer look would have, like the split-second exposure of a photograph. The whole room glittered with moonlight. Mariah was sitting slouched against the wall; by this point I doubt she could have supported her own weight. I couldn't tell which of her injuries were from the broken glass and which were self-inflicted later, with her knife. The top of the deer's skull was balanced on her head, a few stray maggots dropping onto her hair. Her face was a mask of joyous spiritual rapture. And in front of her lay her creation. It was the deer, or it once had been. Mariah had added to it. Its head was a sheep's; its back half was a dog's. One of its front legs had been replaced with a thick black snake. And along its back, roughly sewn on, were three pairs of what I now think must have been vulture wings. Mariah was singing it a wordless hymn of adoration. The thing was covered in her blood.

I took the stairs two, three at a time; I leapt down them. I wrenched open the front door, left it ajar, and sprinted into the woods, my face cut by thorns and my hair snagging on low branches. I was desperate to get as far away from the house as possible. Not because I thought Mariah or her angel would come after me, but because I knew that if I didn't leave immediately, while my resolve was strong, I was going to turn around, run back into the trees, and join them.

The house was demolished shortly after the discovery of Mariah's corpse. I mourned the building as I mourned my friend, all its paintings and wooden babies and bones. All that remained of the house were the tapes, still hidden in Mariah's armchair, waiting to be rediscovered. It used to bring me comfort, their survival. Now I can only hope they got thrown out and are rotting with her. I know, deep down, it's what she would have wanted.

The Revellers of the Rift
Marty Young

'You're desperate to believe me, that's why you're here,' the woman said. The edge of her left eye spasmed. She blinked, blinked again, then turned away to stare towards the door of the cafe as she rubbed at the twitch. 'You wouldn't have come otherwise.'

'Fair enough,' Jacob said, holding up his hands in surrender. 'Sorry. You're right. Okay, so let's go take a look, then.'

She picked up her phone without looking, as if some psychic link let her know where it was at all times, and climbed awkwardly from the chair.

Florence 'Flo' Patterson was a frail thing, pale skin stretched over fragile bones. Her hair was messy but clean, the whites of her eyes free from evidence of drug use—when they weren't twitching—and they fired up pretty well when she was pushed.

There was enough vibration in some of her words to resonate at the same frequency with the vibration within him too, the one always thrumming, always on. Enough to pause before hitting delete on that first email she'd sent.

Enough to re-read it again, and to reply.

Was she telling the truth?

She certainly believed what she was telling him, that was for sure. He'd been able to tell that from the short phone calls they had shared before he drove the six hours out to this hidden town. Dunestead, so named due to the sand dunes on its eastern flank. The desert was beyond, with searing heat and little rain.

Yet here…it was a haven of sorts. Oh, the desert's influence was clear enough, with battered and worn-down buildings, brown grass and dead bushes, but there was also a vibrancy here, as though the town didn't fear the heat or the dry and knew cooler, wetter times were always close at hand.

And there was life, too. He'd noticed that the moment he climbed from his parked car. Beyond the townsfolk and birds that cawed exhaustedly across the sky; life in the buildings themselves, in the ground surrounding them, just waiting to rise once the rain returned. To rise once more and swell with vivacity.

Red flags hung from the streetlights, languishing in the breeze and promoting the *31 Parade from 9pm*. Beneath the words was a close-up picture of a man with a huge smile and white paint in jagged streaks up and down his dark-skinned face. The teeth were sharper than normal.

It was the reason Jacob was here. The Halloween parade, although as he had looked over the town when he had first arrived, there were no pumpkins to be seen. No giant spiders and pretend cobwebs draped over houses or shops. No witches or skeletons. None of the usual paraphernalia.

Just those posters.

Some houses had painted their windows black or taped black paper over them. Even some of the doors were black, all painted in three rough broad stokes.

He finished off the lukewarm long black, wiped his lips and gathered his own phone from the table, hitting pause on the recording before following after her. 'Wait up.'

The stares from the others in the cafe weren't overt or threatening, just...shifty. A flicker his way before a hand rose to cover eyes, pretending to scratch the side of a face. The barest hesitation as someone turned around to look at something past him.

Obvious despite their covertness.

Okay, he thought. *Interesting*. He added that to the mental notes he was taking, surprised as how long that list was quickly becoming.

On purpose, he took his time at the door, patting his hip pocket as if to check for his wallet. As he did, he smiled at the old couple nearby. A man, bald, and a woman, with long grey hair. Both smiled back at him, not a hint of unwelcome in their faces.

'Are you here for the parade?' The woman asked him.

196

'Yeah,' he said. 'Got to sort out a few things first, but I'm hoping to stick around for it.'

'Oh, you definitely should, it's well worth it.'

The tone was inviting, but there was a gleam in her eyes. The old man's too, when Jacob looked over. Something more than just excitement.

'Happy Halloween,' he said, letting the door close quietly behind him, but not before he caught the woman's reply: 'Oh, we don't say that here.'

Flo was already twenty paces up the road and showing no signs of slowing. He hurried to catch her.

'So, I'm the only one to take you serious, huh?'

'I don't blame them,' she said.

'How did you find me, anyway? It's not like my name is...' He didn't finish. Didn't want to.

'The mainstream newsletters wouldn't take my calls. No one would. So, I tried a different route.'

'The Borderlands.' The magazine he wrote for—not even close to being a reputable gig. It was where all journalists went to die. Still, at least it paid, even if barely.

Another patch of graffiti marred the building they passed—Specs for Sure, an optometrist. A small circle with the bottom drooping as though seeping down the wall. A single dot in the center. It was painted in yellow.

'What is this?' He asked Flo. 'It's the third time I've seen this since hitting town.'

Flo's step stuttered, then she picked up her pace. 'We have to hurry. That starts appearing when they get close. I don't know why. It's like a reaction to...*him*.'

A strange sensation rose up over him. It wasn't fear and it didn't elicit goosebumps, and nor did his heart race.

Happy Halloween...

He couldn't describe it; not fear, no. But something akin to that ancient emotion.

Oh, we don't say that here.

The street was a street, complete with the occasional car, other people out walking, shops open for business—everything a small outback town was supposed to be. More of those strange, covert stares, but enough warm smiles to make them forgivable.

'Hurry up,' Flo said, and he was shocked to realize she had stopped almost fifty feet ahead of him now.

He flinched; behind her, a glimpse of something more. Something…

What was it? A person? Was it even alive? It shifted, then. Took a step towards him before spinning away, a dance of merriment as it shimmered from sight.

He stumbled back a step, his mouth coming open but not yet working.

'Please,' Flo called, either unaware of what had been behind her or knowing and hurrying still - or because. 'We have to hurry!'

Jacob opened the camera app on his phone and took a photo of her. Then he took another, zoomed in a little more.

Neither photo captured what he had thought he'd seen. On instinct, he took several more shots of the town around him, but again…nothing.

'Jacob!'

'Okay, okay.' He switched off his phone and went after her, watching, always watching, the space beyond, but whatever he had seen didn't reappear.

#

Flo led them out of town a ways, out to where the sand took over. Further ahead, the dunes rose up like strange mountains. Closer, small hills spotted the foreground, dome-like structures with low rounded tops.

'They come from here,' she said, staring out across the ocean of sand. Weird scrubs - perhaps spinifex, though he wasn't sure—grew randomly and there was a stark absence of trees. 'Shimmering into sight like they're a mirage, and the first time you see them, that's what you'll think. That they aren't real at all, or that you're suffering heat stroke, or, or, or that the rhythm of the drums is causing you to hallucinate. But…but…as you watch, as you watch…they…'

Her words fell apart into a broken silence punctuated with groans. Jacob thought the sounds were coming from her, but they weren't. Somewhere further off into the sand, that was their source. Out beyond the first mound, just out of sight.

A small plume of smoke rose into the air.

'They've lit the fire.'

'They have,' said a voice behind them.

Flo flinched and spun.

'Hello, Flo,' said a small woman of medium build. The raised mask on her head was the same as the face in the posters about town. She wore denim coveralls and a cotton shirt, despite the heat of the late afternoon. Her hair was grey and short but kept tidy.

'Miriam,' said Flo, and Jacob noted the small step she took away from Miriam.

'Won't you introduce me to your friend?'

Flo met Jacob's eyes and he could see a conflict of emotions within them. Without making her endure more suffering, he smiled and extended his hand. 'Hi, I'm Jacob.'

Miriam's grip was firm. 'Are you a friend of Flo's? Here for the parade?'

'That's right. She's tried to get me here before, but I've never been able to make it,' he said, finding the lies coming easy.

'I'm Reverend Miriam Langley. It's lovely to meet you and I'm glad you could be here for Flo. I know it's a difficult time for her, after last year. Flo? How are you? Are you okay?'

She sounded sincere but things were vibrating within Jacob again, a clear sign something was off.

'I'm fine,' said Flo. She glared at the woman, not hiding her disdain.

'That's good, that's good. You'll still be joining us tonight, won't you?'

'Do I have a choice?'

Miriam laughed. 'Oh Flo! Of course you do! We all do. We always have.'

Flo went to say something but didn't. She turned away, back towards where the bonfire was. The plume was thicker now, and occasionally a red lick of flame rose above the top of the mound obscuring it.

'The parade is an interesting one,' said Jacob, watching the woman closely. 'I couldn't find anything about it online. Who's the face in all the posters? And why do you cover your windows and doors in black? Three thick strokes. It's not a Halloween tradition I know.'

Miriam was still smiling and it was as genuine as they came. Rapturous, even. 'That's the Herald. The leader of the parade. Our otherworld emissary. *Aos sí*. He leads his kind across these lands and leaves happiness and prosperity in his wake.'

'That's…err…' He didn't know. 'How does that marry with your own faith?'

'Oh, it's God's will. He dictates the way and we all follow, even our Herald.'

Flo laughed, then. But hers was nothing like Miriam's had been. 'Keep telling yourself that if it helps you sleep. It doesn't me—and it didn't my dad.'

Miriam grew serious. 'Flo, I know this is a difficult time for you but it's been a tradition in Dunestead for longer than I've lived here, and I've lived here longer than you've been alive. I'm sorry about your dad, I truly am, but it was his choice last year. His and his alone.'

'It wasn't his choice! It was our guilt he couldn't live with anymore!' Flo shoved the other lady, making her stumble backwards. Then Flo stalked off, back towards town.

Jacob didn't know what to do. He started going after Flo but then stopped and checked on Miriam. 'Are you all right?'

'Yes, yes, I'm fine. I'm just worried about her. Please, keep an eye on her tonight. It's an emotional time for her.'

'Yeah, I will. That's why I'm here.'

'Good.' Miriam continued to smile at him, otherwise not moving. Her blinking had slowed.

'Well,' he said, wanting to ask her what Flo had meant but unable to. He wanted to ask if he could take her photo but didn't do that, either. 'Happy Halloween.'

'Oh, we don't say that here,' she said, still with her smile. 'We celebrate a different part of Halloween.'

He turned and went after Flo, forcing himself not to turn around because he knew Miriam would still be there, unmoving, watching him with her dead smile as though her batteries had run out and she'd frozen in place.

Flo hadn't told him much about her dad other than he had gone

200

missing this time last year. She had alluded to some connection with the parade but that had been as much as she had told him.

'I'll tell you more once you get here,' she'd said over the phone.

He hurried after her, catching up just as the sand became concrete footpaths and roads again. 'Hey, hey wait.'

He grabbed her arm, but she shrugged it off.

'Flo, please. Stop.'

She did, and as she did, all the anger and fight drained away and she slumped.

'What's going on? What aren't you telling me? What did you mean back there?'

'They'll want you to join this year.' She didn't look at him.

'Join what? The parade?'

'But it will have to be your choice. They won't force you. No one can force you.'

'Okay,' he said, not following.

'And you'll be tempted. You have nothing else.'

The harsh truth blasted him.

There were drums in the distance now, a rhythmic thrumming based on a wild beat, one that raced like a heartbeat before slowing and then skipping forwards again. There was merriment to that sound, something that promised so much happiness.

'Oh no, already?' Flo said. She turned back to face the way they had come. Miriam was out of sight over the first mound. The smoke was thicker still, steadier.

The air shimmered, a heat haze no doubt due to the fire and amplified by the setting sun, but even that thrummed with the beating of the drums, as if there were figures hidden within, dancing.

'What happened last year?' He pushed. He needed to know. He needed to know what he was walking into tonight before the darkness fell across town and joined with the painted doors and windows.

'Miriam was right. My dad chose to join them,' she said, and her words were quiet, so weak and heavy with pain. 'He...he just... That morning, he put on the clothes he wore to church on Sunday, turned to me, and said, 'Today's my day, Flo. Enough's enough.' That's all he said.'

She paused, watching the smoke, swaying slightly to the beating drums that rose and fell in volume. 'Then he hugged me and walked out the door. I couldn't stop him.'

'I don't get it. What did he mean? What's so dangerous about a parade?'

The questions caused her to flinch again. She stared at him and he had to look away, uncomfortable under its weight, thinking of Miriam and her weird run-down smile. 'You wanted to see where it all takes place before it gets dark, but now we should go. It gets cold out here once the sun sets. Despite it all.'

'You never told me what happened after the parade. Why didn't your dad just come home again?'

'You don't leave, once you join. You don't want to, even as you peel apart and lose your humanity and become something else.'

She headed off again, back towards her old Subaru parked outside the cafe, and as she walked away from him, the heaviness of her step changed. Lightening. As if the joyous melody from the drums had pushed aside her pain and anguish and filled her with merriment. Just a touch of it, but enough to be noticeable.

Jacob didn't go after her, though. He found he couldn't move.

'Fuck me,' he whispered. *Just what the hell had he stumbled upon? This was pure Wicker Man shit—and that hadn't ended well for the protagonist, either.*

But was this finally something real? Something he could capture and show to the world, to prove he wasn't a fool chasing shadows and whispers. He had gone so far out into pseudoscience that no one would even take a call from him anymore, let alone publish anything he wrote. He had all but ruined his career chasing the impossible. Had become stained with it.

If none of this was real, then he was done. For good.

His hands had become clenched at some point while he watched Flo walk away, and he kept them that way, squeezing them tighter until they ached. There was something here, he was sure of it. He could *feel* it. The whole of Dunestead was in on it, whatever *it* was.

And he would fucking reveal it to everyone, prove to all the naysayers that he wasn't a hack.

#

'Tell me about the parade,' he said as she put on a coat and zipped it up. Jacob was recording the conversation on his phone, occasionally switching to the camera app to snap a shot, or even a short video clip.

She paused, mid-zip. Then resumed, slower than before.

'Miriam said it's been going for decades, although if that's true, I'm surprised no one else has ever posted about it.'

'It's been going for decades because no one wants to share it. Look around; this town is wonderful. It's an amazing place to live. Part of our reward for allowing the Herald his trespass across our world.' Her voice had slipped into a dream-like state as she spoke, her eyes glazing over. She continued dressing but on automatic. 'Our otherworld emissary. Aos sí. It's always new people who join in, caught up in the euphoria. Those who live here know better.'

Aos sí. Miriam had said the same. He knew the words but couldn't remember their meaning. 'What made your dad join, then?'

She froze again, the words getting caught in her mechanisms. Her daze was gone, though, and her brittleness was back.

'And why keep living where they celebrate the same thing every year? All that will do is cause you to relive it over and again. That's not healthy. You shouldn't even be attending this year.'

'I…'

He waited but she just stared at him, whatever words she had wanted to speak also gone.

'Miriam said you celebrate a different part of Halloween here. What did she mean? What does Aos sí mean? All I have are questions, Flo. You said you'd tell me what was going on once I got here, but you haven't.'

'You'll join them,' said Flo, and the dejection in her words was palpable. 'The parade. I know you will.'

'Not before I publish the story,' he said. 'With or without your help.'

'It won't matter once it starts. It never does.'

'We'll see.'

'We should go,' she said. 'It's time.'

#

Caught up in the euphoria, she had said, and he understood now what she meant. His heart hammered like he couldn't remember it ever doing before. But it wasn't the beating of panic and it didn't cause him to fear a heart attack.

Instead, it thrilled him entirely. He couldn't have stood still for the biggest front-page grabber in the world. His body simply no longer knew how to.

And that desire to prove himself to the world had been burned from him, seared away in an instant as soon as they had entered the flickering light of the bonfire, no longer mattering in the slightest. Even the idea of taking out his phone to record what was happening was abhorrent to him. He would miss too much if he did.

It was a drug beyond all drugs. At once so completely overwhelming and all-encompassing, and yet it left him more clear-headed than he had ever been.

He whirled and carolled, lost in the rhythm of the drums and the merriment of those around him. It was contagious. People wore Herald face masks, and the jagged white paint and permanent sharp smile weren't threatening in the slightest. How he wished he had a mask of his own.

Flo was next to him and she was likewise lost under the enchantment. She spun, throwing up her arms and her head back, letting loose a wild yell of delight. She was one of the few without a face mask, and there were tears in her eyes.

Jacob glided closer to the shimmering void hovering above the bonfire. It drew him in, irresistible. He had no idea what it was, had never seen anything like it. He rubbed his eyes, but the blurry spot remained.

'Wait,' Flo said, reaching out to grasp one of his arms.

'No,' he said, laughing off her concern. 'It's okay. It's beautiful!'

'Don't,' she said, twirling with the beat.

'Why wouldn't I?'

Townsfolk danced, they waved their hands high above their heads, bouncing from foot to foot, spinning and dipping, prancing and cheering. Laughter rose with the beat and fell with the drums. Shadows matched their movements, but flickering in the light of the bonfire, they were more erratic.

'I don't know why I wanted it so much. It's such a wasted life.

None of that matters, does it? Not when you have this.' He indicated with his hands towards the people before them.

'It's not what you think it is,' said Flo, but the strength was gone from her argument now.

And there they were, the parade, led by the Herald himself - itself. Because there was little humanity in its form, despite how human it looked - no, it was completely human, but the energy coming from it screamed alien.

Screamed…something, for even the word *alien* felt wrong.

The Herald, all twelve feet of it, danced a merry jig as it came into view, materializing from the foggy void that continued to shimmer above the bonfire. It stepped out into the air and then down towards the ground, where it kicked up a blast of sand before skipping ahead, spinning around and tipping its top hat to the surrounding townsfolk.

It wore a dazzling outfit, some strange blend of theatrical flair and commanding presence. A red tailcoat with ornate gold embroidery, black riding trousers and knee-high boots. Beneath the coat was a pale cream vest and white shirt. Around its neck a small red bow tie. Its face was exactly as it had appeared in the posters about town and the face masks the revellers wore.

A huge cheer rose from the townsfolk and they joined the Herald's dance, if not the parade itself—because that was one thing Jacob noticed, despite his rapture. They might dance and laugh and cry with delight, but they kept away from the Herald, and from those shimmering forms growing into being behind him.

They kept to the edges, careful not to get caught up in the wake of the parade - and Jacob was sure that was it, that to get too close would cause you to get swept up in the slipstream of the otherworldly dance and be lost.

He didn't know how or why he knew that, but he did. Like humanity had once known when to fight or when to flee.

And yet… And yet that knowledge did little to stymie his delight. Because the option was there should anyone want it. To join the parade. Surrender their humanity. Flo had said as much, and he could hear it from the Herald itself.

'Come,' said the Herald, smiling at him, speaking to him only. 'Join us and laugh! Dance!'

Reverend Miriam was there, dancing with the rest of the

townsfolk. She saw him and raised her mask, laughing louder, but it wasn't directed at him. More shared with him.

He found himself laughing back, and Miriam encouraged him on, even as she spun away from him.

Go, she said with movement. *Join them.*

'Join us,' said the Herald, extending a hand towards him.

Something flared a warning deep within him, something primal slowly waking up from evolutions of slumber. This was the story he had hunted all his career, a ticket so golden it was impossible. Presented before him, nothing hidden about it.

Step out, become the observer. Record it all.

He would be famous.

Instead, he stepped closer, his head bopping now, catching the rhythmic beating and weird unified thrumming of voices from this world and beyond. His arms rose, his hands dancing their own jig at the ends of their extremities. His legs too, now they bounced him closer and he was twirling and spinning like everyone else, and before him was the Herald, majestic and surreal and imposing and welcoming, leading them across the land towards a second swirling foggy spot a hundred feet ahead of them. A migration across worlds.

The forms following were human and yet they weren't. Some— and he recognized Flo's father from the photo she had shown him— were more human than others. Some had two arms and two legs but that was the extent of any relationship. Every other aspect was twisted into something else, something different. Revenants, wraiths, echoes—there were no faces on the most extreme ones, no ears or hair. Those ones had run out of their humanity and were little more than husks, spectres. But there was laughter—

'Jacob, I'm sorry,' Flo said, suddenly next to him, swaying alongside and not resisting the pull. 'No more blood on my hands.'

She shoved him, hard. He lost the beat and tumbled away, thrown out of the whirlwind and onto the sand.

'No,' he yelled, but it was too late. The Herald laughed as she joined with the rest, still dancing, unable to stop. But the tears were spilling freely now.

The townsfolk whooped and swayed to the drums, keeping pace with the parade as it moved ever onwards. They clapped at Flo, cheering her on as Jacob climbed back to his feet, already the drums finding him again, instructing his heartbeat.

He screamed back at the townsfolk, imploring for help, that deep primal warning ringing loud in his head, even if he remained ignorant as to why. Miriam laughed with him—because somehow he *was* laughing, despite his panic—but there was a flash of anger, of anguish, in her masked eyes, too. She condemned him as she reached for his hands and spun him in small circles. Soon he was swallowed up by the townsfolk again, all of them skipping over the mounds and down into the valleys, parallel to the parade, waving to the Herald and he waved back, always laughing, his extra sharp teeth glinting in the light.

'No!' Jacob cried out, laughing aloud. He pulled from Miriam but then sought her out again, only to push her away once more.

The urge was back, the wanting need to join the Herald, to join those with him. An urge that was rapidly outweighing his fear. There was such euphoria in Flo's face, in her movements, even in her voice. Those with her, the ones most human and the ones who had pretence only, took turns taking her hands to spin with her, dip her, to hug her. And she revelled in it all.

Each leap of joy took him closer and closer to Flo and the fey wanderers, those vestiges of humanity. Miriam was again at his side, encouraging him onwards. Never pushing him, never demanding. But that was worse because the rapture in her face made him want it even more. The Herald face mask she wore, and those around him, were somehow alive, the sharp wicked smiles larger than before, expression lines evident, cheeks glowing red.

Somewhere, some other world or existence, Flo called out to him but her word—'Don't!'—was a whisper dissolving beneath the drums, beneath the stamping feet. Pure elation enveloped him and drew him into the Herald's fold.

Miriam held onto his hand, and this time her expression was one of terror—*don't*, her eyes said, but then that emotion was gone again, lost beneath the surging tide of joy.

And as he got closer, and closer, dancing towards Flo, and as he heard Miriam call out his name—

—and he felt the ground tilting more steeply beneath him, speeding up his jig towards the parade, he heard the cries and screams beneath that laughter, beneath the thrumming tune of merriment.

The anguish.

Despair.

The pleading for salvation. For death—or something more final than this version of death.

He heard Flo once more, 'Oh, Jacob…'

The whirlwind had him, turbulence pulling at him, spinning him around and around and around—

And then the Herald paused, turning back to the township to give one final wave. He raised both hands and the town cheered again. He removed his top hat and gave a small bow, then turned towards the shimmering spot and stepped out of sight.

Those echoes of revelry under his banner screamed and howled and screeched out for release but they danced and swayed and bopped onwards, stepping through into the second void with limbs almost disjointing themselves in an effort to cling onto the world, and vanishing for another year. Flo was there, just behind her father, and they were both torn through into the void, howling and howling.

Jacob was the last, and he saw Miriam and reached out towards her in desperation because he could feel it now. The claws, the skinning, the drinking of his soul. She waved back, still giggling and cheering. Crying and sorrowful. Her gesture alternated between a goodbye and a final attempt to save him, her merriment dissolving under ever-growing guilt.

Then that world was gone.

Clyde
Tom Rimer

In that barren waste of rot and grime, the color red stood out like a beacon.

Clyde should have recognized the warning for what it was.

He didn't, but he should have.

He shifted in his sodden waders and took a few trembling steps forward.

'Now, who'd a left dat der?'

The white face looking back at him didn't blink, didn't cease its grinning, didn't speak any sort of audible answer.

Clyde lifted his woolen hat for an instant to scratch at a place on his head that used to have hair. He thwacked it back down and it slurped into position. The shivering ghost precariously balanced himself on the uneven walkway as he gawked at the listing, forgotten, canvas and the painted-on face that leered at him from the shadows of the alley—its eyes unnaturally bright, even in the descending gloom of that late October, Cape Cod, nighttime.

'Well, halloo to you too.'

The being in the painting was motionless. Mute. A petrified joker, frozen before its last laugh.

Of course you are, Clyde reassured himself. For some reason, this he didn't speak aloud.

He looked over his shoulder, in the direction of the now completely empty pier, and then back toward the dark crevasse that ran directly parallel to his own street. He was alone in the deluge.

Alone on All Hallows' Eve.

Alone with a painting of a smiling clown.

At first Clyde, a man always in search of his next dollar, was struck by the shining, golden frame. For the briefest of instants, his jaw dropped, but he quickly snapped it shut before his hand had even a moment to investigate. A puddle of a similar hue littered the ground beneath the portrait, revealing a wooden frame—

Not gold.

—in its place.

Again, Clyde searched through the raindrops for anyone peering back, as if someone might suddenly call out or curse the skinny specter for getting too close to what did not belong to him.

Aside from the patter of the rain and a distant rumble of thunder—or perhaps an aluminum boat that'd come too close, too swiftly, to a dock—there was nothing else to be heard.

Few ventured out after dusk at the Olde Sandwich Pier, in the Olde Sandwich Towne.

Once satisfied that no one was paying him any mind, the part-time lobsterman with the waterlogged hat wrapped both of his calloused, prematurely-gnarled, hands around the gold-painted trim of the portrait.

It blinked.

Clyde gasped.

The clown fell face down onto the grey stones of the road.

'Holy Mary mother'a—'

He stopped himself before finishing the unnecessary plea and began to laugh uneasily at himself.

Clyde—who'd, in his shock, fallen ass-first into a puddle reeking of weeks old haddock—slowly struggled back to his feet.

''Ya dumb fool. It's just a paintin'. A paintin' of a circus clown, for Chrissakes. Prolly some rascal's idear of an 'Allows' Eve prank. Nuffin' more.'

Despite the self-chastisement, he hesitated before slowly lifting the rectangular piece of artwork upright again.

All appeared well—just as it had before—aside from a fresh smudge to the paralyzed mime's left eye. As if the demon had only just begun to cry, a rivulet of blue paint now streaked from its infected oculus, all the way down to the frilled red and white collar that encircled its throat.

Clyde gulped.

"Spose yer no werse fer wear. Yer comin' home with me now, ya sad feller.'

And then he gulped again. There was something almost—*familiar*—about the depiction gazing back at him, but he wasn't entirely sure why. There was no reason it should have been, not that he could think of.

'Hmmpf.'

Without another thought, Clyde was moving on home, toward the small brownstone that'd been passed down to him from his quite dead folks, toward the door that only had one key, one person who possessed a copy, and one person who ever turned it.

Clyde.

He was at that very door in less than a minute, fumbling in his pocket for that very key. He pulled the cold brass out into the colder night air and quickly inserted it into its place. The oaken entrance with the peeling blue paint swung inward with a groan and the sodden man trudged inside, dragging his newfound guest into the bowels of the domicile.

He leaned the painting against his favorite chair—the leather one with the nail-head trim. It was the color of wine and had an imprint of a dead man seared into its flesh.

'You wait der, feller. I'll be right b—'

Lost in his own thoughts, he didn't complete the sentence as he made his way toward the clawfoot tub in his bathroom. He often spoke aloud to himself and regularly didn't finish the things he was saying. Whether it was out of an embarrassment and a realization that he was holding a conversation with an empty apartment or because he simply didn't care, he didn't know. And no one else did either, because—well—no one else was around.

No one else was *ever* around.

The pipes squealed as warm water rushed into them. Steam

quickly fogged up the spider-webbing cracks on the antique glass mirror over the sink and Clyde stripped out of his wet clothes. With a loud sigh, the scrawny man slunk into the bath and let his eyes fall shut. Though the once-white porcelain was long since stained with red, he didn't care and it didn't prevent him from quickly falling asleep in its embrace.

In fact, it never bothered him.

Why would your blood bother me? I put it there. Remember, Marion?

Clyde rubbed his long nose, with the salt of the day still crusted around his overstretched nostrils, and—before long—he was snoring.

A scream sliced through the serenity of the man's slumber and he lurched forward choking on the dirty, now cold, bathwater. Clyde had apparently fallen under the surface, but for how long he couldn't be certain. If not for the wail—one that sounded as if it'd been vomited up through the vocal cords of a dying, strangulated cat—who knows how far under he might have sunk.

'Hullo?' he whispered, balancing himself precariously on bony elbows out into the air of his unheated apartment.

Of course, no one responded—

No one ever does.

—because there was no one there.

There never is.

Clyde stood up and let the water escape his filthy naked torso. He grabbed an old towel with dark brown handprints smeared all over it and covered himself up. He poked his wrinkled nose and wrinkled face out through the bathroom door.

'Hullo?' he tried again, this time a bit louder, a tad more confident.

The room, the only other beside the bathroom in his place, was empty. Save for one grimace.

The clown painting was facing him. It hadn't been before.

'Jeesssus H—' he started and caught himself. 'Nope. *Nope.* Not gonna cuss. Marion doesn't like that. Clyde's gon' do right by my Marion.'

I always do.

He cracked his neck.

Well…almost always.

He sniffed. He was quite certain he'd left the portrait facing the main entrance, but shrugged it off. Things had an odd way of happening on their own in that apartment, regardless of what Clyde wanted. It'd been so for some time. Lamps knocking themselves over. Water running without a hand turning a faucet. Food tumbling out of the icebox.

The fireplace lighting itself.

Clyde blinked. That thought hadn't been his own. The voice, unfamiliar to him. A stranger violating a space it didn't have the key to.

Because no one had a key to Clyde's place.

No one other than Clyde. Not anymore.

Not since Marion—

He hit himself in the left ear. 'You knock that off, Clyde,' he said to himself. 'You just knock that right the hell off—'

He turned his head to the bathroom door frame—there was no actual door there anymore because, as Clyde saw it, there was no further need for any sort of privacy—and ran his index finger around the edges of a heart carved into the wood. The symbol of long-dead love wreathed a simple message.

'C + M. 'Til death.'

Marion had always thought the last line 'Til death' had been a bit morbid. 'You think we be needin' that, Clyde?'

He'd laughed then—and so had Marion—though, as he stood there drying in a towel stained with her blood, realized that maybe she'd been right.

'Because, maybe,' he said aloud, 'Maybe 'til death' just isn't long enough.' He looked back toward the bathtub. 'Nossir. Love shouldn't be given no expiration date.'

A tear formed in the corner of his eye and he quickly swatted it away, his fingernails still black with the grime of a long day of work. He took a few steps toward one of his only pieces of furniture—a mahogany bureau that'd likely been sitting in the same spot for over a quarter-century—and yanked open a drawer. Quickly dressing into dry, clean-ish, clothing, he tossed the hand-printed towel back into the bathroom behind him.

'Now then,' he stretched his hands over his head. 'We gots to find a good place to hang *you*.' He approached the clown, nodded a few times, and then lifted it up and onto the mantel over his blackened

213

fireplace. He leaned it back to rest against the brick stone wall and, in the process, knocked a few of the baubles and framed memories aside as he made room for the gaudy, water-damaged, spectacle.

'There we are,' he said, stepping back and admiring his handiwork. 'A place of honor. Marion will love this. Marion always says she wants—'

Clyde turned and looked back toward the bathroom.

'No,' he shook the bees out of his brain. 'No, *no*. Marion is gone, Clyde. Marion is gone. Been a year tonight, it has. It's 'Alloween again, it is. You're all alone now.'

He looked up at the painting. It leered at him like a king staring down at a sniveling subject who was unsuccessfully pleading for clemency.

Clyde wiped at his hands, even though there was nothing to wipe off. 'Well, then,' he said, eventually unlocking his eyes from the gaze above the fireplace. 'My belly needs fillin'.'

He dug around in his only cupboard, pulled an unlabeled tin from the depths of the makeshift pantry, slammed it down onto a small corner table, and pulled a Swiss Army knife out from a kitchen drawer. He flicked through all the small metal appendages—several of which were crusted in something dark, something long since coagulated—until he found the can opener. He pried open the beans and then grabbed a spoon. Taking his dinner with him, he sank into his favorite chair—the one with the dead man imprint—and brought a mouthful of the cold molasses concoction to his grey, peeling, lips.

And right then, Clyde began to choke.

There was a fire burning, brightly, underneath the mantel. Flickering orange lit the white-painted face. It continued to grin, haloed in a hellish glow.

Clyde spat his beans onto the floor.

He knew he hadn't started the fire, but that's not what alarmed him. After all, *things had an odd way of happening on their own in that apartment, regardless of what Clyde wanted.*

He looked up again at the portrait.

And then he remembered.

'No,' he stammered. 'It can't be. How'd you find me? How'd you get here?'

The flames quivered and popped below the maniacal sneer of the jester.

Clyde lifted a warped finger toward the mantelpiece. 'You bastahd. You followed us here. You followed us home. I always knew you was trouble. But, Marion—Marion wanted to take you home dat day. Now, I remember. Last 'Alloween. Marion thought you was cute, she did. Marion begged me. Pleaded. But, I said no. *No*, I told her. You—you shouldn't be here. We left you in dat shop. The one up in Ogunquit. Yes, dat little expensive joint with da door dat chimed like angels' wings when we entered. Dat's what Marion said dat day. Can you believe dat shit? Angels' wings for Chrissakes. And da owner—da one with da scuffed tophat and da red, soiled, ringmaster lookin' coat. I remember him, I remember *you*, and I remember dat day, because dat was da day we came home from our trip. Da only trip we ever took. I remember dat day, yah bastahd, because dat—dat was da day that my Marion—dat was da day I—'

Clyde looked behind himself, toward the open bathroom door.

Toward the white tub with the dark-red stain.

He clenched his fists and turned back toward the clown. Fifty dollars was what the con-man wanted for it. Fifty whole dollars. That would have been at least a week's worth of pay for Clyde—back when he was working full time, that is—and he'd laughed right in poor old Marion's face. She'd cried all the way home. She'd cried when they stepped over the threshold later on. She cried as her trembling hands lit the jack o'lantern in the kitchen window. And she was still crying as she slunk into her steaming bath that night.

I just wanted her to stop crying.

Clyde swallowed the memory down. Pushed it inside, like he always did.

'What do you want with me?'

There was no answer. The flames continued to lap at the stack of firewood that Clyde had no memory of stacking.

'Answer me, ya smirkin' fool! How'd ya find me? After all dis time. How?'

There was a loud pop and Clyde jumped up out of his chair. A spark danced away toward the rafters of the home, escaping to safety and away from the madness playing out down below.

Clyde followed the drifting ember until it burned away into nothingness and then he called after it. 'Is dat you Marion? Did you bring dis onto me? Fer what? You think you can just leave me here with—with dis? With *him*?' He pointed up at the clown face. 'You know it was an accident. You know I didn't mean to do it. What— are you tryin' to punish me? Well, it ain't gonna work, Marion. I'm sorry I didn't recognize it afor I brung it indoors—I don' know how I missed dat. A momentary lapse of m'brain, perhaps. But I'm takin' it back outside.'

He started to walk toward the fireplace and then stopped, as if something had caught his attention back on the ceiling. He threw his head around, frantically searching, standing on his tiptoes, and leaning an ear toward his drafty roof.

'Huh? What'd you say, Marion? Speak up for Chrissakes.' He appeared to listen to the silence. 'No, you can't keep it. I told you dat afore. It's creepy. Gives me da chills. I saw it outside and I thought—oh, hell, I dunno what I thought. The smile looked different. Friendlier. Something made me want to bring him in.' Clyde again pointed a finger toward the portrait, all while keeping his gaze on the ceiling. 'He *made* me do it, Marion. Bewitched me, he did. An 'Allows Eve jinx it is. Marion? *Marion*? You know I wouldn't lie to 'ya? You know I hated dat bugger afore, right?' He strained to hear a response. 'No, I—*no*, Marion. For Chrissakes, I'm not tryin' to replace ya? Who could ever replace *you*? Oh, Marion. My beautiful, beautiful, Marion. I'll take him outside. He's a goner. I promise. Just you watch. You'll see.'

Clyde reached up and yanked the painting from the mantel. A small glass figure of a humpback whale, blown just down the street at the town's artisan glass factory, smashed onto the wooden floorboards. Clyde groaned but continued his purposeful stride toward the front of the house.

He threw open the door and stepped out into the night.

A flash of lightning welcomed him back into the darkness. The moon, likely obscured by rolling thunderheads, provided little to no illumination. Clyde braced himself for the boom, counting down like a child, 'One Mississippi, two Mississippi, three—'. A loud crack from above caused him to duck his head. 'Yer close!' He screamed up into the inky black. 'Musta missed you sneakin' up on me whiles I was asleep in my bath! But I hear 'ya now! I'm ready fer 'ya, 'ya bastahd! Der's no surprisin' ol' Clyde!' With a grunt, he chucked the ghastly canvas as far as he could into the alley and, by the time he'd slammed the door behind himself again, his clothes were—once more—completely drenched.

As if that weren't the case, and as if he were still dry as a bone, Clyde plopped himself back down into his wine-colored, dead-man chair, in front of the fire that he himself could not possibly have lit.

He closed his eyes.

'Oh, Marion, Marion, Marion,' he mumbled to himself. 'Couldn't leave well enough alone, could 'ya?' He chuckled. 'Just tryin' to have a quiet night at home, Marion. I don't need these sorts of reminders. You understand dat, right Marion? *Marion*?'

No one responded, because no one ever responded to Clyde. Not ever. Not, at least, since—

Marion.

Clyde's eyes got heavy and, before long, he'd once again fallen asleep.

A low chuckle—born from depths so dark, so evil, so far beneath the ground mortal men tread so ignorantly upon—rippled underneath the dead man chair and directly into the soles of Clyde's bare, begrimed, feet. The tremor awakened the slumberer, whose eyes immediately widened upon seeing the tableau before him.

'No!' he wheezed, breathing too deeply of the black smoke that poured from the fireplace and into his shack. 'You!'

The clown painting had returned to its perch on the mantel, streaks of wet paint and mud confirming it'd recently been out in the elements. The figure, now deformed and void of any merriment, peered down at him—a ghoul freshly sloughed of its carnival attire for an oozing mange.

'Begone! Get out of my house, ya devil!'

The clown-demon remained frozen, unmoving, but another subterranean chortle shuddered through the cottage.

Clyde whimpered and jumped to his feet. 'Beast! I knew what ya were when I first saw 'ya! I tried to warn, Marion. I *tried*, but she wouldn't listen to me. She couldn't hear my plea and den it were too late fer her. You did this! Dis is yer fault, yah bloody bastahd! You *made* me hurt my Marion!'

Again, a low guffaw rumbled under his feet. From the clown's eyes poured two blue tributaries, which had—at some point—begun to form a puddle on the mantelpiece.

217

'Say somethin'!' Clyde pleaded. 'I ain't afeared of no stinkin' circus freak! Ya can't hurt ol', Clyde. Nossir. Say somethin' or be gone with 'ya!'

But this time the clown didn't laugh. It gave Clyde none of what he desired. It sat quietly—patiently—waiting for the man's next pathetic act.

Clyde covered his mouth with a forearm and lunged toward the fireplace. With a bare hand, he reached in and grabbed a flaming log. Screeching, he kept his grip and held the burning piece of timber up to the malevolent painting. As the flesh on his hand began to sear and bubble, orange flames licked the bottom-most edges of the heinous work of art. Clyde wailed and the clown wailed and one of them knocked the red-hot wood to the floor. Immediately, a throw rug with scarlet splatters ignited and flames slithered toward the feet of the man's beloved chair.

Clyde howled and the clown howled in turn.

Grasping at his hand, the lobsterman scarecrow amalgamation burst out the front door of his home and allowed himself to collapse in the brick-walled clutches of the adjoining alleyway. Gingerly, he laid his hand into a murky puddle and imagined he could hear the cool water sizzle.

The fire inside his rotten house burned brightly and coated the night in a stench of chemically-treated wood and death.

Clyde took a deep breath of both.

Before long, the volunteer fire brigade and the town constable arrived with wooden pails, axes, and calls directed toward anyone who might still be locked away in the belly and remnants of Clyde's scorched, smoldering life.

It's all gone, Marion. Everything we worked so hard to build all these years. Gone. All because of you—you and dat smirkin' bastahd.

A face peered around the corner after a time and the human attached to the face squatted beside him.

'Clyde?' it said. 'He's here! Over here!' The soot-stained firefighter shouted for help. It turned back to him. 'Clyde? Can ya hear me, man? What happened? Can you tell us where Marion is? Is she still inside? There's blood, Clyde. Stains on the carpet. On the walls. Blood and—'

But Clyde couldn't hear him. The mirthful intonations of circus

218

music flooded his ears and he clamped his hands over both. He flopped onto his side and writhed as if the melody was acid being injected into his veins.

Been gone fer a year and no one's even noticed. Marion deserves so much more. Marion deserves not to be forgot.

The man placed a glove onto Clyde and then turned to dash back into the home. Whistles and shouts for more hands polluted and covered over the typical sounds of an evening by the canal. But Clyde could hear none of that.

'Get outta my head, ya bastahd,' he whispered, climbing to his feet. He stumbled around to the front of the home. There were folk passing buckets of water in a makeshift assembly line, folk chopping furiously to create a second entry point into the home, and folk dragging out as many of Clyde's possessions as could possibly be salvaged. Everything was singed, still-smoking, or soaked. A pile, debris from a life gone bad, formed out on the cobblestone walkway. Aside from an old Clydesdale still attached to the fire wagon, there were no other sentinels keeping guard of his belongings. All were busied with the task of preserving what they could and what they believed was still hidden inside—

Marion.

But their work and efforts were all for naught. Marion wasn't there and hadn't been for some time. They wouldn't find her.

Not inside that hell-hole—

And then Clyde saw it.

Teetering at the precipice of the rubble, and the mostly destroyed vestiges of his existence, was the painting.

The clown painting.

The one Marion had begged for.

The one Marion had cried for.

The one that, unlike Marion, would just not die.

Clyde crept up to the pile. Plucking the tainted piece from its perch, and garnering only a half-hearted snort in response from the Clydesdale, he slunk away before anyone else could take notice.

The night was crisp and Clyde's breath hung in the air ahead of him. He limped at a steady clip, knowing exactly where he was headed.

I'm coming, Marion. I'm ready to finally give you what you want.

I remember now. Ol' Clyde didn't forget.

The shouts emanating from his house quickly faded, as did the orange fireball and the orange-tinted smog that covered the nightscape.

'Fools,' he mumbled. 'Weren't nuthin' in der worth savin' to begin with.' He huffed and winced at the cold under his bare feet. 'Never were afore and der certainly ain't now.'

Clyde approached the dock at the canal. His little rowboat teetered in its usual spot, moored with the careless angler's knot he'd grown accustomed to employing. It was loose—nearly freed from the load and responsibility it'd tolerated for so long.

He threw the clown in first and then jumped down after it. The current, as always, was strong and Clyde knew he had to be careful not to tumble in. No one could swim it and survive. No one could resist its death pull.

He braced both sides of the gunwale until it ceased its rocking and, after a moment, undid his lazy coil and let the invisible drift of the waterway take him.

Clear of the dock, Clyde casually inserted each oar into its respective crutch and began to row. It was an exercise he'd done daily for over thirty years and required less mental effort than it had to open that can of cold beans.

For the first time since grabbing it off of the refuse pile, Clyde glanced down at the face at the bottom of his boat. It stared dumbly back up at him, the bobbing and dipping of the dinghy giving the illusion that the fiend was nodding and plotting, plotting and nodding, with each crest and subsequent crash.

'We're almost der, ya monstah.' He hocked a huge ball of phlegm out into the darkness. 'You're both gonna finally get what yas have been askin' fer.'

The slapping of his oars almost lulled him to sleep. It was late and the strain of that night, those months, those years, was finally getting to him. A blood-red buoy dipped up and down ahead and, quickly, he sidled up to it.

With the hands of a man who'd done the task many times before, Clyde easily anchored his vessel. Cautiously, he peered over the edge as if expecting something might suddenly burst forth and pull him under.

Nothing did.

And so Clyde, right then, pulled on his moldy pair of canvas gloves and began to haul up the lobster trap. This creel, in particular, was heavier than his others, but he bit down hard and yanked up on the fraying, seaweed-covered rope.

From the depths, bubbles rose. It wouldn't be long.

'Soon now, Marion. So soon.'

He continued to tug and the sinewy lines of his forearms bulged under the burden. Just as the skies reopened and began depositing pelts of icy rain onto his back, the wooden crate, shrouded in green webbing, rose from its watery grave.

Clyde dragged the box into his boat, careful not to jostle its contents.

'Hullo der, Marion.' He sniffed. 'My beautiful, beautiful, Marion.'

The skeleton inside was folded in half, its bones covered in only a few stubborn, stringy, scraps of flesh and fabric. Wisps of dark hair lay flat over the creature's skull and Clyde brushed them away to get a better look at the caverns that'd once been her eyes.

'I brung him to ya, Marion.' Clyde let his head hang and he fought to see through the pools of hatred forming under his eyelids. 'You wanted him, so I brung him. And now,' he cleared his throat and belched a deep, guttural, snarl. 'Now you two bastahds can be together. For ever.'

And then, with the same exuberant facility with which he'd folded up his late wife, Clyde bent the clown in half. He lifted the lid of the lobster trap and placed the evil thing on Marion's chest, crossing her lifeless limbs over it.

Clyde wiped the back of his hand over his leaking nose. He closed the lid of the trap then and whispered once more to his love.

'Goodbye, Marion.'

Without looking at it, he kicked the coffin back into the canal and waited until the gurgling ceased before sitting fully upright again.

Clyde sighed and looked up at the night sky. The autumnal rain continued to pour down on top of him, but he didn't care. The droplets were refreshing, rejuvenating even, and he breathed in deeply. For the first time in a long time, Clyde slowly inhaled and felt his shriveled lungs fully inflate.

Untying the rowboat from the buoy, he let himself drift with the current. He had no intention of returning to his old dock, his old town, or his old house. That life was over and he was ready to pick up and move on. Though he'd no possessions, Clyde had never really needed much to get by. He'd start again, somewhere else. The Cape was small, but not so small that he couldn't find another cut-off community to hole up in. He'd been resuscitated, been saved, and he knew Marion and her clown were finally gone for good.

After a short time, Clyde's rowboat exited the canal and he was expelled out into the wide-open Cape Cod Bay. Hugging the coastline, Clyde passed the infamous town boardwalk and eventually allowed himself to cruise into Morton's Creek. It wasn't a permanent terminus, but until morning it'd be a familiar—and secluded—rest stop for the weary traveler.

He heard the bow crunch and sink into a welcoming sandbar and hopped out. The frigid water bit at him, but he didn't care. He tugged his craft up onto land and then collapsed into a dune.

Clyde.

Grassy, spectral, fingers tickled his bony cheeks and he sat up. Unsure if it'd been seconds or hours since he'd laid down, he quickly investigated his surroundings. It was still the darkest part of Halloween night and the moon remained completely hidden. He could hear the lapping of waves as they met the underside of his boat and Clyde crawled on all fours to the water's edge. His face felt raw, covered in blood, sweat, and exhaustion.

Leaning out over the edge of the creek, he splashed the cold saltiness over himself. It stung in some places, but Clyde didn't mind. He'd been pained by far worse.

As the ripples in front of him settled and the reflection finally took its true form, Clyde gasped. Frantically, he began thrashing at the face in front of him and, when that did nothing to change the sickening grin peering back, he started to claw.

At his own flesh.

At his own eyes.

At the red nose.

And at the blue, still-smudged, makeup that would never wash away.

The Hollows
C.E. O'Conaing

Alicja couldn't tell why the suburb looked different, but it did.

In the years that followed, that question would surface in her head every Halloween night. Was there something about the strip of identikit bungalows and lawns that should have set her off? Wasn't there a feeling of unease as she rounded the corner and began to wheel downhill, the slow curve of pavement leading to a row of quiet, dark houses?

But Alicja knew there wasn't a weird, eerie feeling, even if there should have been. That's what was so strange.

Cillian ran on ahead, gangly and energetic. At twelve, he was the oldest of the group, and there was an unspoken understanding that this would be his last year trick or treating. However, this meant he was old enough to be considered a chaperone, so the group got to trick or treat independently for the first time ever.

This was no big deal for Cillian and Aoibheann, his nine-year-old sister. Alicja was consistently amazed at the level of freedom the pair enjoyed. Not merely allowed to watch whatever movies they wanted, they also sometimes had the house to themselves when they came home from school. Alicja was jealous, but the siblings were

223

her best friends in the neighborhood. They never made fun of the way Alicja pronounced things and once, when an older boy had said her name was stupid, Cillian said he'd 'Batter the fuck outta him.' The older boy had just laughed, but he still didn't make fun of Alicja again.

The trio had tried every house in their estate and the two neighboring estates, fancier neighborhoods with newer houses that had more elaborate, individual designs.

'That's how you know if the sweets are any good,' Cillian had insisted.

Aoibheann nodded along, having heard Cillian's theory before, but Alicja was enthralled. It was 2004 in Ireland, the height of the Celtic Tiger, and suburbs grew like weeds around every city, town, and stop sign in the country. That's why they'd moved from Poland, because Alicja's dad had said Ireland was trying to build a whole other country on top of itself. New developments popped up on a weekly basis near Alicja's seaside hometown, the small community branching further and further into the surrounding farmland with each passing month. Alicja's father joked that there were fewer trees and more houses every time he took the five-minute drive into town. She never understood why grownups found that so funny.

Work was the only reason Alicja's mother had agreed, with some degree of trepidation, to let Alicja go trick or treating with Aoibheann and Cillian. Her mother had a shift cleaning at the posh school in town and her dad wouldn't be back from work until late, so Cillian had convinced her that Alicja would be fine to trick or treat with him, Aoibheann, and their mam.

As far as Alicja knew, their mam was never going to join them.

'Sure she'll only slow us down!' Cillian insisted, 'Halloween's once a year, we've to make the most of tonight.'

This meant continuing past the neighboring estates and out onto the main road for a short stretch. Alicja felt her tummy tense, self-conscious of her wheelchair as cars whipped past in the darkening dusk. If Aoibheann and Cillian had any idea she was nervous, they didn't share the inkling. Instead, Aoibheann pushed her chair while Cillian charged ahead, both girls listening to his latest soliloquy. Alicja didn't need any help with her chair, but she had a feeling

Aoibheann wanted to slow down and was using this as a convenient excuse.

'And then in Castlebar, Jaysus, you'd be laughing,' Cillian continued, 'They've estates that go on for miles! And they're all mad rich.'

He looked over his shoulder as he turned off the road and onto the thin footpath that led down a steep hill.

'Course they're all shitebags in Castlebar, though,' he added, 'But like, you'd go there tonight. If you could.'

Alicja and Aoibheann nodded in agreement. They would, if they could.

The rate of local development was prodigious enough that the group weren't all that surprised when they found a neighborhood they'd never seen before as they reached the bottom of the hill. They were even less surprised to find it was composed of a few dozen wide, beige bungalows in neat rows. Some of the houses looked like new builds, with the same stray sheets of plastic on unfinished windows that Alicja was used to from her dad's work. Others were lived-in, full of light and cluttered, mismatched furniture, and belongings. But there was no movement coming from any of them.

'Do you know anyone who lives here?' Aoibheann asked.

Alicja could hear her voice shake a little as she spoke. She pushed Alicja's wheelchair down the paved path, and Alicja became certain Aoibheann was doing this to avoid being at the front of the group. Before Alicja could respond, she heard Cillian calling from a few houses ahead, ignoring his sister's question.

'Lads, these people are *loaded*,' he said, 'We're gonna do amazing here, just wait.'

Cillian forged on ahead, as if searching for the perfect house. Alicja watched him, curious. She wasn't sure how this neighborhood could be so promising when Cillian's earlier claim was that big, different houses guaranteed more diverse and generous sweet selection. Still, his enthusiasm was hard to reject.

Cillian passed the short, paved paths leading to each front door and seemed to consider them, steeling himself, before walking onto the next one. Aoibheann was silent and Alicja said nothing, especially since there weren't many lights on in any of these homes. It wasn't like they were missing a goldmine, so there was no point asking what exactly Cillian was waiting for.

'This one,' he finally announced.

Cillian ran up the path and rang the doorbell. For a gut drop instant, Alicja imagined him running off and Aoibheann following suit, leaving her to heft her chair back up the hill alone while an annoyed homeowner chased her. But Cillian just stood at the door, bobbing his head. His homemade Cat in the Hat costume wasn't perfect, but he did have a hat, and Alicja had done her best to draw whiskers on his face before they left the house. Cillian said they looked 'Unreal' when he thanked her. Aoibheann said they looked more like cat turds.

No one answered.

Cillian rocked on his heels for a few more moments before walking back to them, offering a loose shrug. He tried the next house, and Alicja noticed Aoibheann glancing around. The sky was growing dark, the evening's blanket of navy-blue cloud turning to black night now. The weak orange glow of the street lights lit the way ahead of them in small pools, the lawns outside its bounds now a blur of dark green shapes.

'Anyone home?' Cillian yelled, his voice emerging as more of a squawk than a yell.

Alicja giggled but Aoibheann full-blown howled at her brother, receiving a dirty look for her trouble.

'Ah fuck this,' Cillian said, 'Sure we came all the way here!'

Cillian tried a few more doors, still receiving no response. The sky seemed to darken by the minute. Alicja and Aoibheann glanced at each other, then down at their heaving grocery bags full of assorted mini bars. It did seem fruitless to continue the search, and some vague faraway part of Alicja's mind felt paranoid that, somehow, they might lose all the goods they'd already earned if they kept going.

'Cillian, we've to turn around,' Aoibheann cried.

Cillian stopped walking but didn't turn to face them. Caught between two of the street lights, his figure was obscured by the darkness. Alicja expected Aoibheann to blame her, to say 'Alicja's mam won't let her go too far!' or 'She'll get tired in her chair!' but no such comment came. Aoibheann folded her arms, planting her feet on the pavement, and Alicja felt a shiver run up her back.

Cillian threw his hands up as he walked beneath the street light's pale glow.

'Yah, grand, fine so,' he said, crestfallen, 'There's no one home here anyway. Weirdos.'

Alicja heard it before she saw it. The creak of a door swinging open, almost inaudible. She looked to Cillian and Aoibheann, expecting confirmation, and the three stared at the house beside them. Cillian had tried their door maybe a minute earlier, although Alicja was sure the sky had somehow grown darker in the intervening time. No one had answered.

Now, though, it creaked open.

Cillian stuck his arms out, a pantomime of curiosity, and began walking up the paved path backward. Still facing the girls, he pulled a face and shrugged before turning to walk to the door. Alicja could see him square up his small shoulders as he walked. Aoibheann didn't move, but Alicja wheeled her chair onto the path. Once she was outside the street lamp's little circle, it really was night-time. Dark, and blue everywhere. Hard to discern.

Alicja followed Cillian to the doorway, moving slower than she needed to but unsure why. Cillian pushed the door open and stared inside the house. The walls were bare and beige, looking freshly painted. A hallway with a carpeted floor lead into three rooms, but only one door was open.

To Cillian's left, about halfway down the long, narrow hallway.

The greenish glow of a TV's light emerged from the doorway and splashed across the hallway, throwing shadows on its carpet and wall. Alicja hadn't noticed a TV in the dark living room as they went up the path. Cillian took another step inside as Alicja pushed her wheelchair onto the single concrete step leading up to the doorway. Dad had said that they weren't allowed put those steps on new houses now, because they meant people with chairs like Alicja's couldn't get in.

Alicja felt something behind her back, pushing her up onto the step.

She gasped, but the scream she felt in her throat didn't come out. Aoibheann had shoved her chair up onto the concrete step. Evidently, she had decided she was better off nearer the house and the others than on her own on the pavement. Cillian was halfway down the hallway, his hands in his back pockets, when he turned to face them.

'No one's fucking home,' he protested.

For the first time, Alicja heard real unease in his voice. It wobbled as he forced a confused smile, throwing his long arms out. The hallway was silent, the flickering light of the TV illuminating the darkness in momentary, uneven flashes.

Alicja saw the kid emerge from a doorway behind Cillian. A kitchen door, must have been. The door opened without a sound and the kid crept onto the carpet, the soft steps of sneaking downstairs once parents were asleep.

At least, Alicja thought it was a kid.

It was smiling a broad smile, its dark eyes wide. It couldn't have been older than Alicja and Aoibheann, a skinny nine-year-old carrying a large plastic bowl full of sweets. In the years that followed, Alicja reminded herself they *had* to be sweets. Just a multipack of mini bars. But no matter how many times she told herself this, she remembered seeing something dark writhing among the wrappers.

The kid's black hair was plastered to its forehead, its grin wide and unmoving. Its skin looked so pale that it was almost translucent in the pale light of the next room's television set, but its eyes were what made Alicja's stomach drop. They weren't a single colour, but fuzzy, every shifting shades of grey. TV static.

The kid walked toward Cillian with slow, deliberate steps, a toddler learning to walk almost a decade late. Alicja grabbed the wheels of her chair and pulled back, but the movement was too frantic. The chair toppled on its side, throwing her between the paved path and the damp grass of the lawn. Alicja screamed. Cillian looked around, dazed, and bolted, running back through the hallway toward the door. The hallway seemed impossibly long as Alicja watched him run, prying herself off the rough ground. Behind him, the kid kept coming, still smiling its empty rictus grin.

Cillian grabbed Alicja, yanking her by the shoulder and depositing her back in her chair. He grabbed the handles and shoved as she started spinning the wheels, frantic and panicked. The kid got closer to the doorway. Alicja heard her heartbeat pounding in her ears.

As it reached the doorway, the kid dropped the bowl.

This was where repeating the story always became tricky, because

228

there *couldn't* have been spiders and cockroaches pouring out onto the carpeted floor in a great deluge. There couldn't have been maggots and small black snakes curling on the carpet. Alicja couldn't have seen baby teeth among the bars, bright white even in the nighttime darkness.

Maybe it was a prank, a bowl full of novelty scares, and time and imperfect memory had turned it into something more traumatic. But Alicja could never convince herself that the boy's mouth hadn't opened when he reached the door, a maw full of fangs too big for his young, gaunt face.

The bang was so loud that even the thing in the house was startled.

Cillian slammed a banger into the carpet and followed it with another, throwing away the fireworks he had cherished all year in a puff of smoke and ear-splitting noise. The thing flinched, confused enough for Cillian and Alicja to skid down the paved path and back out onto the street. The orange glow of the street lamp felt like safety but, the moment they reached it, this irrational idea evaporated. Safety meant getting back up the hill, out of the estate, getting back home with the doors locked.

Cillian didn't look over his shoulder as he pushed Alicja up the hill, but she did. In the years that followed, they rarely ever spoke about that night, save one or two drunken late-night conversations. From what she could remember of them, Alicja was jealous of Cillian not looking back. He could tell himself that was 'mad fucking weird,' and leave it at that. Alicja couldn't forget the kid standing on the step front of the house.

Not chasing them, not screaming or cursing, or gnashing its teeth. Just smiling.

Alicja never found that estate again in the broad light of day, but it wouldn't have mattered anyway. The historic boom and bust and boom again meant that houses, buildings, entire developments and neighborhoods were built and torn down, repo'd, replaced, and resold before any of them turned twenty. She couldn't have found that estate any more than she could tracked down Tír na nÓg.

That was what made the kid's smile so strange. He was so placid and accepting, unbothered by their sudden, explosive exit.

Like he knew they'd be back someday.

The Day You Die
S. B. Watson

I. Le Bateleur

My name is not important. It hasn't been for hundreds of years. All that matters is the pain my soul has suffered, the pathways between worlds I've walked, the sacrifices I've been made to give. All that matters is that the end of my suffering is in sight. My escape. My release. All that matters is the day you die, when I will finally be free.

In 1796 I was a printer of books in a lonely village in Georgia. I had a little shop, a quaint, two-story cottage. The press was below, my chambers on the second floor. In those days, America was growing. You could sense it in the swaying fields of summer wheat, planted larger from season to season. Could smell it in the fireplace smoke that hung in the Autumn air, could hear it in competing church bells, pealing sharp and clear across winter hills, and could feel it in the rolling hum of Spring oxcarts coming to market.

My press started small, but was growing, just like the country. I took orders for books, pamphlets, and notices. I printed bulletins and newspapers. And, as the election between Adams and Jefferson began, political records and documents.

So, when the old hermit who lived out of town stepped across my lintel, I looked up to greet him as any other customer, notwithstanding the rumors that hung about him like a corpse's pallor. They said he'd murdered an old woman who lived up the road. Murdered her and fed her soul to the devil. Of course, I didn't believe that. To me, he was just another customer.

The hermit was a dark man, perpetually stooped, his skin wrinkled and browned like the rotten flesh of the medlar fruit, his eyes deep set, with ragged whiskers the color of blanched snow. His cloak was threadbare, clothes rags, boots disintegrated to leather husks. In one hand, he grasped a knotted walking stick—in the other, an oilskin-wrapped parcel, which he dropped on my desk.

'Keep this for me,' he said, eyes following me as I came out from behind the press, wiping inky hands against my apron. Already, the tug of apprehension began to weigh in my breast.

'What is it?' I asked, reaching out to take the parcel. The knotted staff smacked across the table, pinning my hand against the oilskin.

'I'll pay,' the man said, his voice creaking like the music of the wind through old, dead tree limbs. From his cloak he took a rotting sack, which he dropped to the table. I heard the clink of coins. 'More gold than you'll ever earn in this lifetime.' Slowly, he removed the staff from my hand. Carefully, a tremor in my grip, I undid the brittle latigo fastening the oilskin parcel and laid it open.

Inside was a book. I picked it up but dropped it immediately back to the table—there, in the pitted leather of the cover, near the corner, was a human nipple.

The hermit spilled the rotten bag open. Old coins, dark and lumpen, their gold obscured beneath what seemed centuries of tarnish and wear, hundreds of them, printed in runic figures I'd never seen before, danced across the table and rolled to the floor.

'For how long?' I murmured, reaching for the coins.

'One week,' he said. 'Lock it up. I will return for it, last day of month. On Samhain.'

I'd never heard the word before—sounding like *saa-win*, as he said it, a deep lilt twisting his croaked words—but before I could regain my senses, and refuse, he turned and hobbled to the door, chanting softly beneath his breath, the only word I understood the strange one he'd just defined—Samhain. Over, and over, and over.

IIII. L'E'mpereur

It rained that night, wind gusting down the chimney of my cottage, whipping candlelight into dancing figures against the walls. The next day was chilly, the sun hidden behind a skein of grey clouds. For seven days, the air grew colder, crisp with the damp smell of Autumn leaves. For seven days I tried to work...but couldn't. The book lay heavy upon my mind.

I'd locked it up, in a heavy, iron-banded chest, at the back of the printing room. Every night I dreamt of the chest, sitting alone in the darkness below. In my dreams, it breathed, like a caged animal. Every morning, on my way down from my chamber, I passed the chest quickly, trying not to look in its direction. And every day, bent over my presses, I felt a presence behind me, as though I were not alone, as though someone stood and silently watched me work.

Finally, the last day of October arrived. Samhain, as the hermit called it. The morning broke cold and clear, and for the first time I saw an end to my strange, creeping terror—the hermit would return, I'd give him that infernal package, and never do business with him again.

But the first customer who entered my shop, a councilman from the village, dashed this expectation—the hermit was dead.

They'd gone for him in the night. A few councilmen, a few respected men of the village, and a few farmers. They'd tried him by Witch Swimming, for the murder of the old woman, right there in the bog by his hut, just outside of town. Tied him in a hemp bag and dropped him into the water—the councilman said he floated, proving his guilt, even as he drowned.

I closed the shop and barred my windows, a dull panic tickling the edges of my resolve. The book was mine, now. But what to do with such a thing?

In the broken light that seeped through my shutters, I opened the chest. The parcel sat upon stacks of business papers, and a few bags of coin, deceptively still and quiet. Gingerly, I unwrapped it, trying not to look at the parched nipple jutting from the sandy cover of human leather. Every instinct told me to destroy it. To throw it into the fireplace and kindle the logs hot for seven days and nights, until every spark and remnant of its soot had been ejected from my home. But my fingers strangely itched for the touch of that leather, and I still couldn't fathom what was *inside* the pages.

And so, I opened it.

There were twenty-two thickly pressed papers of rough parchment, and on every page was an illustration, like large cards, faced with cruel and fantastic figures. They were all titled. Strange names—*La Force*, *La Maison Diev*, and *Le Diable*. I stopped when I turned to *Le Hermite*, and saw the full-page picture of a cloaked man, stooped, holding a knotted staff.

I slapped the book shut. The nipple brushed my fingertips. Hastily, I wrapped it back in the oilskin, threw it in the chest, and locked it tight.

That night, the wind was quiet outside. The very air seemed taut,

233

coiled, ready to snap with nervous tension. I went to bed early, after generously stoking the fireplace downstairs. I must have lain there for hours, listening to the muted crackling of the logs, trying to fall asleep. And then, just as my eyes grew heavy, I heard a sound from below.

Hands trembling, dressed only in my nightgown, I lit a candle and tiptoed to the landing of the stairs, and listened. From below, in soft gushes, came the sound of breathing.

VII. Le Chariot

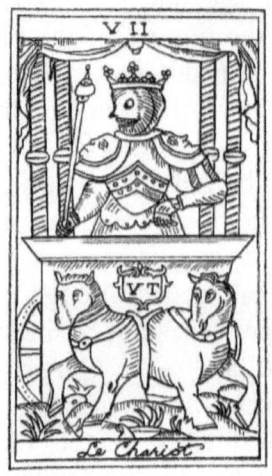

Slowly, I descended the stairs, the candle shaking wildly in my hand.

The candle-flame caught the water before I could clearly make it out, reflecting wet-orange across the face of the silty pool that had flooded the entire printing room floor. Standing at the foot of the stairs, I held the candle out, peering aghast at the transformation of the room.

Dark, opaque pools covered the floor. A swamp-smell hung heavy in the air, full of decay, pungent with the reek of oily mud and dead water. A diaphanous mist fell in slowly curling drapes from the rafters, obscuring the perimeter of the small room. The printing presses and my other equipment loomed in this vapor like menacing scaffolding in a cemetery-fog. I stepped down into the water and my bare feet sunk into a fine silt before settling against the coarse wooden planks of my floor.

I stood in silence, frozen in place, the candleflame flickering like a corpse-light in the wandering mists. Not a sound stirred in the impenetrable haze, other than the soft bubbling of strange gasses from the muddy waters covering the floor. No movement met my stricken gaze, save the slow churning of the mists.

And then, just as rational thought began to return, from low in the murky water beside me, the half-submerged chest breathed.

I spun round, casting the light upon it in time to see a gush of dark water spurt from the old, cracked wood, its hiss sounding like the breath of a living creature. Fear gripped my bosom. I tried to back away, but in the continuing hiss of the water words seemed to form, instructing me, *commanding me*, to unlock the lid and open the chest.

My hands shaking, I took the keyring from the wall—the keys rattling against each other and breaking the deathly stillness in the room—and forced the skeleton key into the padlock. It turned with a grating squeal. The lock snapped open. I dropped it into the bog around the chest and threw open the lid.

Water poured from the mouth of the chest, streaming down the sides, full of small, creeping things that struggled in the sludge, crawling away from my light. The dark water inside seemed bottomless, its depths gurgling with deep currents. My gaze was held to that oily abyss, and I peered into the rolling swells that splashed and frothed onto the printing room floor. Try as I might, I could not tear my eyes from that foul water, even as a shape began to glisten in the darkness—a writhing mass of naked skin, folding upon itself, twisting and turning like a coiled rope as it came ever clearer into view, coalescing at the last moment into a solid form as the hermit's book rose to the surface.

With one hand, I took the book and pulled it from the chest. Water streamed from the human-leather. And then I turned and looked across the room.

The hermit stood at my desk, wreathed in the mists. My candlelight glittered upon him, giving his outline an emerald glow, and passed right through him. 'Bring the book.' His voice was a strangled whisper. 'It is time we played our game.'

235

I put the book on the table.

'I don't want to play with you,' I said. A dark feeling took hold of me, trembling in my bosom. I already knew I had lost.

'There are twenty-two fortunes in the Book of Colmcille,' said the hermit, emerald reflections rippling within him, as though he were submerged in water. 'Choose a number of fortunes to read.'

'Who are you?' I asked, still trying to resist.

'Any number,' he whispered.

'Please, tell me who you are? What Hell have you come from?'

The ghostly eyes drifted, then, their gaze shifting far into the distance, and the weight of what they might be seeing struck me with cold horror. '*Cúl Dreimhne*,' he said. 'I come from old lands and old ways. They wouldn't convert. They wouldn't believe, but in vain those druids tried to curse me. In vain they wove their spells— The Church protected me. But at *Cúl Dreimhne* I was forsaken. I was tricked. The blood I spilled was used against me, as a pagan human sacrifice. I was profaned to my Lord, cursed by my people, and banished by the druids to wander the earth. They stole my name, stole my book, and cursed me to walk the world between worlds, for ever.'

'What is this book?' I asked.

The dead eyes shifted back to me. 'It's a battling book, my

cathach, a book of prayers, of pasts and futures. Now, choose your fortunes.'

'Eight,' I said.

'Open the book.'

Placing the book with its binding against the table, I pulled my hands away and let the covers fall open. *Le Hermite* grinned up at me in the candlelight. The ghostly hermit spoke again—'Turn the pages—one fewer times than fortunes you chose, however you like.'

Hand trembling, I took the edge of the page, and hesitated. I had chosen eight fortunes, so I turned five pages to the left—*La Justice, La Movreux, Le Chariot, Le Pape, L'E'mpereur*—and turned two back, to *Le Chariot*, seven turns in total. The ghost reached out, and tore the page from the book, letting it fall to the waters beneath him. 'Again,' he said.

Time after time, I turned the pages, seven at a time, and every time the ghost tore the page I landed on from the book. In a panic, I watched as the pages of The Devil, of Death, of The Hanging Man resurfaced more frequently. I dodged them every time. Halfway through the strange game, it struck me to land *on* one of these ill-fated pages, to bait the ghost into tearing *them* from the book. But, try as I might, I never could hit them. With growing terror, I began to see a pattern. A bottomless gnawing chewed into my stomach as *La Mort* passed in the turned pages again and again. Page after page fell to the torpid waters below the apparition, until only two pages were left, and the ghost tore the final page from the *cathach*, revealing my final fortune.

Death.

X. La Rove de Fortune

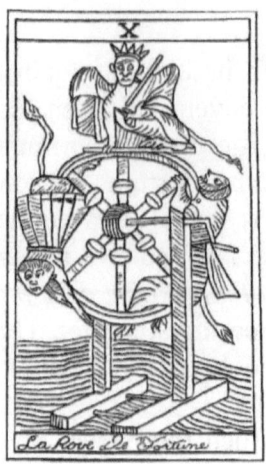

My skin began to soften, loosening from my muscles and bone, liquefying beneath my very eyes. Swamp water fouled my tongue. My lungs filled with fluid, which I vomited through chattering teeth, only for my breath to be taken away again. The vapors in the room shimmered, as though the light from some dark sun was breaking under rippling water.

'What have you done?' I screamed.

The hermit laughed. And yet, though it was *he* who laughed, I felt *my* lungs quaking with each vile exhalation. The hermit spoke that same weird language as before, and I felt *my* water-logged tongue, swollen and cracking, voicing the words. And then, as green mists rose before my eyes, I stood looking at myself. The printer was now across from me, wearing my nightgown and cap, *my* face twisted in some perverse enjoyment as it spat out the druidic incantations, laughing all the while.

I looked down to see my hands, ghostly emerald, shimmering in the underwater light. Old, cracked, pitted skin, my nails long and hooked, split at the ends, my robes torn like the frayed hem of a forsaken scarecrow. Under my gaze, my green body began to dissolve, settling down like poisoned rain into the book on the table, drawn into the page that was Death.

The skin-cover of the *cathach* writhed and shuddered as it took the green mists. In my head I heard a distant scream, the howl of an old woman, beating against my temples, its pulse growing louder and more desperate as my body slowly fell into the book.

I looked up at the printer as I dissolved downward, my vision fracturing into the amorphous vapor. The last thing I saw was my own face with the dark, devil-eyes of the hermit, gazing down at me as he closed the skin-cover of the *cathach* and pitched me into darkness.

And yet, true death did not come. The beating of a woman's heart, the sinuous struggles of her taut skin, bound me within a human prison. Endlessly, her suffocated cries resonated in my head. The beating of her pulse, the feeling of bony fingers wrapping her throat, coarse knuckles pressing into her flesh as she struggled her final battle against death. I was stifled as her neck broke beneath the hermit's murderous grasp. The panicked tattoo of her heart rattled in my mind, over and over.

Gradually, although this endless torment imprisoned me, I came to know other things in the darkness. Crawling things, that slithered across the book's skin-cover, maggots that burrowed the flesh, the press of watery currents, the migrations of silts and river stones.

Slowly, as the druid's spells weakened, light penetrated the corpse-skin book. Eels chewed the human leather, fishes picked at the rotting nipple, and the old woman's cries of terror fell silent below the murmur of swampy water. Two centuries passed as the enchanted book rotted away in the bog where the druid had thrown it, but finally, one day, the woman's cries fell away entirely, and I was bathed in light, and my spirit slipped from the tattered remnants of her bound skin and rose from the waters.

The village was gone. The farmlands were gone. In the sky, a metal cylinder with fixed wings crept through the clouds, a parched white trail stretching in its wake.

XVIII. La Lune

Everything around me was drawn in a diaphanous vapor. Trees loomed like vague skeletons. The sky glowed dimly with a wan, grey light. A long, paved road wound through the glades where once a wagon-path had been. Slowly, as though lofted on some invisible wind, I shifted down this road, following it towards my village, but it was not there. Only knotted trees, wound tightly together by mosses and vines. Here and there, I recognized the shape of old buildings beneath the forest cover. Here and there, an old foundation stone jutted from marshy tree roots. But there was nothing left but wreckage, now.

I returned to the road and travelled until a city rose before me.

Tall buildings glittered darkly below the veiled sun in the sky. Great metal beasts roved the streets—of course, I soon learned they were cars. I saw people walking on cement sidewalks, electric billboards penetrating even my between-world with their neon glare. Smog and soot scudded the air, music echoed from distant speakers. Television sets glared in storefront windows, replaying what they saw outside, in the streets, in real time. When I passed these, they grew dark, their screens fuzzy with static.

Under my dead gaze, lovers on park benches turned around, looked over their shoulders. Squirrels dropped their nuts and bolted for trees, dogs whimpered, and the busker at the corner drugstore became suddenly morose, playing a sad song he'd never heard before—it had been one of my favorites, you see, from two centuries earlier.

No one saw me as I wandered. Just felt me upon their skin, creeping like a cancer as I passed. There was nobody else in the dark-sunned world I'd been born into. Just strange, directionless winds and the soft whispers of other lost souls, drifting across time like a spectral radio station that never ceased its broadcast.

Day or night, my strangely lit view of your world never changed. Always, it glowed with the same color-bleached glare. For years, I wandered this barren landscape, alone, searching for any trace of the hermit who damned me to this private Hell, attempting to learn the secret to the magic of my imprisonment. Vague memories haunted me. Words, the old man had said. Gestures he'd made, as he incanted in my printing shop.

These memories took me all over the world. To Africa, Spain, and England. In Ireland I found an answer in the form of their patron saint—Saint Columba, Colmcille, the victor of the Battle of *Cúl Dreimhne*, a battle fought in 561 over the forgery of a holy book of prayers. Tradition says the man was banished afterwards, and lived the rest of his life in Scotland, revered as a seer, a man of God, a sage. But I'd met the man himself, two-hundred-fifty years later, and I knew the truth. Colmcille never went to Scotland—he was banished, cursed by the druids, and an imposter took his place, and his magic book.

Yet, this was only part of the answer. Decades more I wandered, across Ireland and Scotland, studying the standing stones on their ancient moors. I haunted the parlors of mystic charlatans in Paris, and frequented dark secret societies in India and Egypt. I gained knowledge. I was insatiable. I stopped at nothing. Threads of power, stitched between worlds, had been woven back then, when I was imprisoned. Threads that ensnared me like a fly in a spider's web. Threads that all congealed into that one unholy book... Just as they do now, in *this* one.

The Deck

Reader, had you forgotten that this story started with you? That everything revolves around the day you die? What would you do if I told you I knew when that would be? Would you laugh it off, and go about your day, forgetting everything you read here? Would you smirk, and play it cool, pretending not to be disturbed, even though your flesh tingled with vague unease?

Probably neither. You'd likely smile, and think, 'this writer is trying very hard, but it's entertaining, let's see where it goes.'

Either way, here you are, still reading. Bravado? Skepticism? Lurid fascination? Fear?

Fools are easy to sway. The simpletons at Black Beacon Books never knew what possessed them—it was easy, forcing myself upon them. Likewise, S. B. Watson, the man who's cursed fingers typed out these words for me, was perhaps the cheapest fool of all. And all for this one copy to be printed, this very copy of *Samhain Screams*, that you now hold in your hands, with these words written for you.

And yet, you *still* don't believe me. So, let's play a little game, then.

Here with me in the ether is a deck of cards I have crafted. Unbound to the old hermit's physical restrictions, *my* deck is infinite. A tarot, just like the hermit's, comprised of twenty-two Major Arcana, repeated over and over. You can't see it, but it's here in front of you, right now. Reach out. Take any small number of cards, carefully. They spell your fate, you know. Now, take that same number again and add them to your deck, and hold it in your hand.

Now it's my turn. I'll select a few random cards as well… Twelve. And add them to yours. Can you feel the weight of them, pressing against your palm? I can see them, even if you cannot. Now, put the book down, and shuffle them all. Shuffle them well.

Once you're satisfied, count your deck, and then remove exactly half the number of cards. Throw them away. Then, remove the original number you had chosen, the first time you took from my deck.

You should have a small set of cards in your hand. To be exact, six. *L'E'mpereur, Le Bateleur, Le Chariot, La Mort, La Rove De Fortune,* and *La Lune.* The exact six cards that have headed each section of this story. And now that our game is set, and your cards have been spread, let's tell your fortune, shall we?

You chose six cards. Turn back and start at the first—*Le Bateleur*. Just as the hermit bade me, now I bid you—turn in this book from card to card, five card choices, back and forth, however you like. Once you've finished, rip out *L'E'mpereur*, or fold the page in half to cover the card, making the crease sharp and deep. If that was your selection, I salute you—you have won. Burn this book, and forget I ever existed.

But of course, *L'E'mpereur* was not your choice, was it? Then we play on... Turn the pages again. Five times. It's your own fate in your hands, so choose carefully. Once you've finished, rip out *Le Bateleur*.

Have you bested me yet? Have I lost? I think not. Turn the pages again, five times, five card choices, back and forth, spelling your fortune. Once you've finished, rip out *Le Chariot*—no use, this cat-and-mouse ploy, I know it wasn't your selection. Rip it out, and make five choices again, counting each movement one-by-one.

When you've finished, rip out *La Lune*. No moon of rejuvenation for you.

Now, we have two cards left. You can see where this is heading, can't you? Even so, you must make the moves. Turn between the cards, five times, back and forth, making your final selection, ending on your fate—Death.

Did you ever really think it would end any different, when I told you, from the very beginning, that I live on the day you die?

The ritual is cast. You fool. You should have thrown this book across the room the minute I began speaking to you. You should have burned it, from the very beginning. But, just like the fools at Black Beacon Books, just like S. B. Watson, you dismissed me.

What you hold in your hands is a cursed book, Reader. Soon to be even further enchanted, by the gift of your own blood.

I will come for you. I will come on the day when the veil between worlds is at its thinnest, when only a vapor separates the realm of the living from all the creatures of Hell, from principalities and powers, from wastrel spirits and evil forces—this Samhain, you will die. You will die, and I will be free to follow Colmcille, to enact my revenge.

But don't worry, I've discovered deeper secrets than Colmcille ever knew—I don't need to steal your pathetic body to loose myself from this eternal torture. I don't need a form to possess, or a magical tome of human skin. All I need is your soul, bound eternally to take my place in the dimension of dispossessed spirits. Your soul, which you have just forfeited.

On the day you die—Samhain—don't look for a ghost in the wind. Don't seek me in the creeping shadows of the witching hour, or the rustling of autumn leaves down the sidewalk. No, I'll be in the truck that wanders into your lane before you can swerve, in the tree branch that tumbles unexpectedly on your head, in the hard candy that lodges in your windpipe. Or, perhaps you will choose to make it easier for the both of us. The bridges near your town are high enough, are they not? The knives in your kitchen would be so soft and smooth against your wrists…

And don't think you can get out of it now. You've already cast your lot. Run, if you like. Or hide. Burn this book, it makes no difference. This Samhain, you will die, and I will be ready for your soul.

Author Biographies

Jacy Morris is an Indigenous author. He is a registered member of the Confederated Tribes of Siletz. At the age of ten he was transplanted to Portland, Oregon, where he developed a love for punk rock and horror movies, both of which tend to find their way into his writing. He has written several novels, including the *This Rotten World* series and the *One Night Stand at the End of the World* series. His latest novel, *We Like It Cherry* was published August 2025 by Tenebrous Press. His next work will be the novel *One-Shot* from Torrid Waters (November 2025). *jacymorris.com*

Mia Dalia's tales of horror, noir, science fiction, mystery, crime, humor, and more have been featured in dozens of anthologies, magazines, literary journals, online, and adapted for narrative podcasts. Her stories were voted Top Ten of Tales to Terrify 2023 and shortlisted for the Crime Writers Association's Daggers Awards 2024. She's the author of novels, *Estate Sale* and *Haven*, novellas *Alakazam, Tell Me a Story, Discordant, Arrokoth, Do You Know The Muffin Man?* and the collection *Smile So Red and Other Tales of Madness. daliaverse.wixsite.com/author*

DJ Tyrer dwells on the misty northern shore of the Thames estuary, close to the world's longest pleasure pier in the decaying seaside resort of Southend-on-Sea, and is the person behind Atlantean Publishing. They have had stories in such anthologies as *Alone in the Borderland* (Belanger Books) and *Chilling Horror Short Stories* (Flame Tree), and issues of *Occult Detective Magazine, parABnormal,* and *Weirdbook,* and in addition, has a novella available in paperback and on the Kindle, *The Yellow House* (Dunhams Manor). *djtyrer.blogspot.co.uk*

Nick Manzolillo is the author of the novel *Moon, Regardless* and his short fiction has appeared in over seventy publications, including: *Night Frights*, *Switchblade*, *TQR*, *Red Room Magazine*, *Grievous Angel*, and *The Tales To Terrify* podcast. He has an MFA in Creative and Professional Writing from Western Connecticut State University. Nick lives in Rhode Island with his wife, son, and three well-read cats.

Matthew R. Davis is a Shirley Jackson Award-nominated author and musician from Adelaide, South Australia, with over one hundred short stories and seven books published to date. His latest releases are the horror collection *Songs of Shadow, Words of Woe* (JournalStone) and the non-fiction *The Cure On Track: Every Album, Every Song* (Sonicbond Publishing). He was the bassist/singer/songwriter of *Blood Red Renaissance* and the bassist/backing vocalist of *icecocoon*, amongst other projects. He lives in Morphett Vale with the award-winning artist Meg Wright, aka Red Wallflower, and her cats Juniper and Lexi. *matthewrdavisfiction.wordpress.com*

Darren Todd is a freelance book editor for Evolved Publications, and his short fiction has appeared in more than sixty publications over the years. His short story collection, *The Ugly Mug and Other Stories*, is available on Amazon and Audible. While some of his works fall under the literary umbrella, he often returns to genre. His style and reading preferences tend toward the psychological, as he enjoys stories that linger in the imagination long after he's closed the book on them. He lives in Asheville, North Carolina with his son and girlfriend.

Hannah Baxter is a horror and fantasy writer from Omagh, Northern Ireland with an MA with distinction from Queen's University, Belfast. Her work has been featured in *The Martello Journal*, the Dark Poets Club's *Dark Poets Prize Edition II*, *Spellweaver Magazine*, Writefluence's *The Other Side*, *Drawn to the Light Press #13*, and *New Isles Press #2*. When not pounding out a new story on her laptop, she can be found with a good book, a hot cup of tea and a cat on her lap.

Tom Coombe is the author of *The Clown King and Other Stories of the Pre-Apocalypse*, a collection of short horror stories and weird fiction published in the summer of 2025. He lives in Pennsylvania's Lehigh Valley with his girlfriend and their cat, and is mentioned on the Wikipedia page for Santa's Little Helper from The Simpsons.

Daniel Fox is a writer of horror, thrillers, fantasy, and children's books. He also created an online Choose-Your-Own-Adventure horror video game called *Ocean of Death*. Wow, he should really focus.

Kevin M. Folliard is a Chicagoland writer whose fiction has been collected by The Horror Tree, The Dread Machine, Demain Publishing, and more. His work has been collected in *The Misery King's Closet* and *The Misery King's Country*. Kevin enjoys his day job in academia and membership in the La Grange Writers Group. *kevinfolliard.com*

Arthur Goodhill is a writer from Midlands, Ireland. He enjoys writing horrors, mysteries and anything you might call "weird". His work has appeared in Timber Ghost Press' *Dead Stars and Stone Arches* anthology, he has published poetry books and a novella, and he is currently working on his first novel. When he is not writing, he can be found exploring the lake of Lough Ree and its islands. *instagram.com/arthurgoodhill*

Perth writer **Martin Livings** has had over a hundred short stories in a variety of magazines and anthologies both locally and internationally. His first novel, *Carnies*, was first published by Hachette Livre in 2006, and was nominated for both the Aurealis and Ditmar awards, and his short story collection, *Living With the Dead*, was published in 2012. Both are now available from Amazon, along with the follow-up collection *Light Falling From a Long Dead Star*, novellas *Rope* and *The Final Twist*, and novels *Skinsongs, Sleeper Awake, An Ill Wind, The Temp* and *The Obituary*. *martinlivings.wordpress.com*

Em Starr is an Australian horror writer. Her work has appeared or is forthcoming in numerous places, including *The NoSleep Podcast*, *Flash Fiction Online*, and publications by Underland Press, Flame Tree Press, and Eerie River Publishing, to name a few. Her short story *Red Dirt* appears in *The Black Beacon Book of Ghosts*. Hailing from the beautiful Mornington Peninsula (Boon Wurrung country), Em is a lover of animals, beaches, blossom trees, and bloody good coffee. *emstarr.com.au*

Epiphany Ferrell lives near the Shawnee National Forest in southern Illinois. Her horror stories appear in the Stoker-nominated anthology *Shakespeare Unleashed* and forthcoming in Ellen Datlow's *Best Horror of the Year, vol. 17* and elsewhere. Her flash fiction is in *Best Microfiction*, *Best Small Fictions*, *Wigleaf*, *Ghost Parachute* and other places. *epiphanyferrell.com*

Brian Moreland lives in the Texas Hill Country, where he writes a blend of mystery, horror, and dark suspense. His short stories have appeared in several horror anthologies. His books include *The Devil's Woods*, *The Witching House*, *The Seekers*, *Darkness Rising*, *Shadows in the Mist*, *Tomb of Gods*, *Savage Island*, and *They Stalk the Night*.

Elle Jones is a writer, circus acrobat, and student. Her work focuses on the horrors associated with femininity, shame, and faith. She lives in Athens, Georgia.

Marty Young is a Bram Stoker-nominated and multiple Australian Shadows award-winning writer and editor, and sometimes ghost hunter. His fiction and anthologies have been nominated for and won numerous awards, while his essays on horror literature have been published in journals and university textbooks across the world. Marty was also the founding president of the Australian Horror Writers Association from 2005-2010, and one of the creative minds behind the internationally acclaimed Midnight Echo magazine, for which he also served as executive editor until mid-2013. His last novel was *Gutterbreed* (2020), which was nominated for an Australian Shadows Award and an Aurealis Award for Best Horror Novel. *martyyoung.com*

Tom Rimer is the author of *The Glowing* Trilogy, *Malevolent Nevers*, *Odious Ghouls*, and *Buoygeist*. His work can also be found in a number of anthologies including *13 Tales to Give You Night Terrors*, *The Nightmare Never Ends*, and *Dreamcaught*. He is a member of the HWA.

C.E. O'Conaing is a writer and poet whose work has appeared in *Sad Girls Club*, *Smitten Land*, *Nanoism*, *100 Foot Crow*, *The Weary Blues*, *HCE Review*, *The Occulum*, *NonBinary Review*, and many more reputable locales. Born in Ireland, they now reside in Edinburgh, where they spend their time at work and, occasionally, hacking away at a perpetually unfinished novel.

S. B. Watson lives near the coast of rainy Oregon, where he writes tales of crime, mystery, suspense, and the macabre. His works have appeared in *Spinetingler*, *Punk Noir*, *Mystery Tribune*, and *Mystery Magazine*, as well as various anthologies, including *The Black Beacon Book of Pirates*, *Crime Wave*, and *Crimeucopia: Through the Past Darkly*. sbwatson.com

Greg Chapman is a horror author, editor, and artist based in Brisbane, Australia. His fiction and art has received wide acclaim from readers and critics of the horror genre since his first publication in 2011. In 2024, his collection *Midnight Masquerade*, published by IFWG Publishing International, won an Australasian Shadows Award, and he was a finalist for the 2016 Bram Stoker Award with his debut novel *Hollow House*. His most recent short story collection, *Black Days and Bloody Nights* is also a finalist in this year's Australasian Shadows Awards. His artistic endeavours include designing book covers and creating illustrations for various publishers and authors in Australia, the United States, and the United Kingdom, including. He was recently named as a finalist in the Best Artist category of the British Fantasy Awards. The first graphic novel he illustrated, *Witch Hunts: A Graphic History of the Burning Times*, written by Rocky Wood and Lisa Morton, won the Superior Achievement in a Graphic Novel category at the Bram Stoker Awards in 2013. Greg was also the President of the Australasian Horror Writers Association from 2017-2020. *darkscrybe.com*

Cameron Trost is an author of mystery, suspense, horror, and post-apocalyptic fiction best known for his puzzles featuring Oscar Tremont, Investigator of the Strange and Inexplicable. He has written three novels, *Flicker*, *Letterbox*, and *The Tunnel Runner*, and three collections, *Oscar Tremont, Investigator of the Strange and Inexplicable*, *The Animal Inside*, and *Hoffman's Creeper and Other Disturbing Tales*. His short fiction has appeared in numerous anthologies and magazines in Australia, the United Kingdom, the United States, Canada, and France. Originally from Brisbane, Australia, Cameron lives with his wife and two sons near Guérande in southern Brittany, between the rugged coast and treacherous marshlands. He is a registered heritage tour guide (guide-conférencier) and runs the independent publishing house, Black Beacon Books. He is also a lifetime member of the Australian Crime Writers Association. Never without a project on the go, Cameron is currently adding the final touches to *Dead on the Dolmen*, the first mystery novel featuring Oscar Tremont. *camerontrost.com*

Also Available from Black Beacon Books

The Black Beacon Book of Horror features dark and disturbing tales
from some of the most original and imaginative authors writing in
the genre today.

For news, reviews, competitions, author interviews,
and exclusive excerpts

Visit our website
blackbeaconbooks.com

Like us on Facebook
facebook.com/BlackBeaconBooks

Join us on Twitter
@BlackBeacons

Find us on Instagram
instagram.com/blackbeaconbooks

Subscribe on Patreon
patreon.com/blackbeaconbooks

Discover All our Social Media Links
https://linktr.ee/blackbeaconbooks